LEAGUE OF INDEPENDENT OPERATIVES
BOOK 3

MASTERMIND

KATE SHEERAN SWED

To Lynn
editor extraordinaire

SLOANE LEAPT over the broken window of the hotel lobby, barely clearing the ragged edge of glass that still clung to the sill. She could catch Oliver. She had to. Alex and Hilda were struggling behind her, but she couldn't turn to help them over the ledge. A single beat of delay, and Oliver would get away.

Her translation app stuttered a continuous scroll of words across her vision, making it harder to focus on her target. As if she cared about what this world's strangely frozen billboards had to offer. Sloane attempted to shut off the scrawl with a verbal command, but the app ignored her.

They'd come to this planet to steal the Blade of Starlight, turn it in for its hefty bounty, and get back to their home galaxy. Until Oliver had betrayed them, leaping in front of Sloane to close the Blade in a fancy box. All of which had happened about thirty seconds ago. Maybe a minute.

Sloane wasn't exactly sure what she'd do when she caught him. Tackle him to the ground. Force an explanation. Take the Blade herself, if she could.

Strange trees with fringed leaves lined the strange planet's streets, their skinny trunks swaying in a dissipating breeze. Oliver's sandy head streaked across the street before her, vehicles honking as he darted in front of them. Not one of them seemed to stop automatically, as they would have on any planet in the Parse Galaxy; instead, people sat behind each control deck, their hands holding onto wheels. A man in a red, open-topped vehicle shouted after Oliver, and Sloane's translation app gave up, simply informing her that he'd used an expletive.

She followed Oliver across the street, ignoring the enraged shouts of the man in the vehicle. There were faster ways to move, even on an unknown planet, but Oliver had yet to bust out his hov-tiles. Briefly, Sloane wondered if he somehow knew more about this place than he'd let on, but the thought evaporated as she swerved to avoid the wide-open back doors of a parked cargo vehicle. She tripped up onto the curb as Oliver streaked across her peripheral vision. Luckily for her, his body armor stood out on this planet like a blood leaf in a vat of cream. The way people stopped to stare at him helped, too.

Sloane wished she could risk hov-tiles, but Oliver might be avoiding flight for a reason. If so, she'd also risk losing him if she tried to use hers. She cursed and ran harder.

Oliver took a sharp turn and darted along a path laid between two rows of those strange, skinny trees. He, at least, seemed to know exactly where he was headed. He clutched the box as he ran, the one he must have obtained in that back room at the black market they'd visited together. The one that now held the Blade of Starlight. He'd been so apologetic, heading into that secret room without her. How many lies had the asshole told?

Plenty, clearly. Most importantly, he'd screwed his crew out of the largest bounty ever known to the galaxy—galax*ies*?—and Sloane intended to find out why.

The path opened into a wide plaza, where a long rectangular shrub seemed to act as a fence. It looked like a green box, all flat lines and corners. Was it cut, or did it grow that way?

Not important. Sloane started through the gap in the plant-fence, determined. She was going to get the Blade of Starlight back from Oliver and turn it into a bounty that would let her bid this crew goodbye, for good. Not a betrayal, but a promise—one only she could fulfill. She'd return them to her uncle, and she'd go back to her old life. Her real life.

And no one would stop her from doing that. Not even her treacherous former security officer, slash thief, slash sort-of boyfriend. *Ex*-boyfriend.

A pair of hands grabbed her by the shoulders, pulling her to her knees behind the plant-fence. She pivoted, prepared to attempt a punch while also trying to remember whether she was meant to tuck her thumb inside her fist or wrap it around the outside.

Luckily, the need to take a fifty-fifty chance on breaking her thumb could wait for another day. It was only her pilot, Hilda, who'd caught up with her and now crouched behind the green fence, breathing hard. Alex, the ship's scientist, sat red-faced on the ground beside her.

"Let's find out who he's meeting, eh?" Hilda said.

See, this was the problem with Sloane's crew mates. They always wanted to stop, to think things over. To consider a situation before they started punching overly muscled betrayers in the face.

Sloane peered through the plant-fence's leaves. "He could disappear."

But Alex shook her head, coughing a little. "Not without a wormhole, he can't. And the only wormhole generator in existence is back on the *Moneymaker*."

It seemed a little presumptuous to assume that the only wormhole generator in *all* of existence, across the *entire* universe, was the one Alex had invented and left behind on their spaceship. On the other hand, Oliver's boss hadn't teleported him away, which must mean said employer had no access to a wormhole. Besides, Oliver had clearly wheedled his way onto their crew for reasons beyond regular paychecks (which Sloane couldn't provide) and the captain's charming smile (which Sloane *had* provided, without hesitation).

Maybe Alex's wormhole research had been the whole reason for his presence.

Oliver stood in the middle of the plaza and touched a fingertip to his temple. A com implant, if Sloane had to guess. Had he had it the whole time? Had someone been listening? Because that could potentially be embarrassing. Very.

Hilda was leaning so close over her shoulder that Sloane could feel the pilot's breath hot against her ear. She was about to elbow the woman for some space when the air in front of Oliver... shimmered.

That was the best word for it. The air shimmered, and a ghostlike figure appeared in the center of the plaza, not five feet from where Oliver stood. Long, fat curls fell to the man's shoulders, and his face wore deep lines across the forehead and sprawling out from his eyes. A cloak drifted over his torso, the fabric clasped at his throat with a broach in the shape of a beetle. Fitting, really for someone looking for a weapon called the Blade of Starlight.

"He even dresses like an epic-vid elf," Sloane muttered, and Hilda elbowed her in the ribs with a look that Sloane interpreted as *Shut up and don't get us killed.*

Oliver gave the elf a bow. Sloane couldn't see his face, only the back of his head. "I have the Blade," he said.

"You've done well," the elf guy replied, his voice somehow resonating across the space. Sloane had never bothered much with understanding the physics of an open-air holo-meeting.

What did this guy do, hijack local tech? She glanced around, wondering if this world even *had* tech. "As soon as you transmit the wormhole ship's coordinates, we'll commandeer the vessel and bring you home."

Like hell, Sloane thought, though she wasn't sure what she could do to stop them from here. At least it confirmed that Alex was right; these people couldn't create wormholes on their own. Why hadn't Oliver gone directly back to the ship, then? He could have leapt back through the portal, surely. She doubted he'd have been able to shut it down before Sloane and the others followed him through, but he was the only real fighter among them. Surely he could have coerced them into anything.

With his back to her and no tech-enhanced volume, Sloane couldn't hear Oliver's reply. She thought she could make out the timbre of a question in the muffled tone of his voice, a feeling that was enhanced by the way he hung back, fingers wrapped tightly around the Blade-holding box. As if he did not entirely trust this person. It was, Sloane supposed bitterly, a natural approach to these kinds of underworld dealings. Maybe Oliver thought the elf intended to stiff him on his pay.

In answer to Oliver's mystery question, the elf grinned, his wide mouth stretching uncomfortably far into his cheeks. At least, it looked uncomfortable to Sloane. "Ah. He did say you might ask."

Sloane glanced at Hilda, who shrugged. Alex's lips were twisted in concentration as she squinted in Oliver's direction.

Oliver startled, then fumbled his tab out of his tool belt with his free hand. The elf blinked almost lazily, folding his arms. Waiting. Sloane assumed that whatever Oliver was reading so intently on his tab, his employer must have sent it. The seconds stretched as he stood unmoving for so long that Sloane wondered if the elf emissary had somehow frozen him in place. She wished she could see his face, wished she could somehow gauge his reaction to whatever it was the elf had given him. Information? Payment?

The elf cleared his throat. "Is there a problem?"

Oliver looked up, finally. Even at a distance, the tension in his arms was more than obvious. The hand holding the Blade box shook.

He didn't say anything more. Instead, he whipped around, shoving the box under his arm, and ran back toward the leaf-fence where Sloane and the others were hiding. His eyes were wide as marbles in his handsome face, his lips parted in shock and fear. Whatever he'd seen on his tablet, it wasn't good.

The elf sighed, shaking his head, and drew something out of his cloak pocket. Surely these people couldn't do anything to hurt Oliver, Sloane told herself. Not here.

Oliver made it halfway across the plaza before he fell, his limbs convulsing.

Before she could think, Sloane ripped her arm out of Hilda's grip and ran to him. She could hear Hilda and Alex shouting behind her, but it was too late; her feet were already carrying her across the plaza. Her heart squeezed painfully in her chest, and not from the exertion of the run. It was the sight of Oliver seizing on the ground, his mouth twisted in pain, that sent fear trilling through her veins.

Heroics weren't her thing, not usually. Not ever. But this was Oliver. Their friend. Her lover, for stars' sake. Lies or no, she'd help him if she could.

Sloane ignored the ghostlike figure of the elf, still hovering in her peripheral vision as she fell to her knees beside Oliver. Blood leaked out of his ears, his nose, and she could see the delicate veins in his cheeks, standing out against his paper-white skin. Yes, he'd betrayed her. But he'd also shared her bed. She touched his hair, hands shaking, and he opened his eyes.

"Sloane." His hand reached around feebly, fumbling along

the plaza pavement until his fingers closed on the box. He shoved it into her hands as the whites of his eyes turned red with blood. "I'm sorry. I didn't know."

She wanted to ask what he hadn't known, and why it could possibly matter so much. But the man was dying. Or would, if she didn't get help soon. "We can get you to a med center," she said, pushing the box aside and trying to speak in a soothing tone. She wasn't a doctor yet. She had no idea what the elf had done to him, or what kind of healing tech this world had, or how to get back to a halfway civilized planet. It made her want to weep with frustration.

Oliver pushed the box harder, and Sloane took it back, if only to spare him the effort. He licked his lips, coating them in blood. "The Fleet said... I told him... sever it..." He shuddered, his limbs convulsing anew, and streams of blood poured from his nose and mouth. He took a breath, and his throat rattled. Even if this planet had decent medical facilities, it was too late. She could tell it was too late.

Sloane gripped the blood-slicked box with one hand, tears blurring her vision as she caressed his hair with the other. She didn't think he'd be able to speak again, but when he let out the breath, she made out one last word: "Run."

MARY WAS after the aliens before they'd reached the shattered windows of the hotel lobby. She paused for a beat before jumping after them, to make sure that Eloise was breathing—which she was, though she'd probably regret having landed on her knees in all that glass—but still, the aliens moved way faster than Mary could have anticipated.

Yes, she'd just finished packing away the Trap and the other league retirees in a major fight. And sure, they'd poisoned her only a few days ago, after which she'd spend several nights designing tech to help beat them—which meant her body sorely lacked appropriate levels of sleep. So yeah, she might not be operating at prime efficiency.

Still. These newcomers might look human enough, but they had to be aliens. And the aliens moved *fast*.

They'd all shown up to steal the Pearl Knife, with their armor and their strange translating tech, and then one of them had seemed to betray the others. That was all Mary had been able to make of the strange conversation in the hotel lobby. Aliens. Betrayal. Stolen Knife.

Just once, she'd have loved some breathing time. A day to sit by the pool after taking down a formidable team of rivals. An hour, even.

Outside, she could see no trace of the aliens, only the back-end of a red convertible as it sped through the snarl of traffic in front of the hotel. Taking a guess, Mary rushed across the street, earning numerous curses from the cluster of stalled cars. She paused on the opposite sidewalk, scanning her surroundings for any sign of alien activity.

It would make sense, really, if she failed to find them. If she failed to get the Pearl Knife back for El. Lately, it seemed that failure was Mary's default.

No handy signs marked where the aliens had gone. Behind her, the traffic was already sorting itself out. Pedestrians had stopped to peer past the cordons at the destroyed hotel lobby, and to crane their necks toward the clouds. The strange, stormy weather that the LIO retirees had drummed up for the fight had melted away into L.A.'s typical sunny day. The weather worker was still at large, and the animal whisperer. And Dolly. Talk about failures, letting Dolly disappear like that.

Mary's head pounded as she forced her thoughts into the moment, and onto the task at hand. She squinted, half aware of cars stopping yet again on the road behind her. Noticing her. Taking photos. Or maybe just flipping her off. Was it weird for her to wish for the latter?

A pained cry echoed from the direction of the concert hall plaza, and Mary took off through the gauntlet of palm trees that led in that direction. She hoped she'd find the aliens there, and not some poor victim they'd left behind. Her blood jittered through her system, doing its best to raise the last dregs of adrenaline she had left after the fight.

As Mary headed for the hedges surrounding the plaza, a woman started to scream. She picked up the pace, bursting through the narrow gap and ready to fight. As ready as she could be, under the circumstances.

A few steps past the hedges, she stopped. The man who'd presumably betrayed the other aliens lay sprawled on the ground in a pool of blood, so much blood that little rivers trickled between the plaza's mosaic stones. The dark-haired woman bent over him, her face contorted in grief, and Mary questioned her interpretation of what had just happened. *Had* this guy betrayed her? What was going on? The alien with the gray braid yanked on the younger woman's arm, trying to pull her to her feet. When she resisted, the third alien joined in.

A movement behind them sparked Mary's attention, and she glanced up to see a misty figure hovering in the plaza. As soon as she noticed it, the figure blinked out of sight.

Mary resisted the urge to squeeze her eyes shut. She could worry later about whether she was seeing things. For now, she had to deal with what was right in front of her. Namely, the box with the Pearl Knife, which the screaming alien still held tightly under her arm. These people weren't fighters—or at least, Mary didn't think they were—and they were distracted. There were three of them, yes, and Mary had just come out of a major fight. Still, she thought she could take them.

And yet, she stood rooted to the plaza, unable to convince herself to act. She'd hurt Goldi in New York when she'd accidentally shot her grapple hook instead of her stunner, and she *was* tired. It could happen again. The Trap was one thing, and Monster; they were fighters.

These people—these aliens—were something else. And one of them was bleeding. Mary had been born to vigilantism through fire and blood; violence didn't stop her, not anymore. Yet the woman alien's screams echoed in her ears, twisting with the memory of Goldi's pained cries, and the sight of the man's blood burned her eyes like an accusation.

So Mary hesitated. Out in the open. With the Pearl Knife mere steps away. Time seemed to slow, but it couldn't have been more than the space of a heartbeat, or maybe two. Enough time for the older alien to notice her.

"Sloane!" the alien cried, and the dark-haired woman's head whipped up. She met Mary's eyes.

"Stop," Mary said, because she didn't know what else to say. She should shoot a sedative dart—three darts—but she couldn't get her hands to move to where she'd clamped the weapons under her sleeves. She was frozen. Useless. "We can help you."

Right. They'd help the people who'd just stolen from them. If that didn't sound like a trap, Mary didn't know what would. And she couldn't think of anything that would make her sound more convincing.

The dark-haired woman—Sloane?—staggered to her feet, tears streaming down her face. She glanced back across the plaza, to the spot where the ghost figure had disappeared. And then her shoes... melted.

It was the best description for what happened next. The alien's shoes melted, the soles flattening until they met one another in the middle, forming a kind of board. Like a tiny snowboard. In the middle of L.A.

But not even Mary could make a joke about it. With a gentle hum from her now-connected shoes, the dark-haired woman lifted off from the ground and flew away across the plaza, with her friends following behind her.

Dumbstruck, Mary watched until they'd disappeared. Hover boards. They had hover boards.

On most days, she'd have been impressed. She'd have taken what she'd seen to the lab, or HQ, to consult with the engineers there. She'd have tried to build something.

Today, as her enemies retreated into the sky with the Pearl

Knife in their clutches, she could only see defeat.

———

Mary wasn't sure she'd ever felt tentative about anything in her life, unless she counted swimming lessons at the age of three, when she hadn't wanted to get into the pool. And she couldn't even remember that herself. Only her parents' stories about the SoCal girl who hadn't wanted to get wet.

Now, she was home—or she was about to be. Not in California, but rising through the floor of the garage behind Niagara Falls in the back of the unmarked sedan that had picked Mary and El up from the airport.

The headquarters of the League of Independent Operatives. The place she'd been raised. The home she'd abandoned for the last four months while she tracked down the league's retired members and tried to bring them to justice.

For years, she'd longed for this place. When she was off 'playing' in her celebrity persona—formerly her secret identity —for weeks at a time, or when she'd been assigned to months of stakeouts, she'd longed for LIO HQ and its cave-like garage, its titanium corridors, its labs and sparring rooms and libraries. She'd always felt most comfortable here, like she belonged. She'd been homesick for this place more often than she could recall.

And now she felt *tentative*, of all things. She could have avoided the feeling, since El had wanted her to stay in L.A., but she hadn't been willing to leave her sister alone. She hadn't wanted to be alone herself.

Now, she almost regretted her choice. If she'd had something handy to punch, she would have. As the car shuddered up the final incline, she had to work not to hold her breath.

"Home sweet home," Eloise said, and Mary jumped. Her

sister had barely spoken on the cross-country trip back to HQ, merely assuring Mary that she was still OK before lapsing back into silence.

When Will had parted Dolly from the Knife and transferred its powers to Eloise, Dolly had gotten sick. She'd aged prematurely, her hair wiped from brown to white. She'd gone *blind*.

Now, the Knife had been wrenched from Eloise's consciousness, and Mary was here worrying about whether HQ was still home. Not only was she a failure, she was a selfish one. Excellent.

Eloise's eyes were bloodshot, puffy bruises pooling beneath them, her dark complexion paled to ash. Mary practically expected her sister to age twenty years before her eyes. Wasn't that what Dolly had done, when she'd given up the Knife? Slowly, yes, but still. When Mary looked at her, though, Eloise attempted a smile.

Mary grabbed Eloise's hand, resting on the seat between them, and gave it a squeeze. "We're going to get the Knife back. Wait and see."

"Not sure I want that smartass back in my brain," Eloise said, but Mary just squeezed her hand again. She couldn't pretend to understand El's relationship with the weird Knife that gave her powers, but she knew it was important. And she was going to help, in any way she could. Tentative as she felt, the thought of leaving HQ—of venturing back into the world— made her hands clammy, and she hoped El wouldn't notice. Or that she'd chalk it up to homecoming nerves.

The car doors swung open, letting in the musty, cave-like air of the garage. Mary took a deep breath and let go of El's hand.

The garage looked the same as it always had, with rows of vehicles ready to bust out on a mission at a moment's notice. It smelled like water and oil, and damp rock. A hundred memories crowded through Mary's mind—lying on her back under SUVs to equip them with tracking devices, bending beneath sedan hoods to upgrade engines—and she blinked them away.

The place looked the same as it always had, except for one thing: Nathan Pearce was here.

Ex-cop, ex-boyfriend, and now, a LIO initiate. She was well aware of his presence here, though she hadn't expected to see him so soon. But here he was, in dark jeans and a leather jacket, leaning against the hood of her favorite silver smart car. The sight of him tugged painfully at her chest, as if someone had caught hold of her ribcage with a fishhook and was attempting to yank her across the room. Toward him, away from him, it hardly mattered. Pain was pain.

At least he still had a fading bruise around his eye, from where she'd punched him in Long Beach. A small comfort. He deserved bruises, after the way he'd abandoned her.

Nathan cleared his throat, and Mary turned to offer Eloise an arm for support, which her sister rejected with a small wave of her hand. Mary hung back beside her, in case El should stumble. In case she should change her mind, or need anything at all.

"I heard you were coming back," Nathan said. His voice was deep, the Northern English accent as strong as ever. "Thought I'd meet you."

What, so he could torture her? Regale her with tales of her failings? Or maybe betray her again? That would be a nice twist, only she wouldn't fall for it. Not ever again. Yes, Mary was back at LIO, but that didn't change the fact that Nathan had chosen the league over her, right after she'd learned of their involvement in her parents' deaths. It didn't change the fact that he'd left her.

Eloise paused, and Mary's determination to stay beside her

sister faltered beside her desire to escape this room, and Nathan's presence, as fast as she could. But if he thought he could intimidate her into running, he was dead wrong. She might have to fight the urge, but she'd stay at El's side. Where she belonged.

And she wouldn't look at Nathan, though she felt his eyes boring into her. She only looked at El.

"Nathan," Eloise said, her voice a quiet rasp where it usually sounded clear and strong. "Everyone made it back safely?"

Mary kept her gaze locked on Eloise, but Nathan must have nodded, because El said, "Good. Get Ire and Steve. Gail and Pete, too, but no one else. Tell them we'll meet in half an hour."

Eloise had instructed Mary not to tell anyone about the Pearl Knife's disappearance. Not yet. And now she was assembling her closest allies, only the most trusted. Mary tried not to balk at the idea that 'most trusted' included Nathan. This was league business, and whatever she felt about it, Nathan was a part of it now. Mary could only blame herself for getting him involved with LIO in the first place.

Did Eloise really intend to keep the Knife's disappearance a secret? Mary tried to glean the answer from El's expression, but her sister had shuttered her intentions behind a wall of eerie calm. When Eloise didn't want to be read, there was no point in trying.

"Your office?" Nathan asked.

"No," Eloise said, "bring them to my room."

Mary blinked, startled. Eloise never held meetings in her room. She held meetings in her office, where she could use all her intimidating props and hold court in front of her huge video screen. A fresh surge of worry clenched at Mary's stomach, and she had to stop herself from reaching out to make Eloise accept her help.

As if she'd ever had any success making Eloise do anything.

"Will do," Nathan said, and Eloise started walking again. Mary stayed at her side, ready to leap in if she missed a step. If she so much as sneezed.

"Are you just going to ignore me?" Nathan asked, and though Mary didn't turn, she knew he was speaking to her.

Mary didn't answer. If he expected her to forgive him for leaving her in October, he'd be waiting a long time. She might be willing to work with LIO again, but that didn't mean she trusted him.

She didn't know how to deal with him being here. She would, in all likelihood, have to speak to him eventually, though she didn't know how she'd manage it without losing her temper. Or her composure.

Eloise glanced at Mary, lifting her eyebrows slightly, but Mary just shook her head. She didn't have to speak to him now. She had to help El to her room, help form a game plan, and help get the Pearl Knife back.

NATHAN HAD NEVER SEEN the inside of Eloise's bedroom before. She might be LIO's leader, but her quarters shared the same layout of the others he'd seen, and the one he called his own: a small seating area that shared the space with her neatly made bed, a mini refrigerator, a wall-sized screen that mimicked a window with a garden view. Simple. Clean. The setup always reminded Nathan of a hotel room. As little as any of them were in their rooms, in did make sense.

He'd felt awkward stepping inside, as if he might accidentally find his boss in her nightgown. He'd never had any qualms about knocking on her office door, but this just felt... strange.

He was the last to arrive, since Steve had sped ahead instead of keeping him company on the way here—possibly, Nathan suspected, in hopes of stealing a one-on-one moment with Eloise. He was aware of them all, in his peripheral vision, but his treacherous eyes were drawn immediately to Mary. She lounged in a flower-print armchair that looked as if it hadn't been reupholstered since the 1970s, at least based on its orange and pea-green color scheme. She had her feet sprawled out as if she meant to look casual. To Nathan's eyes, she simply looked exhausted. She didn't acknowledge his entrance, any more than she'd acknowledged his greeting in the garage.

Not that he blamed her. He probably shouldn't have imposed on her return to HQ like that, but he still thought it was a better move to get the reunion over with, rather than dreading a public meeting in a random hallway.

Or a public beating. Because the last time they'd met, when he'd helped save her from the Trap's poison-torture session, Mary had tried to kill him. Or she'd attacked him, anyway. She might not have intended to murder him, though he wouldn't have placed a strong bet on that. At the very least, Nathan was certain that only Mary's weakened state had prevented her from breaking his arm.

He deserved it, of course. Still, he wished she'd give him a chance to explain, to apologize. The sight of her there, as comfortable back at HQ as she was in any room she entered, ignited an ache of regret in his chest. So many mistakes.

But she wasn't the only person in the room. A heartbeat, two, and he forced himself to look around. Steve, Nathan's former police colleague—and a former LIO operative—sat on a loveseat that matched Mary's hideous chair. Nathan hadn't expected Steve to return to HQ with them after the fight, given how little he trusted the league. Yet here he was, his striped fedora tipped at an angle on his head.

Steve's father, Flick, had helped them to win the fight in L.A., but Nathan had no idea where the elder super-speeder had vanished to after that. Had he gone back to his hiding place? Or was he simply absent because Eloise hadn't summoned him to this meeting?

After the battle in L.A., Nathan had been tied up with the Wave operatives he'd freed from LIO's prison. He'd seen them off, and he'd come straight back here with Steve. He had no idea what had gone wrong after that, or why Eloise hadn't simply filled them in through coms or video chat. Whatever it was, though, it had Mary glancing frequently at Eloise, worry pinching her bloodshot eyes.

Nathan settled himself beside the door, leaning back and scanning the room in an attempt to hide the way his eyes kept darting to Mary. Against his will, too. Like she was a magnet, and he was nothing but a poor, subservient splinter of metal.

The league's public liaison, Gail, sat beside Steve, her red hair twisted into a messy bun, while Ire leaned against the wall beside the couch. The huge man practically looked wedged into the space. And finally there was Pete, the head of surveillance, who perched on the couch's arm, clenching his hands in his lap. Nathan wondered if he, at least, had an idea what this meeting could be about, or why it couldn't have waited until everyone was rested.

Because they clearly needed rest. Eloise was sitting on the edge of her bed, hands on her knees. Her face was drawn, almost as if she'd lost weight in the half-day that had passed since the fight with the LIO retirees. They'd returned here victorious, having captured most of LIO's original members, and yet... and yet, something serious must have gone wrong. What the hell had happened back there?

Eloise cleared her throat, as if to quiet a room already silent with dread. "There's a reason we're meeting here, rather than in my office." Her voice sounded soft, as if the effort of speaking was almost too much to handle. "This news is for the people in this room, and no one else."

She took a deep breath, and Nathan had to fight to keep from holding his own breath as she gripped the bedspread in her fists. "The Pearl Knife was stolen," Eloise said.

Steve leapt to his feet, nearly upsetting the coffee table. Ire straightened from against the wall, his face red, while Pete's drained of all color. Gail began to cry.

Only Mary sat unmoved by Eloise's words. She'd been there. She already knew.

Nathan rested a hand against the wall behind him, anchoring himself as best he could while the world turned somersaults around him. He'd been trained to remain calm in stressful situations. He ought to be able to summon the skills now, and yet somehow he felt an inch from breaking, his heart making a bid to pound its way out of his chest. The Pearl Knife was the center of everything they did here, the powerful yet enigmatic engine that drove the League of Independent Operatives. Without it, what were they?

But that wasn't why Mary was staring at Eloise, muscles tense. Like she was ready to leap up and catch her sister if Eloise somehow toppled off the bed, lest she shatter on the floor.

No, Mary wasn't concerned about the league's greatest asset. Nathan knew her, and he knew she had to be thinking of what the Knife's absence had done to Dolly. What it might do to Eloise. Nathan clenched his fists, unable—unwilling—to picture Eloise wasting away as her mother had. She was too strong.

"Was it Dolly?" Ire asked, practically baring his teeth. Nathan half expected him to storm out the door to drag her back here at Eloise's word, old woman or not.

"How?" Steve breathed, still standing between the couch and the rickety coffee table. He, too, looked ready to leap out the door. "No one can touch it but you."

Eloise looked at her hands, and Nathan could see tears glittering in her eyes. Did she feel the Knife in her mind, at a distance? Or had she been completely severed from it? "They had a device."

"We're dealing with powers we didn't even know existed," Mary said, her voice as quiet as Eloise's. With his full view of the room, Nathan watched the attention shift from LIO's leader to the reckless operative who'd gone rogue. Again, he had to fight to keep breathing. Would they listen to her, after she'd ostracized herself from the league? Worked actively against them, even? Nathan, for one, hadn't been at all certain that Mary would agree to return.

Mary shook her head, as if she couldn't quite believe what she was about to say. "Aliens. They look like humans, but they came through this golden portal. They locked the Knife in a box, and they ran. I tried to catch them, but..." She shook her head again, wedging her bottom lip between her teeth.

But they'd gotten away, and tenacious, over-confident Mary had let them go. Or so she seemed to view it. Nathan had spent weeks by her side, watching her make one reckless choice after another as she crashed after her enemies. Mary didn't just let the bad guys go—not without a fight—and she certainly didn't blame herself when they slipped through her fingers.

Mary made plans. She assembled tech. She gave orders.

This Mary was different. This Mary looked defeated. Nathan steadied himself as best he could, stifling the urge to go to her. She wouldn't thank him for that.

She leaned forward in the chair, gripping the armrests as if expecting everyone to start making accusations. "I think they might be stuck here. On Earth."

It should have been a hopeful statement, one that made them all sit up. Gail should be getting out a notebook. Pete should be ready to chime in with ideas for surveillance-based mission assistance, and Ire should be relaxing back against the wall.

Instead, Mary's words were met with silence, everyone too stunned to move. Tears still streamed down Gail's cheeks.

"What makes you think so?" Steve asked, and Nathan

caught the coldness in his tone. The protectiveness. As if he half suspected Mary of losing the Knife on purpose.

Nathan knew better. What did the others think?

"They'd have gone back through their portal if they could have," Mary said. "But it closed, and they didn't reopen it. They're trapped."

"And that means we can find them." Eloise sat up a little straighter on the bed, her voice picking up a hint of its former snap. "I'm sending you out in teams, as soon as everyone gets a few hours of sleep. Steve and Nathan together, and Mary and Ire. Gail and Pete, I need you on surveillance, reviewing the tapes, looking for clues. You can use my office instead of the main lab. I'll join you when I can. Dad's on his way, too."

Nathan glanced at Gail and Pete, but they didn't seem at all startled to learn that Eloise's father had mysteriously returned from the dead. She must have filled them in, at some point.

Mary sat up in her chair blinking as if she'd just woken up from a long sleep. "I'd work better from HQ."

Nathan couldn't keep his jaw from dropping as he stared at her, his brain struggling to compute. The Mary he knew was all action. When she wasn't moving, she planned. When someone held her back, she shattered her restraints. Up until now, Nathan might have been able to blame Mary's defeat on her concern for Eloise, and her obvious fatigue, but planning to stay at HQ, instead of heading into the field? Six months ago, that suggestion from someone else would have earned them a defiant look, and possibly a punch in the face.

And he wasn't the only one who thought so. Everyone in the room was looking at her, this time with expressions of shock. These people all knew how unlikely it was that Mary would rather stay put than go out on a mission. An important one. They'd just heard news of aliens and a missing Pearl

Knife, yet they still had the capacity to look surprised. That was how out of character it was, as if she'd just announced her intention to live forever in her celebrity persona, or join forces with the Trap.

Why was she sidelining herself? Or trying to. Based on the way Eloise's lips thinned, Nathan wondered if Mary would find herself shoved out the door, anyway.

If Mary noticed their surprise, she didn't let on. "I can help with surveillance. Gail's too busy to add another job to her plate, especially if we're supposed to be keeping this a secret. And whoever finds the Knife may need a device of their own, for transportation. In case something happens to that other box. I can work on that."

There was a beat of silence that stretched a little too long for comfort. Eloise was studying Mary as if her face might give something away, but Mary just looked back at her calmly. "Are you sure?" Eloise asked finally.

Mary nodded. "Positive. You need me here."

Nathan found himself wishing she'd allowed Eloise to convince her. He didn't understand what she could be thinking. He didn't understand her at all.

Eloise let out a breath. "All right. Ire and Steve, you two will head back out to California."

Ire glanced at Steve, frowning, while Steve merely continued to watch Eloise. Interesting dynamic there. Nathan knew why Eloise wouldn't have paired him with Mary, but he wondered if she'd also been looking to keep those two apart.

Eloise ignored their suspicious looks, or pretended not to see them. "They don't know this world, and they likely don't have IDs or money. They shouldn't have gotten too far."

"Except that they have hoverboards," Mary said.

Steve sat back down on the couch and leaned his elbows on his knees. "They have *what?*"

Mary sighed. "They pulled a *Back to the Future* on me. That's how they got away."

Nathan studied her face. She couldn't possibly be blaming herself for this. Could she? For a few weeks, he'd felt like he knew her, and pretty well, too. Now, she almost seemed like a different person.

Eloise stood. "Let's assume they ditched the... hover-boards... as soon as they could. If they want to stay off the radar on Earth, they'll have to walk around like everyone else. And if not, we'll see it on the news soon enough. Get some rest. We're going to need it."

The others recognized Eloise's dismissal and headed for the door. Nathan considered trying to catch Mary again, but before he could move toward her, Eloise called him over.

"What happened to your Wave operatives?" she asked, and Nathan felt Mary's steps slow as she followed the others toward the hall.

Up until yesterday, the league had been hiding a few dozen wrongly accused Wave members on their prison level. After learning the truth of their innocence, Nathan had released them. They'd helped in L.A., but they were gone now. Which was as it should be, of course.

Nathan slipped his fingertips into his pockets, hoping this wouldn't be an issue. Eloise had seemed supportive of the move, at least after the fight. "They wanted to go back to Wave. So I sent them back."

At that, Mary whipped back around. "You did what?"

Not the moment he wanted her attention. Although it might be safer to assume she'd never pay him any unless she could yell at him. Maybe it was best to get it out of the way. "I sent them back to Wave," Nathan said. "Where they belong."

Mary's cheeks flushed red, but she just shook her head and

hurried out the door. As if she wouldn't have done precisely the same thing. At least she'd spoken to him?

"All right," Eloise said. "Not what I'd hoped, but I get it."

"If I hadn't let them go, they'd still be prisoners." When he'd released Dr. Gordon, Jo, and the other Wave operatives, he'd promised them they'd be free. Really free, not indentures to the league.

Eloise sat back down on her bed, and Nathan understood he was meant to go now. Instead, he said, "I think we could team up with them. Maybe open up a line of communication with Wave."

She was willing enough to work with Wave operatives outside of formal negotiations. Why not contact Wave directly? See if they could make amends?

Eloise leaned her hands back on the comforter, propping herself up to look at him. "And why would we do that?"

Nathan did his best to make his expression casual. "It's like Mary said. We're dealing with powers we didn't know existed. Maybe it's time to see if we could find some common ground."

Eloise took a deep breath. Let it out. "I can't risk it. They chose to go back, and that's fine, but it also means no contact. Understood?"

Nathan opened his mouth to argue, but Eloise looked so exhausted. Not fragile, exactly, but this was not the time to push back. He nodded. "Understood."

4 / ELOISE

ELOISE'S MIND felt like an underwater cavern. It was like coming home to a space she'd known all her life, only to find it transformed into a limitless network of dark tunnels. As if something crucial had been ripped out, taking a piece of her with it. When she closed her eyes, she could practically see the dangling roots, the sparks. The damage.

The whole meeting had happened underwater, too, or so it felt to her. Like a dream. People spoke, expressed shock, and she'd had to strain not only to listen, but to process. To respond like the leader they expected her to be.

The Pearl Knife was gone. Eloise didn't know what sort of box that man had trapped it in, only that it had cut off her connection with the blade as though it had never been there. Except for the damage, the dangling tendrils of neurons or whatever the fuck happened in the brain that had made it expand around the Knife's consciousness. What mattered was that she could *feel* it, reaching for nothing.

She wished Agnes were here. But Eloise had dissolved that bridge once and for all by refusing to trust the former league scientist after the Las Vegas fight. How could she, with Agnes now working for Wave? Their sworn enemies?

Whatever Nathan believed, the bad blood between LIO and Wave went too deep for healing. LIO had spent too long framing Wave for crimes they hadn't committed—like the murder of Mary's parents—and for all of Dolly's admittedly numerous sins, Wave was hardly blameless. Eloise couldn't bring herself to trust an organization that had only protected certain areas of the world from rampant terrorism, like a bodyguard shielding only their clients. Even if she could, it was impossible to see past some of their tactics. Like sending a thirteen-year-old Nathan Pearce into an office building with a bomb.

They'd never find common ground. The prisoners' return to Wave only underscored that fact. Not that Eloise didn't understand their decision, but still.

The sound of running water snapped her bedroom back into focus, though her eyes hadn't been closed, and she blinked. Steve Taylor stepped out of her tiny bathroom, using his enhanced speed to leap across the room and hand her a cool washcloth. She took it, though she glared at him while she did. Or at least, she tried to; her body felt sluggish. Slow to react to her reeling brain's commands.

Steve knelt before her and lifted her washcloth-holding hand to her forehead, and Eloise realized she'd just been sitting there. Staring at it. The thing was pink. How had something *pink* made it into her rooms?

"I won't pretend anyone was fooled by that performance," Steve said, his baritone voice laced with worry. He'd shed all his affectations, his fedora—it was sitting on the coffee table—and his fancy clothes. He was just... Steve. "Your acting skills are abysmal, as always. They might be afraid to ask, but I'm not. Are you all right?"

The cloth was cool against her skin, so pleasant she wanted to weep with the relief of it. She'd practically felt her colleagues

—her friends—recalling the images of her mother's failing condition as she talked. Gail's tears, Pete's solemn stare, Ire's furious shock. And Mary, with her vigilant worry. As if Eloise herself now teetered an inch from death. *Don't you?* A voice in her head whispered, but she shoved it away. There was too much to do.

"They're worried about the Knife," she said, the lie bitter on her tongue.

"They're worried about *you*." Steve hadn't removed his hand, and she realized he was rubbing her back, gentle. Eloise wanted to lean into it, to breathe the light spiced coconut smell of his cologne, to bury her face in his neck and cry. Or sleep. Or both.

Startled by the instinct to lean on him—on anyone—Eloise lurched away, scooting farther down the foot of the bed. Steve dropped the cloth, and it fell to the carpet with a wet smack. What was it about him that made her feel so off balance?

"Sorry," Steve said. "I'm sorry, El, I didn't mean—"

"You should go," Eloise said, doing her best to summon a businesslike tone. Whenever she did that, though, her voice rasped out of her throat as if she'd spent hours screaming. To the best of her knowledge, she hadn't.

Steve stood, swooping to retrieve the cloth and return it to the bed. "And you should rest." He wiped his hands on his pants. "Deal with the rest of it later. We can hold down the fort."

Especially with Mary determined to stay here. What was that about, anyway? Mary had never turned down an opportunity for a mission, for action, in her life. Eloise's head spun, and she pushed the thought away. Later. She'd deal with it later.

Steve stood there, thumbs jammed through his belt loops, as if waiting for her to promise she'd sleep. The joke was on him; Eloise wasn't sure she could do much else.

The Pearl Knife was gone. Her power, her companion, her... well, her friend. Gone.

Eloise's phone buzzed with an incoming call, and she stood to retrieve it from her bedside table. Before she could take a single step, Steve was blurring across the room to snatch the device ahead of her. Of all the enhanced abilities to contend with, his speed could definitely be the most annoying. Useful, sure. Until he decided to use it against her.

"Travis Bertram," Steve said. "The government liaison kid?"

Eloise nodded. She didn't have the energy for Travis right now. "I'll call him back later."

Steve nodded, and a tightness around his mouth relaxed a touch. As if he'd expected to have to fight her on that.

The phone stopped ringing, and Steve set it back on the table. It shook with the notification of a voicemail—no doubt a huffy and demanding one.

As Steve made his way to the door, at normal speed this time, the phone gave a double buzz. Travis had texted her, too?

Steve, of course, got there first. "'Call me back within the hour, or expect a visit in the morning,'" he read. "That little— What are you doing?"

"I'm standing," Eloise said, though now she was moving toward her closet to retrieve a suitable jacket. She could toss it on over the clothes she was wearing now; Travis knew she'd just returned from a mission. He *was* a little... whatever Steve had been about to say.

"You should be resting," Steve said. "You're in shock. Your body is in shock. Let us—"

"You can't talk to Travis Bertram," Eloise said. "And he can't know anything is wrong, which means I can't call him from my bedroom. He'll expect a video call, as usual, from my office."

Steve pressed his lips together. "At least take it slow. He said within the hour."

Eloise jammed slippers onto her feet and made for the door. At her current pace, the trip might take her a full hour.

To her dismay, Steve followed her down the hall as she left the comfort of the residential wing and turned toward her office. The halls were quiet, and she realized she had no idea what time it was. The slippers suddenly seemed like a foolish choice for someone who wanted to keep the disaster a secret, but the few team members she passed only nodded to her respectfully and continued on their way.

They were probably just hoping she wouldn't stop them with a last pre-bedtime assignment. Or pre-breakfast. She started to glance at her phone, to check the time, but Steve still held it.

"You can go," she said, holding out a hand for the phone. He didn't give it to her. "Aren't you supposed to be packing for your trip?"

"Yeah, about that." He lifted a hand to scratch his head. "Ire doesn't exactly like me. We kind of got off on the wrong foot when I burst in here last month—"

"Whose fault is that?"

"—and I was thinking it'd be better if you paired us each with one of the new recruits. You know. Cover more ground that way, like you said. Before Mary bailed."

Eloise stopped at her door and snatched the phone out of his hand. If Ire was annoyed with Steve, it probably did stem from the fact that he'd tried to sneak into HQ through the back entrance. Earning himself a nice, violent welcome. "I don't know the recruits well enough yet to trust them. They haven't even seen HQ, and in case you've forgotten, there's an organization out there creating temporary abilities. They could have a plant working with the recruits. I can't tell them about the Knife."

Steve, of course, didn't even want to be a part of the league. Technically *wasn't* a part of it, and hadn't been for a long time. He didn't like them, claimed he didn't trust them. But he was still here, accepting missions, handing her cool cloths, and sticking to her heels like a worried grandmother.

He could remind her of those things, argue that perhaps he shouldn't be trusted himself. Instead, he just nodded. "Right. Of course. We'll make it work."

Because Eloise did trust him. In fact, she didn't know what she'd do when he finally decided to leave for good. All the more reason to keep her distance. Not get attached.

"You do that." She went into her office, shutting the door and drawing the lock without waiting for Steve's response.

Immediately, she wished she hadn't. It was a near thing, keeping herself from opening the door to call him back. Because her office was her office, the same as it had always been —with one glaring exception.

The glass case beside her desk held all her blades, the ones she'd practiced with for years in preparation for taking over her mother's title as the Pearl Knife. Now, the top shelf sat empty, its occupant dragged away by strangers. It felt more like a kidnapping than a theft, more like grief than any sort of material loss. The Knife spoke to her, sang to her, coordinated with her in a language she couldn't have described to anyone else. It was... well, maybe not a person. But an entity, capable of thought, of independence. Personality, definitely.

To be in her office alone, without the Knife... it felt like a hot poker in her gut.

Eloise took a moment to compose herself, walking around to the chair side of her desk to where the wall-sized screen showed Niagara Falls. The water gushed as it always had, oblivious to the tumult behind it.

Eloise leaned back against her desk, resting one hand on the back of her chair, and readjusted the web cam so that it faced her while also cutting out Travis's view of the knife case. She doubted he was observant enough to notice its absence, but she didn't take chances. When she was ready, she checked her reflection—tired, but acceptable—and took a final breath.

Travis answered so quickly that she thought he might have been sitting there with his finger poised over the screen, ready to accept her call. He still looked like a boy playing dress-up, too young and blond for the suit he wore. He'd fit better at a beer pong table. Or a daycare.

"Where the hell have you been?" Travis said, and for the first time in their brief acquaintance, he wasn't sitting with a pile of papers in front of him. He was actually looking at the camera.

At least his level of respect was about the same as always. "I've been on a plane from L.A."

"Planes have phones," Travis snapped. "Planes have email. I expect mission reports after you and your colleagues destroy an entire hotel. You're to keep me in the loop. It's part of the deal."

"I'll have to review the contracts," Eloise said dryly. Travis seemed to think LIO operated as an arm of the government now—one he controlled—rather than a separate, sanctioned entity. Which had been the original agreement. "Mary owns the hotel. Everything's fine."

"You think that stops the authorities from investigating? You think it stops the press from pounding on my door?"

Eloise rested a hand on her desk. Talking with Travis Bertram was like trying to reason with an angry two-year-old. "The press knows what happened. They were in on it."

Travis adjusted his perfectly straight tie, which merely made it crooked. "And now they're asking for comments. From me. *I* want to know what happened."

"And you'll get my full report in the morning," Eloise said, anger rising in her chest. "Forgive me if I'd like to get some sleep after saving the world. Again."

Travis tapped his fingers on the table. "My ass is on the line here, Ms. Reyna."

For god's sake, he talked like a cardboard department head in a political drama. Didn't the boy have a manager? A supervisor? Or had he won his job through nepotism? It was clear he had no idea what he was doing.

Before Eloise could form a response, Travis was talking again. "I'm coming to Niagara Falls. It's time I inspected your facility, and I want an in-person meeting."

"I hardly think that's necessary, Travis."

He glared at her, as if he expected her to call him 'Mr. Bertram.' Or 'sir.' Eloise narrowly stifled a snort at the thought of calling this kid 'sir' without breaking down into laughter.

"You do not understand the severity of the situation," Travis said. "I'll be there as soon as I clear the travel expenses."

"Well, enjoy the Amtrak from D.C. What is it, twelve hours? Thirteen? That's a long trip, to waste your time."

Travis actually stuck out his bottom lip. "I expect them to *fly* me there."

"On a government budget? Good luck." She shouldn't goad him, she knew that. Usually, she stuck with formal, blandly civil replies. But she was too tired, too grief stricken, to force herself tonight. She could apologize tomorrow. Maybe. For now, she'd enjoy it. "Thank you for your call, Travis. I'll talk to you soon."

"You'll *see* me soon," he said, like a correction.

Eloise ended the call, contemplating the disappointing lack

of a receiver to slam down for her own satisfaction. Video calls just weren't the same. She shut down the program and logged out of her system. As soon as everything was secure, she left her office, dreaming of bed and trying not to feel like she was making her escape.

Travis Bertram stared at his black computer screen, trying to tell himself that Eloise Reyna hadn't just hung up on him. She wouldn't dare. The leader of the League of Independent Operatives was reckless, yes, and damned slow to follow his orders, but she usually showed him respect. She understood their relationship.

The woman sitting across from him shifted on the uncomfortable faux-leather seat that served as a guest chair for meetings. "You see?" she said. "The league thinks they're in charge here. They've no respect for you."

Chloe Pearce was not a person he'd ever have expected to allow into his office in the first place. He'd only done so, in fact, because of her connection with the league. Her brother worked for them. Travis wasn't a politician to be lobbied—not yet, anyway—or wheedled into some course of action. But Chloe knew the league, and Travis had always prized his ability to assess the value of a formidable ally.

She was also a leader of the Enhanced Abilities Enforcement Association, an organization with a mission he couldn't help but agree with. Enhanced humans needed oversight, and the EAEA was working to mandate it through legislative channels. Specifically, through Travis.

Chloe leaned forward, her eyes eager beneath her orange-red bangs. "I trusted them, too. I was wrong to. We need to pivot. It's the only way."

Travis glanced down for some papers to shuffle, for something to give him time to form a response, but he'd cleaned off his desk in preparation for the call with the Pearl Knife. He tapped his fingertips on the desk, wondering if his friends would still be out at the bar by the time he finished here.

If Senator Jones would only leave for the night—passing by Travis's door on the way, of course, to see how hard he was working—then Travis would feel comfortable leaving, too. He needed to be noticed. He needed the senator to see him taking this assignment seriously.

Of course, they all seemed to think that assigning Travis to work with the League of Independent Operatives was a boon for him, an easy job with a pretty title to appease his powerfully rich family. LIO, the liaison committee believed, would watch over itself. As liaison, Travis was merely supposed to check up on them. To assist them.

He wanted more. And the league clearly needed a higher level of supervision.

Chloe was still watching him with a wide-eyed look pasted on her freckled face. Travis supposed she meant to look patient, expectant, but the expression made him think of a cat on the hunt. "I don't know enough not to trust them," Travis said finally, stifling a sigh. He tried to imagine cornering Senator Jones with accusations and no evidence beyond a few annoyances. The man would stare him down. Ask if this cake of an assignment was too much for a trust-fund kid to handle.

Travis rubbed his face. "They're highly regarded. I probably ought to cancel the trip."

Or the travel request, since the trip hadn't yet been approved.

Chloe sat back in her chair and crossed her legs. "I think they're hiding something."

"I saw no evidence of that." Except for Eloise's reticence to discuss the L.A. incident. And the shifted angle of the web cam, the slippers on her feet. Slippers! To talk to a government official! Her casual attitude was enough to make him red with rage.

Though even Travis could acknowledge that she had to be tired, as she'd said. And surely that lair of hers had cleaning crews that could knock equipment aside. There *were* explanations. Besides, his bosses didn't want complications and secrets. They wanted *simple*. Perhaps Travis would do well to keep his head down on this, at least until Eloise stepped further out of line.

A pause. Chloe examined her fingernails, eyebrows lifted high. "They don't respect you."

Travis looked down at the desk again. His hands were shaking, a bit. He pressed his palms into the polished wood, digging his fingernails into the scratches that marked this an old piece of furniture, but that only made the shaking worse.

"She hung up on you," Chloe said, and her words meant he couldn't even deny it to himself anymore. She *had* hung up on him. The bitch.

Chloe met his gaze again, her crystal blue gaze cutting across the space like ice. He could see how she'd make a good lobbyist, why her American colleagues had brought her over to help with their part of the crusade. "Think about it. If you prove they're lying—that they've committed crimes, even, which I'm absolutely sure they have—you'll be promoted. Out of this musty office, to a place with a decent view."

Real responsibilities. Staff. Maybe even an assistant, and a working radiator.

She leaned forward again, this time gripping the edge of his desk. "Think about it, Travis. You'll get an official commendation. You'll be a hero."

A hero. Travis did like the sound of that. "In that case, I'd better start packing."

AGNES WOULD HAVE THOUGHT that five-plus years living in LIO's behind-the-falls HQ, followed by four months living in Wave's undersea bubble—practically a small city, really—would have prepared her for any number of surprises, at least on the tech side of things. And it was true that she'd been only mildly surprised to find that in addition to the network of automated tunnels that stemmed away from the ocean hideout, Wave also maintained a fleet of submarines. Even Bradley Archer's midnight appearance at her door last night—this morning, technically—was hardly an uncommon occurrence, though his insistence on whisking her away from the dome had earned him a raised eyebrow from Agnes's wife, Tam.

Now, as the submarine broke the surface, the sight on the view screen before her actually made her jaw slip open.

"We call it the Yacht." Bradley hovered by Agnes's side, shooting her the occasional wary glance. Tam had given him an earful when he showed up, no doubt afraid he meant to tug Agnes away on another dangerous assignment. Only this time, Bradley didn't have a mission for her. He had a summons.

A summons to... a yacht, apparently, though Agnes had never seen anything like this vessel anchored in any fancy

Connecticut harbor. The ship loomed out of the sea before the low-lying submarine, its sides painted in a coating of reflective blue. Had the submarine been even a few hundred yards more distant, Agnes doubted she would have been able to see the thing at all.

And it was big. On one hand, the ship called to mind an aircraft carrier, its front end wide and flat. Good for assembling armies, and landing flying vehicles of various types. It made her stomach twist with unease. In the middle, though, it shifted to something more like a cruise ship, with a window-filled tower that rose gracefully through the center and culminated in a fin-like decoration. Or maybe it was meant to represent a wave.

No name painted on the side, no flags fluttering. Nothing but that blinking blue. Even watching from the screen, Agnes had to squint against the shards of light bouncing back from the sunrise.

"It must be invisible at night," she said, mentally trying to calculate their location based on the rising sun. She'd suspected the undersea bubble was several hours west of California; the ship must be hanging out even further in that direction.

"As invisible as you, when it wants to be," Bradley said. "Let's not keep the Committee waiting."

Agnes could practically hear the capital letter when he spoke. The Committee. After all these months with Wave, was she finally going to meet their leadership?

A short raft-ride later, Agnes was climbing up a rope ladder to stand on the deck of the ship. She could have flown from the raft to the deck, could have used the salty breeze as her escort, but she wasn't much for showing off. Though with Bradley around, she did have to stifle the urge.

As soon as their feet hit the deck, Bradley was moving again, his white-blond hair stirring in the ocean wind. The blue wasn't blinding from the deck; if anything, the sunset painted the ship in strips of sherbet pink and orange. The ocean stretched in every direction, the horizon impossibly far away.

"Why does the Committee want to see me?" Agnes asked as Bradley escorted her up a short set of stairs and into the yacht's interior. She'd been with Wave long enough not to be surprised by their appreciation for luxury; the undersea hideout was more of a resort than a bunker, though she suspected it could withstand nuclear war without so much as a shudder.

The interior of the mystery ship felt fit to entertain world leaders, pop stars, kings and queens. A crystal chandelier graced the entry, its smaller cousins lighting the passage that Bradley hurried down now. Lush carpeting, polished portholes. The smell of sea and chocolate.

Bradley ran his fingertip along the waist-high molding on the wall, as if checking for dust. "I don't know why the Committee wants you." He waved enthusiastically to a crew member in a bowtie who passed them with the barest nod. "I only know when they say jump, I buy a pogo stick."

Now *there* was an image. Bradley stopped abruptly and opened a door. "This is the end of my road. Good luck impressing them."

Agnes never knew if the man was trying to sound sarcastic, or if he truly meant it when he said things like that. Sparing him one last glance but unable to read any clues in his bland expression, she stepped through the door.

The room before her felt... not like a throne room, exactly, but fancy enough for one. Maybe a meeting of Parliament. The walls were lined in wooden panels, the furniture sparse as she made her way across a space that felt too large to be part of any kind of ship. The ceiling seemed low, but aside from the tipping floor, that was the only indication that they were currently at sea.

They'd purposely left the furnishings sparse—at least, so she suspected; a classic tactic—except for a half-circle of chairs at the far end of the room. Five people sat in them, watching silently as she took her time crossing the space. Agnes was half surprised to see their chairs sitting flat on the plush maroon carpet, rather than on a raised platform of some kind, the way royalty might. At least, in Agnes's imagination.

Nerves crawled through her chest, but she breathed slowly and reminded herself that she could turn invisible, fly, and launch things through the air if necessary. She could get out of here, if she had to.

At length, she stood before them. Behind a chair, actually, which faced all five of theirs. Her chair, she supposed. She had to stop herself from gripping the back of it for support. Agnes Jenson was a world-class scientist, an independent operative, and an asset to their organization. She would not be intimidated.

Channeling her inner Eloise, Agnes tipped up her chin and stared over the Committee's heads, waiting for them to speak.

"Go on, girl," someone said finally, and Agnes lowered her gaze enough to see that it was an older woman wearing jeans and a flowered shirt, her short hair dyed electric blue. "Sit."

"She's hardly a 'girl,' Gem." The second Committee member to speak was an East Asian man in an impeccably tailored suit, pocket handkerchief and all. Did he wear that thing all the time? Out here, at sea? Maybe he meant to impress her, though his colleagues didn't seem to feel the need. "You're welcome to sit, Ms. Jenson, or stand. Whatever makes you comfortable."

Agnes sat, smoothing her pants with her palms. "Do you rehearse these interactions," she said calmly, "or have you simply been working together long enough that the tactic comes naturally? Good cop, bad cop? Friendly interrogator versus hard-ass? And what do the rest of you do?"

The well-dressed man—the one who'd invited her to sit—smiled wryly as his neighbor laughed out loud. "Forgive us," he said, with a sideways glance at the laugher. "Especially Cole, for the outburst. They can't help it."

Was this man their leader? Elected, or otherwise? He certainly spoke like one.

"Of course I can't help it," Cole had light brown skin and close-cropped black hair, a notebook propped on their knee. "She called us all out. In the first thirty seconds. I like this one."

Agnes didn't smile back, nor did she relax. These three might be talkative, friendly even, but the other two Committee members had yet to utter a word. A very elderly woman sat on the far end of the group, a cane propped against her chair. She watched her colleagues silently with sharp-eyed wariness. And at the opposite end of the semi-circle, a young man lounged back in his chair, examining his nails as if anything else in the world would interest him more than this conversation.

"We just want to ask you some questions," the well-dressed man said, and Agnes turned her attention back to him. "My name is Jian, and these are my colleagues. Fran, Gemma, Cole, and Matthew. Together, we oversee Wave's operations."

No last names in this room, apparently. Except for her own. Agnes nodded her best 'it's nice to meet you, maybe' nod.

Jian gave her a small smile, as if he understood entirely. She couldn't help liking him, his apparent openness, but still. A little caution went a long way. "You've had recent contact with the League of Independent Operatives," he said.

It wasn't a question. Agnes thought of Eloise's call a few days ago, her request for help in the fight against the rogue LIO retirees. Agnes had refused to help, and clearly they hadn't needed it, anyway. They'd won.

Agnes met the man's gaze. "I won't give you their secrets. That wasn't part of the agreement when I joined you."

The young man snorted, but didn't look up. The blue-haired woman, Gem, barked a dry laugh. A mirthful group, weren't they? "Secrets?" Gem said. "LIO *has* no more secrets. You're here because the Pearl Knife asked you for help, and you spoke on behalf of our organization."

Ah. So this was a disciplinary hearing, then. A wrist slap, or something more serious? "Am I in trouble?" Agnes asked, keeping her voice carefully calm.

She could fly. She could turn invisible. But she couldn't reach her wife and daughter, currently living behind Wave's underwater walls. If Wave held them hostage... she shook her head, willing the panic away. She'd joined up with Wave for a reason, believing in their integrity, and so far she'd seen no evidence of foul intentions on their part.

Glances passed through the Committee members, except for Matthew, who still smirked at his nails. "No," Jian said, after what felt like an eternity, and Agnes had the distinct impression that this had been discussed—at length—before her arrival. "You made the decision we'd have made. But with all the recent commotion, it occurs to us that we've neglected to properly initiate you into our organization."

"You mean you tossed me into a lab and forgot my former employers have the resources to contact me?" Agnes asked.

"Something like that," Cole said.

The older woman—Fran?—hadn't yet spoken. Hadn't made a sound. Agnes imagined Fran and Matthew teaming up against her, and the three in the middle voting them down. If they mistrusted her, she suspected this conversation wouldn't be the end of it, no matter any 'official' decisions.

"I won't give away your secrets, either," Agnes said. "I have no desire for contact with LIO. Eloise just... She was desperate."

Cole tapped their fingers on their knee, watching her carefully. "Oh, we know that. We'd be having a very different discussion if we thought otherwise."

The ship rocked gently, the chandeliers tinkling above their heads, and Agnes had to stop herself from gripping the arm of her chair. It was bolted down, she realized. Made sense.

"We simply felt the need to educate you," Jian said. His shoes shone, and Agnes wondered if he had a more important meeting scheduled after this one. Did the Committee live on the ship? Or did they make their homes around the globe, fitting in with everyday people? "We'd like to learn more about your hopes for this position. To ask your advice from time to time."

Agnes tried to read between the lines, to understand what he was truly saying. Did he mean they were grooming her? That they wanted her for a spy? Or something else entirely? It felt, rather ludicrously, like a review session with the boss. On the whole, Agnes preferred an honest conversation, or even an argument, to this circumspect talk.

She only hoped they wouldn't insist on sending her on missions again. If they did, she'd have to resign. Assuming they'd allow that.

"Eloise will come to us again," Gemma said, and Agnes met the woman's brown-eyed gaze. An enhance ability, or merely a guess? "Do you honestly believe an alliance between our organizations would hurt us?"

Agnes thought of the desperation in El's voice when she'd called, her desperation at not being able to control even her own people. The league left a trail of destruction in its wake, clinging fast to its reputation despite layers upon layers of lies that were destined to unravel, as all lies did. Eloise even accepted the sanctioning of the U.S. government, without bothering to fill them in on LIO's crimes. Or Wave's innocence. She never would.

And Eloise hadn't trusted Agnes in Las Vegas. They'd captured those criminals together—Agnes and Will had done most of the work, in fact—and still Eloise had refused to let Wave contain the threat. She didn't trust Agnes, or Wave.

"I do believe that," Agnes said. "I think a collaboration could mean the end of Wave. For good this time."

Another round of glances traced through the group, and Agnes tried to read who'd fallen on which side of this conversation when they'd discussed it before her arrival. They presented a united front—sort of—but clearly there'd been a conversation. Probably a heated one.

She couldn't read the glances. She didn't know these people. Not half as well as they seemed to know her.

Finally, the old woman on the end stood, swiping her cane from where it balanced against her chair. Deep lines scored her cheeks and forehead, the veins of her hands standing out against her pale skin. She placed her cane down in the carpet with an authoritative thump. "In that case," she said, "I'll be showing you to your new assignment."

As Agnes followed her out of the not-a-throne-room, she couldn't help wondering if she'd just passed some kind of a test.

BY THE TIME SLOANE, Alex, and Hilda made it to the edge of their current landmass to stand on a beach, the sun was sinking toward the horizon, and Sloane had long since stopped noticing the strange looks this planet's inhabitants kept throwing her way. She and the others had stowed their hov-tiles, but there was nothing she could do about their clothes, which were obviously still strange enough for comment.

Hot enough for discomfort, too. The spring-like weather made hours of walking in space-appropriate outfits practical torture. Sloane had contemplated slicing her long sleeves at the shoulder, but she didn't know where they would sleep tonight, or how cold it would be. Small as it might seem after what they'd just endured, she had no more room in her brain for another regret.

She still held the box that contained the Blade of Starlight, had cradled it under her arm as they traversed the strange city. Miles and miles of pavement, often lined with the strange ragged trees, the vehicles coughing off-putting fumes as they whizzed by. This appeared to be a sizable urban center, yet no space-bound ships roared out of hidden ports, and no magna-trains rumbled by overhead. There was nothing more impressive than the occasional atmosphere-tethered airplane.

Sloane's stomach had been growling painfully since well before they reached the coast. No galactic currency here, at least according to the program that scrolled translations across Sloane's vision.

The app knew a few useful things, though. First, that this planet was called Earth. How it could even contain data on the planet's existence, when Sloane had never heard of it—nor had Alex or Hilda—she couldn't begin to guess. Until today, she hadn't realized anyone had ever left the Parse Galaxy at all.

This planet, apparently, made its home in a galaxy called the Milky Way. She'd never heard of it, either.

A row of trucks sat along the edge of the beach, where strange but delicious smells wafted across the sand to where Alex and Hilda cooled their blistered feet in the salt water. The food smelled of sweet pastry and spiced meats, and while Sloane didn't understand the decision to serve these things from the open side of a truck, she'd have eaten anything out of any one of them.

It almost felt like a betrayal to Oliver that she could even think of eating right now, when the box that held the Blade was still smeared with his blood. The box he'd shoved into her arms as if she could save the world.

He'd known her well enough to know that wasn't true. But then again, he hadn't exactly been flush with options.

Sloane removed her boots and joined the other two women in their wading, watching a handful of people as they paddled brightly colored boards out to sea. The boards hardly looked seaworthy, and for a moment Sloane thought this world might have more technology than it originally appeared to.

But then a wave rolled toward the shore, and the swimmers

leapt on to their boards to ride the cresting water back to the beach.

"They look ridiculous," Sloane said.

Alex shrugged. "No more ridiculous than space racers."

She had a point. But then, Sloane had always thought that the people who raced through vacuum on specialized hov-tiles —wearing specialized suits, of course—needed their heads thoroughly checked.

Gray-haired Hilda glared at Sloane and Alex as though they were personally responsible for her aching feet. "We need to figure out what we're going to do."

"Right," Sloane said, running a hand through her tangled hair. "We need food. How do we obtain currency?"

Alex blinked at her. "We're supposed to be thieves."

"Well, I'm not," Sloane said. "I'm a med student."

"You keep saying that," Alex said. "And then you keep trying to steal stuff."

Sloane cringed, thinking of the disastrous attempt on that casino. "Trying being the operative word."

Hilda scoffed. "I mean we need to figure out what to do about *that*." She pointed a shaking finger at the box under Sloane's arm. "About being stuck here, and about finding a way back before Oliver's associates reach the *Moneymaker* and use Alex's wormhole to come after us for the Blade."

"Oh, that," Sloane said. "I figured we'd reach out to Oliver's contacts and tell them the coordinates of the ship so they can let us back into our galaxy. Then we can give them the Blade, collect the bounty, and go home."

It wouldn't be necessary, had Alex created a button or something that could open a wormhole from this side. Though Sloane supposed she *had* pushed the scientist into activating the portal before it was ready, for the sake of chasing this bounty.

It was a really good bounty.

Alex licked her lips and exchanged a glance with Hilda, whose face had gone as gray as her hair. The glance said 'we're really crew, and you're really not, and you have no clue what you're doing.' Even though, to Sloane's knowledge, neither of them had ever stolen anything, either. A strange kind of a thieving crew her uncle had assembled.

That was why they'd had Oliver. The thought of him sent hot bile rising into her throat, and she swallowed hard, pushing the image of his last moments savagely out of her head. "What's the problem?" she asked. "What do we care about this Blade thing? We care about getting home. Someone should collect the bounty."

She hoped she sounded more certain than she felt.

"Sloane," Hilda said slowly, as if speaking to a confused child, "those people murdered Oliver, and we have no idea why. Perhaps we ought to avoid handing them a powerful artifact until we know more."

"Or," Sloane said, "perhaps we should avoid getting on their bad side."

"We don't even really know what the Blade does," Alex added, "or what they want it for. They could use it to hurt people."

"We know it pays well," Sloane said. "That's all I care about." She was all too aware of the fact that only a thin box currently separated her from this potentially dangerous Blade. Whatever it was. She ran a thumb along the markings on the case, trying not to think of the way Oliver had shoved it at her. What had he been trying to tell her, in that last moment? Something about the Fleet, and what had sounded like a plea for her to sever the Blade. But she didn't know what she was supposed to sever it *from*. None of it made any sense.

Hilda sloshed forward and grabbed Sloane's wrist, her

fingers digging painfully into the flesh. "Oliver died rather than give these people the Blade," she said, her voice a low hiss. "He had to have known about that implant, and yet lying, betraying, son-of-a-bitch Oliver chose death over handing it to them."

Sloane yanked her hand out of the pilot's grip. "All the more reason not to take his advice." The words sounded hollow even to her own ears. Oliver, who'd taught them card games, whose cheeky smile had made her weak in the knees. It was hard to believe he was really gone. Impossible.

"We could contact the woman who had it," Alex said. Meaning, Sloane assumed, the woman they'd stolen it from. "And her friend that ran after us. She offered to help."

Sloane looked back and forth between her crew mates, hunger gnawing at her stomach. After five hours of walking, or whatever it had been, these two wanted to go back to the people they'd been running from? The heat had to be affecting their minds.

"I doubt they'll be happy to see us," Sloane said. "And if we go back to them, they'll take the Blade. Our options will be gone."

Alex left the water and plopped down on the beach next to Sloane's shoes. "Then what do you suggest?"

Sloane joined her, setting the box between them on the sand. Was it her imagination, or was it glowing? "We could use it. If it's so powerful, maybe it can get us home on its own."

"Right now, those people can't get to it," Alex said. "Maybe it should stay that way."

Heroics again. Great. Sloane's fingers itched to open the box, to touch the milky white Blade. See what was so powerful about this thing everyone wanted. "Don't you want to get back to your wormhole work?"

Alex hugged her knees to her chest. "Obviously I do."

Hilda had turned her back on them to stare out at the

sunset and the board-riders as if she knew that anything she said would inevitably end with Sloane making the wrong choice, anyway.

And truly, Sloane felt torn. Alex and Hilda might be worried about the Blade's impact on the galaxy, or whatever, but Sloane doubted these people planned to do anything with it that would impact her life in the slightest. With the sound of Oliver's last breaths still rattling in her memory, his blood still drying in the cracks of the box he'd asked her to protect, she had to admit she didn't much want to hand it over to his murderers. Even if she could only admit that to herself.

Without help from those murderers, though, Sloane didn't know how else to get Alex and Hilda home. She might not relish her role as their captain, but her uncle *had* left her in charge of their safety. And she'd accepted the job. Under pressure, yes, but still.

When a shadow fell over her, she jumped in surprise. She'd have leapt to her feet, but she didn't have the energy, so she squinted up at the trio of young Earth-dwellers who were grinning eagerly down at her. One of them wore a silver-painted box as a dress, with functionless cardboard tubes jutting out of the sides. Another had on a black suit that might have resembled her own, sort of, except that the legs were tighter and the cheap fabric crinkled when the girl moved. And the guy in the middle was wearing some kind of a fur suit, a monster head propped under his arm.

If people on Earth dressed like this, she didn't understand why she'd been the one garnering strange looks.

"Take Flight?" the guy holding the furry monster head said, bobbing his head excitedly. The freckles scattered across his nose made him look about twelve, but she supposed he was closer to twenty.

Sloane shook her head, squinting at the translation. "What?"

The girl nudged her friend with an elbow. "Take Flight Comic Con," she said. "Are you going?"

Sloane frowned. Her head still felt murky, but she wasn't sure she'd have understood them in her best moments. She slid the Blade-holding box closer against her side, just in case. "Um, I don't—"

"Yes," Hilda got to her feet and brushed her hands off on her pants, sending bits of sand glittering into the twilight. "That's the plan."

Sloane just stared at her. Hilda wasn't letting the translation app speak for her; instead, she pronounced the Earth words slowly, as though reading a phonetic guide. Which, Sloane supposed, she probably was.

The trio of weirdos grinned. "Thought so," the monster boy said. "Can we snap a pic? Your costumes are epic!"

Snap a pic? Sloane blinked at him, but Hilda grabbed her hand and pulled her up. "Sure," she said.

The boy was practically bouncing on the balls of his feet. "So excellent," he said. He pulled his miniature tablet device out of his pocket and aimed it at them, even with Alex still sitting in the sand rubbing her feet. A picture. He wanted a picture. Why, Sloane didn't know, but as long as it wasn't a weapon, she didn't much care. She relaxed her hold on the box.

"Thanks!" the boy said after a minute. "Maybe we'll see you there!"

And with that, the trio bobbed off down the beach.

Sloane turned to Hilda, who was watching the weirdos with her lips pursed. "How did you know what they were talking about?" The translation app certainly hadn't volunteered any information on that front.

"I didn't." Hilda settled back into the sand. "But I figured we might learn something."

"I learned that Earth is weird," Alex muttered.

With a start, Sloane realized they could have asked the weirdo Earthers for help. At the very least, they might be willing to offer directions, though with the right story—and Sloane was excellent at fabricating sob stories—they might have offered to purchase a meal. She glanced back down the beach, hope rising in her chest, but the trio had disappeared.

Disappointed, Sloane turned her gaze back to the water, watching the board-riding idiots while her stomach contracted painfully. As if she needed a further reminder that she hadn't eaten in hours. They'd need some clothes, and somewhere to sleep. Plus a way to get home. She nearly laughed out loud. Why not ask for a million galactic tokens, while she was at it?

Well, she might not be the best thief in any galaxy, but she was still a thief. Enough of one, anyway, to score something to eat. She looked around the beach, and she started to form a plan.

NOTHING about the engineering lab at HQ had changed. Not really. Mary used to spend hours here, mixing it up with the techs and daydreaming cool ways for the league to win their missions. Why go through customs when you could barrel under the falls in a smart-car-slash-submarine? Though she supposed she hadn't really done any of that designing in here since before she'd started tailing Jenna Carpenter across the country. Coming up on a year ago, that assignment.

Still, the place looked pretty much the same. No one had rearranged the furniture or labeled the tool drawers that she'd always sworn she'd organize on a boring afternoon. Which obviously never came, because there was always something more interesting to do. Unlike the pristine chemistry lab where Agnes had conducted her experiments, this one had posters on the walls—the Rolling Stones, *Star Wars*, and, because of some joke she couldn't quite remember, Cookie Monster—and an espresso machine in the corner. The place even smelled the same, new-car plastic mixed with carbon paper and strawberry Pop Tarts.

It looked the same. It smelled the same. But like the rest of HQ it felt... strange. Mary had woken early, thrown her hair into a bun, and beelined it to the lab to fulfill her promise of trying to find a way for the operative who recovered the Pearl Knife to carry it back to Eloise without burning their hand off. The guy who'd stolen it had contained it, somehow—it didn't feel right to think of him as an asshole, seeing as he was dead now, though that was her first instinct—but Mary didn't understand *how*. Sure, El had that display case in her office. But if someone even tried to touch the case with the Knife inside, it'd sting them. She knew that from experience.

She'd expected a few quiet hours to work by herself, but she'd barely set up a laptop on a central lab table before Luke, one of the team's head engineers, fell in to work at her side. With El's permission, she'd filled him in on the situation; Luke had been a staple at HQ for years. He was as trustworthy as Mary.

And there they'd stood, for the last few hours, poring through the sparse data they'd been able to collect about the Knife over the years. Most of it said stuff like 'the Knife sparked when we tried to get a closer look, and by the way we need a new microscope.' Helpful.

"You think it's about the material the box is made of?" Luke asked, leaning his elbows on the lab table and rubbing his hands over his face without looking away from the screen. While they'd been working, several more engineers had trickled in, though thankfully no one else had joined them. Mary was aware of the others, working on their own projects on the edges of the room. Aware of the constant need to speak cryptically.

Mary knew what Luke was thinking. This was more of an Agnes problem than a Mary-and-Luke problem. Mary wasn't exactly a 'figure it out at the molecular level' kind of girl. If she couldn't solve it with a computer chip or a new engine, she wasn't sure she should be here at all.

But she had to be somewhere. And somewhere couldn't be

out in the field. Yes, she'd registered everyone's expressions of shock during El's bedroom meeting when she'd announced her intention to stay behind. If anything, that only solidified her resolve. They all expected her to demand to be thrown into a fight, to launch herself at the bad guys without thinking.

It was all she'd done lately, and it hadn't turned out well. Not once.

"I still think the Knife is some kind of tech," Mary said. "If it's tech, maybe there's a way to jam it. Temporarily."

"Jamming mysterious space-computer blades. What could go wrong?"

Probably just that the invention would fail. Though she supposed that they risked damaging the Knife, too. She was vaguely aware that the door had opened, letting in yet another engineer who'd be shocked to see her and probably a bit afraid.

Mary scanned the data on the screen, hardly seeing the reports she'd already read a hundred times. Maybe she was thinking too small; the Pearl Knife could create portals—wormholes, she suspected, though she wasn't much of a physicist. What power was the damn thing tapping when it did *that*? If they jammed it, they might accidentally implode the universe.

Suddenly, Mary realized that the calm movement on the periphery of the room had faded. Even Luke was backing away from her, mumbling something about getting a cup of coffee, despite the fact that he'd been the one to install the fancy espresso machine in the corner specifically so he could minimize the need to leave in the middle of a project.

Only one person's entrance could cause them to run like that. They probably feared getting caught in the crossfire, though they needn't have worried; Mary was hardly going to destroy expensive equipment for the sake of lobbing it at Nathan Pearce. As satisfying as that would be.

Mary kept her focus on the screen, on her practically

nonexistent notes. As if looking him in the eye would freeze her in place or something. How mythological. "Authorized personnel only," she said. "Whatever you have to say, I don't want to hear it."

"I promise I've kept all my certifications current."

Not Nathan. Will. Mary's head snapped up, heat rushing into her cheeks. "I thought you were someone else."

Will grinned, and her heart squeezed painfully. She'd known he was alive—her mentor, her surrogate father—but the chaos of the last few days had allowed her to shuffle that truth aside. To pretend they wouldn't be coming face to face sooner than later.

When he'd died, Will had been her hero. Until she'd learned about his role in taking down the plane in the crash that had killed her parents, and left her with permanent scars. And even though she knew he was innocent—that Dolly had been controlling his powers—she couldn't help the wave of mixed emotions that whirlpooled dizzily through her head at the sight of him.

Yes, he was innocent. He'd even transferred the Knife to Eloise. But why had he left them to fend for themselves?

He still stood by the doorway, as if he half expected her to kick him out. He loomed over the space, the tallest person in nearly any room. He had ebony skin, his head shaved, and he looked... Well, as her shock ebbed, she could see the nerves behind his smile. The slight arch to his eyebrows, the too-tight pull of his lips.

Mary had spent the past few months screwing up, failing because she couldn't resist the urge to act before she thought. She'd blamed LIO's old guard for what had happened to her parents. It wasn't that she'd been wrong. But she'd imprisoned at least one innocent guy, and nearly killed someone else. By accident, but still.

She couldn't trust her anger.

Mary abandoned her lab table and crossed the room. When she reached Will, though, she stopped, words dying in the back of her throat.

"I know," Will said. "What does one say in these situations?"

He'd always been able to read her mind. Not in an enhanced abilities kind of way; he was just an experienced teacher. And a compassionate person. "I'm glad you're not dead?"

Mary didn't like the tentative uptick at the end of that sentence, but how else should one greet a resurrected mentor-slash-pseudo-father? Not with anger. He'd been through enough, and so had she.

Will threw his head back and laughed. "Me, too, girl. Me, too."

Mary couldn't help it. She laughed, too. It dispelled some of the tension in the room, and she pulled up one of the lab stools, sitting gratefully. Will remained standing, looking around the lab as if he could drink it in with his eyes. "We're strangers in a familiar land, you and me."

Mary's smile faded, though she tried to keep it pasted on her face. Not that a fake smile would ever fool Will. Not on her best acting day. "I don't know what you mean," she said. "I'm glad to be home."

Will raised an eyebrow. Not convinced. "I'll admit I practically hit the floor from shock when El told me you were still here. Thought you'd be in the middle of the action. Finding that Knife, you know. Or at least, kicking those people who stole it to kingdom come."

"They're aliens," Mary said. "Did Eloise tell you that part?"

He bobbed his head gently, as if to the beat of a song she couldn't hear. "Oh, yes. She told me." He picked a catalog up off the nearest lab bench, a thick selection of tech parts with about thirty post-its stuck into various pages. Someone was about to file a requisition request, clearly. "You thought I was someone else. When I came in."

Mary looked at her hands. "Yeah. Sorry."

He waved her away, still flipping through the catalog. Mary should look through it, too, if they hadn't already placed an order. Maybe it'd give her an idea. Funny, that they still used paper catalogs. She found herself wondering who'd received it in the mail, and what the address had looked like. *League of Independent Operatives. The Hideout Under the Falls. Canada.*

"I hear the boy made a mistake," Will said.

Mary could pretend she didn't know he meant Nathan, but Will knew her too well for that. What *hadn't* Eloise told her father? Apparently he'd gotten the whole soap-opera recap in addition to the important stuff. She didn't like the idea of people gossiping about her, though she supposed it was too late to stop it. "Doesn't matter," Mary said.

Will set the catalog down and came to sit beside her. "I made a mistake, too. A few of them, in fact."

Mary had made nothing *but* mistakes, or so it felt like. A year ago, she'd ignored Eloise's orders and tried to track down a criminal in Reykjavik. She'd failed. Then Eloise had assigned her to watch Jenna—watch, not intervene—and Mary had brought her to HQ. Which resulted in the outing of the league, and all their identities.

Most recently, she'd incarcerated a group of people who, assholes or not, deserved a fair trial.

All Mary had done, from the moment she'd landed in LIO as a traumatized kid, was fail. That didn't excuse Nathan's failures. Not even close. A small part of her whispered that a person who could forgive Will could forgive Nathan, too, but

Mary was nothing if not well-practiced in ignoring such contradictions.

"If you're going to tell me to forgive him, you can stop right there," Mary said. "He abandoned me."

Will leaned his elbow on the table beside them, propping his head in his hand. "So did I."

Mary shook her head, the movement practically involuntary. "It's different."

"Is it? I think I'd be mad at me. In fact, I am mad at me. Livid."

It was true that Will had left them behind, grieving and alone. He'd left the league to splinter in his absence, left Eloise to fend for herself. He'd left.

But Mary had no right to be angry. Not after the way she'd treated Flick and the others. She only shook her head again. "It's not the same thing, Will. It's not."

Will nodded as if he couldn't quite believe her, then hopped off the chair. "I'll leave you to your work, then."

"Maybe you could stop in later," Mary said. "You know a bit about the Knife. It could help."

Will glanced around, and she could feel his unease. It resonated with her own.

"You said you kept up your certifications." She raised an eyebrow. "We could use that expertise."

Will cracked a smile. "You win. I'll check in, promise." He made for the exit, but as he reached the door, he stopped and turned back. "You should know I wasn't going to tell you to forgive the cop. I was going to tell you to forgive yourself."

Before Mary could answer, he slipped out the door. Which was a good thing, because she couldn't do what he asked. She had to remember what she'd done, and rein herself in. If she forgave herself for her mistakes, she might just get someone killed.

No MATTER how long Nathan paced outside the engineering lab, his feet refused to take him inside. The coffee in his hand had long since cooled, his stomach too jittery to accept much of it. He hadn't brought a cup for Mary, given the strong possibility that she'd toss the scalding liquid into his face.

He knew she was in there, working on a solution to the Knife problem. He also knew it was time to offer her an apology, whether she'd accept it or not. She deserved that much from him.

He wasn't expecting to clear the air. He just... He owed her. He wanted her to know it.

Just as he was steeling himself to try, the glass doors to the lab slid open and Eloise's father stepped out. Will Reyna. The Inferno.

"Ah," Will said, with a glance back toward the lab, "I wouldn't go in there if I were you."

"Dangerous experiments underway?"

Will looked him over. The man towered over Nathan, several inches past six feet. Approaching six and a half, if Nathan had to guess. "For you? Yes."

Did everyone know about Nathan's history with Mary?

Well, it wasn't as if Nathan had earned their discretion. Nathan watched Will warily, half afraid that Mary's adoptive father would find it within his rights to punch Nathan in the face. Actually, it probably *was* within Will's rights. Not the way Nathan had pictured introducing himself to one of his heroes. The Inferno. He was a man out of legend.

Instead of hitting him, Will extended a hand to Nathan. "Will Reyna."

Nathan shook it, trying hard not to look relieved. "Nathan Pearce."

Will grinned. "Good, good. We've properly exchanged the information we already know. You're the one who let the Wave prisoners go."

It wasn't a question. Nathan nodded. "I had to."

Will started down the hall, beckoning Nathan to follow. He really was intent on leading Nathan away from the lab, apparently. Well, if Will said this wasn't the day, maybe it wasn't. Nathan tried not to wonder what Mary might have said to Will about Nathan, instead focusing on the encouraging fact that the man had not simply left him to fend for himself.

Mary was as capable of throwing a punch as her mentor. The fading bruise on Nathan's cheek attested to that.

"Of course you had to do it," Will said. A cluster of engineers passed them, hurrying back toward the lab. Group coffee date, apparently. "They were incriminated under false circumstances. It was the right thing."

"Thank you, sir," Nathan said. "I'm glad you think so."

Will waved him away. "No one ever called me 'sir' even when I was partially in charge around here. Don't be so nervous."

Nathan caught himself before he responded with 'yes, sir.' Barely. *Don't be nervous.* Sure. He was only pacing through

LIO's underground hideout with the Inferno. Hero of legends, and a second father to his ex-girlfriend.

Nathan tried to focus on the matter at hand. Surely Will had Eloise's ear; maybe he could help resolve the Wave situation. Hadn't Will been working for them, too? Eloise was right to be cautious, but she didn't know Dr. Gordon, or Jo, or any of the others. She didn't know what strong allies they'd be. And loyal, too.

"Some people think enhanced humans belong behind bars whether they're dangerous or not," Nathan said. People like Nathan's sister, for example. He hadn't heard from Chloe since he'd told her off on the phone. He supposed she must have crawled off to whatever cave spiders like her hid in after their hopes were dashed, though he doubted he'd seen the last of her.

Will shook his head. "That's always been the case, I'm afraid."

Interesting. Apparently Nathan needed to brush up on his history. "You've worked with both Wave and LIO," he said. "What are the chances of a reconciliation there?"

At that, Will paused in the middle of the hall and looked Nathan in the eye. "You want to team up with Wave? Uphill battle, that."

True. "I just... I think we're all working toward the same goal."

"I don't disagree. But there's a lot of strife wedged between us. Going to take more than an olive branch like your prisoner release to win their trust."

And for LIO—especially Eloise—to trust Wave in return. Before Nathan could respond, his com chimed in his ear. Judging by the way Will's head snapped to attention, his had gone active, too.

"We have a situation," Eloise's voice said. Great. Nathan's four favorite words. "We're needed up top."

Will frowned. "All of us?"

"Yeah. And the recruits if they can get here fast enough.

Nathan's heart dropped into his stomach. "What's going on?"

A brief pause. "Oh you know, the usual. Some guy's trying to drive a tourist boat under the falls."

———

Nathan was well aware, as he stood between Eloise and Will on the far side of the guard fence looking down over the falls, that an audience had gathered. There'd been a few people braving Niagara's icy February conditions when they arrived, gazing down at the frosty falls—and the apparently empty double-decker boat bobbing precariously close to the rushing water.

Now that there were three league operatives on the scene, the crowd was thickening with alarming speed.

"The *Maid of the Mist* doesn't operate in winter," Eloise said. "Whoever he is, he stole it and started telling people he was running the first-ever winter tour."

Which meant he had hostages. Great. Nathan squinted down at the little boat. Wherever the tour company stored it, it couldn't have been easy to get it onto the river—which meant they were dealing with someone who had resources. There might be one guy down there, or it might be an ambush.

Eloise seemed to be thinking the same thing. "Could be Wave," she said.

Nathan doubted that. "Or the Enhanced Abilities Enforcement Association." Led by his delight of a sister.

But Will just shook his head. "Too showy. I think it might be a random incident."

Nathan blinked cold spray out of his eyes. When was the

last time LIO had dealt with something that wasn't a conspiracy? Not that he had all that much experience with them, but since he'd arrived, it seemed most of their missions hinged on complex layers of intrigue.

A random incident. Could be refreshing. Still, seemed like an intense one, especially without the Pearl Knife at Eloise's hip. "We may need backup on this," Nathan said.

Eloise nodded. "The recruits are a few miles away, but they're en route."

"And how do we get down there? Submarine car?"

Will chuckled. "Way too obvious. The cars that come up from under the falls are small, and they're not designed to surface. We've been covert for a long time."

Nathan frowned at the long drop, and at the little ship making its slow passage closer and closer to the punishing falls. There was still so much he didn't know about LIO. Someone really ought to write a handbook. "Then how are we supposed to get there?"

Eloise lifted a gloved hand as if calling for a taxi, clenching a fist in open air to grab hold of something Nathan couldn't see. She reached into her pocket and produced a pair of armored gloves, which she tossed at him before raising her left hand with a grin. "We fly."

And then, with both hands high above her head, she jumped off the cliff.

ELOISE HADN'T USED Agnes's zip-line system in years, not since the first rounds of testing. Routine safety inspections had become a checked box, one of many reports that crossed her desk every month. Designed using Agnes's own powers as a template, the ropes and the structures that held them above the falls were completely invisible. It had been one of the scientist's first contributions to the league, an idea she'd apparently gotten while watching a Niagara Falls tightrope stunt.

They'd always known there might be a reason to get down to the water one day, and fast. And secretly, Eloise had always hoped she'd have to use them at some point. Not that she hoped for hostage situations, but as she pushed off the side of the cliff, registering the shock on Nathan's face as she went, her stomach swooped with joy at the thrill of the fall. Cold air whipped around her, sweeping around her masked face—hardly necessary now that her identity was known, but good protection—and pulling at her tucked-in feet. She gripped the invisible handles, savoring the dip of her stomach, the adrenaline-punched joy of a mission in progress.

She only wished the Pearl Knife were here to experience it with her. With the wind pushing back against her fall, she couldn't help that thinking that a good night's sleep seemed to have eased her absent-Knife symptoms. Fatigue still hovered like a specter, but she was functioning at a surprisingly high level. Maybe she'd be able to hold back the uncomfortable physical sensations, the bone-deep exhaustion. Maybe she'd be able to hold out until the Knife returned.

A handful of thrilling seconds, and Eloise landed on the deck of the famous *Maid of the Mist*. Her feet slipped as she ducked into the covered space, her boots sliding on the deck as frost piled up.

Clad in bright blue ponchos draped over winter parkas, boots, and coats, the small handful of tourists who'd bought into the winter-trip lie now stood huddled together in the sheltered part of the bottom deck. Eloise spared them a glance as one of her companions—Dad, if she had to guess—released the zip line and thumped to the deck outside. The hostages just stared at her, wide eyed as cornered animals. Everyone seemed to be breathing. Cold, but breathing.

Eloise darted up the narrow stairs to the top viewing deck and back into the punishing spray. And up to the white capsule that held the captain's wheel.

Dad fell into step at her side, with Nathan following a moment later. "That was weird," Nathan said, breathing hard.

"Welcome to LIO," Dad said.

Eloise opened the door to the captain's area—she didn't know the proper name, and it didn't matter so much right now —and stepped inside.

A man stood alone at the helm, glaring ahead at the rushing white of the falls. He had a few strands of hair combed over his pale, balding head, and he wore a crimson cape with a matching strip of cloth over his eyes. A gray-haired man in sweatpants lay crumpled at his feet. Had this guy also kidnapped a captain? Eloise could only hope the man was still breathing.

The caped guy, as he'd apparently announced on his blog about twenty minutes ago—and sent the link to every news outlet in the country—was aiming the bow directly for the rushing water. And the merciless rock underneath. Did he really think he could drill through all of that with a tourist boat and crash *into* LIO HQ?

"I belong in there," the guy said, as if in answer to her question. He had to shout to be heard over the rushing water and the boat's motor.

"Cool," Eloise called back. "Turn the boat around, and I'll give you a tour. No charge. Maybe you can join up."

The wannabe caped crusader bared his teeth, still staring at the falls like he could make out LIO's hideout beyond. "I said *I* belong in there. Not you."

Great. There were loads of reasons to be angry with LIO, but given that the public knew very few, Eloise had to wonder what kind of conspiracies this man had been dreaming up.

No problem. He was just one guy; Eloise didn't need enhanced abilities to take him down, free the hostages, and get everyone home safe. With Dad and Nathan still flanking the doorway, taking the brunt of the winter punishment—there was barely room for two people in here, plus a passed-out captain—Eloise stepped forward and grabbed the guy by his collar, pulling him away from the ship's controls. As she did, the muscles in her arms started to shake like they might give out, and she gritted her teeth.

She'd just ridden a zip line down to the boat. Her muscles had to be recovering from that. She held on tighter, silently begging her body not to let this guy know how tenuous her grip truly was.

As she dragged him back, he started to laugh, and for a

moment she thought he'd noticed her weakness—*slight* weakness—after all. The collapsed captain on the floor groaned, and Eloise willed him to wake up.

Outside, Dad shouted. Eloise whipped around to see a swarm of black drones dive bombing the deck, a dozen or more, their humming muted by the thundering water. They swooped down as a group, pummeling Will's raised arms, angry hooks tearing at Nathan's jacket. They really needed to get him a better mission outfit.

"This is how you want to be a hero?" Eloise asked as her caped friend tried to scramble out of her grip, still laughing. "Hurting innocent people? Attacking us with drones?"

"I'm demonstrating my genius," he said, half growling half laughing. "I *am* a genius."

It wasn't, Eloise thought, that he wanted to be a hero; it was that he didn't want *her* to be one. He thought he knew better, and he resented the power he perceived in her. In the league. The surveillance team regularly monitored league-related gripes and conspiracy theories, with an eye toward preventing exactly this kind of situation.

Still, this guy had managed to sneak through.

"This isn't an interview." Eloise pushed him outside. She was strong, even without the Knife; she'd trained alongside Mary for years. But her body suddenly felt overcome, fatigue pulsing through her muscles and into the bones, the trembling in her arms spreading into her legs like a plague.

There was no reason for the weakness, for the headache that slammed insistently into her skull. And there was no way she could let anyone see.

She wished for the Pearl Knife, wished for it with every fiber of her being, and not just because she suspected its absence had to do with her physical distress. The Knife would sweep through the air to dismantle those drones in a matter of seconds. She glanced hopefully at her father, but he was staring at the onslaught with the same wistful look she felt in her own heart. As if he could imagine a blast of fire taking them all down.

Instead of unleashing any flames, Dad closed his fists and leapt into the fray. He grabbed one of the drones by its spindly legs and smashed it onto the deck like a football player spiking the ball. It shattered, parts skittering across the deck.

Even without using his abilities, he was pure power.

Dad was already leaping for another drone as the flying machines began to shoot. Not bullets—thank god they weren't bullets—but little silver spikes that lodged in Dad's shoulders, and Nathan's.

"They're more than a mere annoyance," the ship-hijacker said in a sing-songy tone that made her want to toss him overboard. Hijacker? Ship stealer? Whatever. He'd stopped struggling, letting his weight drag. Letting the drones take on the fight. Were the not-bullets poisoned?

"Don't let the darts hit your skin," Eloise called, as the caped guy cackled behind her. Overcome with mirth. Or insanity. Who could say?

She wanted to join the fight outside, to swipe down a few drones of her own—Nathan had joined Dad in that pursuit—but she wasn't sure how long she could stay on her feet, let alone leap into the air. Besides, someone needed to turn this boat around. She dropped the caped hijacker, shoving him out onto the deck, and locked the door before turning to the controls.

She didn't know how to drive a damn boat. She wanted to say 'how hard could it be?' but the murderous falls pounded dangerously close, and it was too easy to picture them all drowning as the ship split apart.

"OK," she muttered. "Let's start with reverse."

The man on the floor moaned again. To Eloise's immense relief, he actually rolled over. Glancing at the falls, which were pushing the boat back as though they had no will to crush it, she knelt beside him.

"Grabbed me in the night," the captain said, grimacing as she helped him to sit. "Pulled me out of my bed."

Eloise looked him over quickly. He had a shallow cut by his temple, and he'd need to be checked out, but for now he seemed OK. "Can you get us out of here?"

The man nodded, and she helped him to his feet. He glanced up at the falls, shook his head once, and took the wheel. Good in a crisis, this one.

Eloise left him to his work, joining Dad and Nathan back on the deck as they battled the drones. The machines seemed endless, ever increasing, and Eloise cursed herself for getting stuck in her ways. They should all be carrying tools like Mary's. They should all be prepared to fight without abilities.

Mary should *be* here, damn it. Eloise hadn't called her. Hadn't wanted to force her out of her self-enforced sidelining, if that were even a possibility. At the moment, Eloise wished she'd dragged Mary out here by the ear.

If Eloise had tools like Mary's, would she even be able to operate them? Certainly not in her current state. Sweat collected along her brow despite the freezing cold, and she blinked away spots that swam into the edges of her vision.

One of the spider-like machines took aim at Eloise's head, snapping her into the immediate fight. She swiped at the thing, grabbing hold of the hook on the end of one of its legs. Her outfit, at least, was fairly impenetrable. Fencing mask, gloves, enhanced bodysuit. *Just try to get through this*, she thought as she slammed the drone onto the deck.

The Knife would be proud of her, if it were here to see. Of

course, if the Knife were here, this would be over already. And she wouldn't be breathing so hard.

On the edge of Eloise's vision, Nathan leapt for a drone, landing against the ship's rail as another swooped up behind him. Before Eloise could call out a warning, the second drone spit out a silver spike, catching Nathan in the back of the neck. He let go of his drone, which flew off drunkenly, its balance upset by the leg Nathan had snapped.

He lifted a hand to his neck, turned awkwardly. Too slowly, as if whatever drug it contained were already taking effect. Another dart sank into his throat.

Eloise ran for him, but a drone intercepted her. She tried to bat the thing away, tried to go through it, but Nathan stumbled. Another drone swooped in, dropping a long hook, and all Eloise could do was scream as it dragged Nathan overboard.

A breath, still full of battle, the smell of burned-out machinery leaking through her mask. Another breath, her opponent drone shattered, another appearing in its place. The spots closed in, as if she, too, had been poisoned. A third breath —what was she going to tell Mary?—another snapped leg.

A wave of ice erupted out of the water, sculpting itself to the side of the boat like a slide. And then two women leapt up onto the deck, carrying Nathan between them.

Eloise really should have spent more time with the recruits. Or any time, really. She'd mainly left their training to Ire. But she knew that one of them wielded ice, and another could jump impractically high. Here they were, looking alive and ready for a fight, with Nathan sagging unconscious from the poison, or the fall. Maybe both.

The fight was over in a matter of seconds. Ice girl made drone-crashing blades by freezing the spray, and jumping-girl leapt after any that tried to escape. The wannabe villain cried on the deck, bemoaning the loss of his precious inventions, his babies, even as he cowered by the rail to avoid them. Eloise found it difficult to summon any sympathy for him as she and Dad restrained him with zip ties and the captain navigated the boat safely to its rightful dock.

⸺

As per usual, ambulances and police crowded the pier as the mission came to a close. A familiar refrain, one Eloise was used to handling without the Knife's assistance. Hiding her physical distress? That was part of the job. Only this time, she'd barely participated in the fight. She wasn't hurt, or she shouldn't be.

Regardless, she couldn't let the local authorities see how weak she felt, any more than she could have let the deluded boat-stealer in on the secret. It might lead to uncomfortable questions. What would she do, if someone in authority noticed she wasn't carrying the Knife?

"Take the others over to HQ," Eloise said to her father as they ushered the hostages down the gangplank. It wasn't common knowledge that Dad was alive; she planned to keep it that way for a while longer. If not forever. "Get Nathan to the infirmary, and make sure those dud darts make it to the lab."

Dad nodded. "The recruits, too?"

"I think they've earned rooms inside the house."

And it would be good to have them nearby. It wasn't only Ms. Ice and Ms. High Jump who'd arrived to help; a water-controlling recruit had stayed on shore, using the falls to help push the boat away from the cliffs, while their x-ray-visioned friend helped navigate everyone from the sidelines and their sticky-fingered colleague hung back as a second backup. They'd all come. And with a plan, too. Ire had taught them well.

For once, the police explanations didn't take long. And at least Eloise could unmask now when she spoke with the authorities. It certainly helped with that trust-building thing. And with being able to breathe. Why was it so hard to breathe? Her lungs felt like they wanted to burst out of her chest, like no amount of oxygen was enough. She held on, hiding her distress with a light hand on the rail. She didn't dare lean against it.

Finally, with the wannabe crusader on his way to jail—regular jail, seeing as he had no enhanced abilities—and the *Maid of the Mist* heading back to its rightful winter slumber, Eloise started up the hill toward LIO's gift-shop entrance. But the road was still clogged with spectators, and she wasn't exactly incognito. Eloise sighed and turned toward to the casino instead, where LIO kept a hotel room—and another secret entrance.

They'd barely won this fight, and a feeling in the pit of her stomach said that they might easily have lost, had the recruits not shown up when they had. They certainly would have lost Nathan, whose heart rate and breathing were steady despite whatever substance the darts had dosed him with. And Eloise felt as if she might fall unconscious at any second as she supported herself against the flowery hotel wallpaper on the way to LIO's permanently rented room in the casino.

Eloise was a strong operative, and a strong leader. She knew that. Without the Pearl Knife, though, she was nothing else. Especially with LIO out in the open, she needed to be able to show her full power. How could she do that, when the Knife's absence had sapped her strength? And how much worse could she expect it to get?

She longed for the Knife, for its friendship. And she longed for its power. So far, she'd gotten off easy in terms of the side effects. Mary would disagree with that, and probably Steve, but Eloise couldn't help comparing her own physical distress to Dolly's situation. But how long would it be before her hair began turning white? Before her eyesight began to fail?

For the first time since Agnes had abandoned the league in favor of Wave, Eloise wished she were here. Oh, she'd missed the scientist's genius more than once in the past few months, but more than that, Eloise felt certain she could have approached Agnes with her Pearl Knife problem without causing a major stir. Agnes would research, test, solve. Agnes would be discreet. And Agnes wouldn't think the whole league was falling down around their shoulders just because Eloise felt a little shaky.

The others? They might. They needed her to be strong.

When Eloise arrived back at HQ, Dad was waiting for her in the hall by the casino elevator. "Figured I'd need the extra-secret entrance?" she asked.

"I had a hunch."

Eloise removed her gloves, more for something to do with her hands than anything else. Dad hadn't used his powers back there, either. She still didn't know if he'd lost them somehow, or if—after years of torment watching someone else control his power—he simply wouldn't risk it. She hadn't worked up the courage to ask him yet.

"I need to get the Knife," she said after a moment. "Steve and Ire might find it, but I can't just sit here. I need to go after it myself."

Mary might be able to stay behind, but Eloise couldn't stand the thought of waiting. Of inaction. Who had a better chance at finding the Pearl Knife than she did?

Dad propped an arm around her shoulders, as if he'd met her here to confirm exactly that. He gave her arm a squeeze. "Glad to hear it. And I'm coming with you."

MARY DIDN'T HEAR about the *Maid of the Mist* disaster until it was over and done with, and the whole team got a situation brief straight from Eloise. Was this how it had always worked, with the team? Blissful ignorance during a fight, video briefing afterward? Usually, Mary would have been up there with them, but Eloise had clearly known better than to call her in. Mary would have refused to go, in any case.

Did that make Mary a part of the engineering team now, instead of an operative? Maybe so. The engineers around her were buzzing with news of the fight, their voices dropping to whispers when they mentioned how Nathan had been injured. Well, so what? Eloise had said he was OK. That he was in the infirmary.

It was the last part of the briefing that tugged at Mary's mind, at her worry. The part where El had said that she and Will were going off on a related mission. Mary had a guess as to what that might be. But why would Eloise decide to go after the Knife herself? Maybe she'd always intended to. Maybe she was feeling better. Or maybe something had gone wrong.

She found Eloise in her room, carefully arranging clothing

in a suitcase that was large enough for a two-week cruise. El zipped her famous suits and jackets into the top portion before starting in on the button-downs and yoga pants.

"Expecting high-level meetings?" Mary asked.

Eloise dropped a pile of socks into the corner of the suitcase. "I always have to be prepared to speak with the authorities."

Mary crossed her arms. "So. You're going after the Knife yourself."

"I have to."

Mary wanted to lean back against the door, to act nonchalant. Like she didn't care. Like she wasn't worried. But everything about this situation made her want to hold on to her sister, never let her go. Mary had abandoned Eloise, left her alone for months here because of the crimes Dolly had committed.

But she wouldn't pretend to be stoic anymore. She couldn't. She crossed the room and came to sit on the bed beside Eloise's suitcase, studying her sister's face for any sign of the sickness Dolly had endured in the Knife's absence. "I don't think it's a good idea. You're not well."

Eloise paused her packing to arch an eyebrow at Mary. "I'm not? I thought I just kicked a tourist-boat hijacker's butt."

Mary would have liked to have seen that. Not that she'd admit it right now. "I saw you after the L.A. fight. After the Knife was ripped away."

Eloise cringed and went back to her packing. "Not the best day."

She spoke as if it had happened weeks ago, rather than a scant few days. Other people might accept her story of a full recovery, but Mary noticed the drawn look around her eyes, the slight tremble in her fingertips. She didn't want to picture El rocking away in a chair like Dolly had, that horrifying deterioration. Still, the images crowded in against her will, of Eloise's strength draining away.

"It was shock," Eloise said, as if Mary had voiced any of these thoughts. As if she'd accused Eloise of something. "That's all."

"OK, but Dolly—"

"—got sick very quickly after Dad broke her connection to the Knife. She knew immediately, Mary. That's why she named me head of LIO right after he died. Her hair was already turning white."

Eloise ducked into the bathroom, re-emerging with a bag of toiletries while Mary stayed on the edge of the bed and put on her most worried expression. It wasn't difficult. "I don't think you should go."

Eloise sighed. And then, she stopped what she was doing and sat down next to Mary on the bed. Packing like a military woman might be Eloise's style, but stopping to listen to Mary? To make a connection? They really had come a long way. "I need my best out there," Eloise said. "Are you willing to go?"

Unfair question. Mary gripped her knees, doing everything in her power to keep her voice steady. "You know you can't trust me. You've always been right about me, El. I make terrible decisions."

"That's not true."

It was easy to call up the list of failures, with so many fresh in her mind. If she tried to tick them off on her hands, she'd run out of fingers. "I screwed up Reykjavik. I brought Jenna to HQ. I chose my secret identity over saving a friend. And—"

Eloise held up a hand. "Everyone makes mistakes. One of mine has been refusing to appreciate your instincts. We're different people, and we don't always see eye to eye. But with more support from me, some of those situations would have turned out differently."

Some. Not all. "Don't go," Mary said. "Please."

Eloise only smiled sadly. "I don't have a choice."

And Mary could see that she didn't. Not really. She bit back further argument, instead just nodding. These were Eloise's powers. It was Eloise's life. And since when had Mary's decisions been superior to her sister's? Since never. That was the whole problem.

Maybe she could have Pete send some direct surveillance to her tablet, help her keep an eye on things from afar. And she could definitely get to work on that box, so if Steve and Ire reached the Knife first, they'd be able to contain it without relying on the aliens' tech.

Mary slid off the bed and headed for the door. At the last minute, she paused. Hesitated. Turned back, to find Eloise back to tucking toiletries and whatever else into her suitcase. Mary cleared her throat, uneasy. "I heard something. About the fight."

Eloise looked up, and the sympathy in her eyes was almost more than Mary could take. "Nathan's fine," Eloise said. "He's in the infirmary."

The infirmary. Sure, people who were fine went there all the time. Mary looked at her shoes, as if they might speak up on her behalf. Help her form the words. Mysteriously, they did not. "If you could tell him—"

"You've never needed a relationship proxy before, and you don't need one now." Eloise's tone was gentle, but her words were firm. "If you want to talk to him, go see him."

Yeah, right. Because it was just that easy. Mary left Eloise to her packing, heading out of the residential wing and back toward engineering. She could take the short loop or the long loop, and she needed time to collect her thoughts before heading back to the lab. Otherwise, she'd be useless once she got there. So what if the long loop took her by the infirmary? It was an unrelated fact. She needed to maintain a calm, steady presence in the lab, for the sake of the other engineers. Injured or not, Nathan Pearce was not going to stop her from doing what she needed to do. In her own home, no less.

Mary knew bullshit when she heard it, even from herself. But she didn't care. So she had to see that he was alive. What was wrong with that? Yes, El said he was fine, but what if something had changed since she'd last checked in? It was entirely feasible.

The route to the infirmary seemed shorter than she remembered. Maybe she'd talk to him, after all, just for a moment. Just to make sure. She didn't even have to be nice, unless he was really sick. And if he was really sick... Well, then she couldn't leave things the way they were. She'd have to clear the air, for his sake.

When she reached the glass doors to the hospital area, though, it was obvious that Nathan was not very sick. Maybe not sick at all, anymore. A little pale, perhaps, but otherwise he looked like himself. He was sitting up on a cot, wearing a white T-shirt and grinning widely at a woman with rainbow-streaked blonde hair, who sat in a chair beside the bed, her hand on his shoulder.

Mary had never seen the woman before, but she had to be one of the recruits that Eloise's brief had mentioned. One of the women who'd saved him. As Mary watched, the woman threw back her head and laughed at something Nathan had said.

Well, good. It was good that the recruits had been there, including this one. Mary ducked out of sight, ignoring the hook that again sank painfully into her ribcage at the sight of him. Nathan wasn't going to try to make amends. Or, if he did try, it would be merely because of his own sense of duty—not because of any feelings he might still have for her. It was a relief, really, to know she wouldn't have to reject any advances.

Mary backed away from the door, breathing through the annoying band of tightness around her chest. Maybe she'd take the short way back to the lab, after all.

THE SUBMARINE DOCKED after surprisingly little travel time, depositing Agnes and her Wave-Committee escort, Fran, on a tidy tropical island. Palm trees, sparkling sand beaches, gentle waves racing each other toward the shore. Spending a few months underwater hadn't bothered Agnes; she wasn't claustrophobic, and was prone to forgetting her surroundings whenever her work absorbed her. Still, the sea breeze felt especially delicious as it teased through her hair, and she found her eyes continually drawn toward the sky. So much space, and so much air. The place was nothing short of paradise.

And yet, Fran had clearly brought Agnes here for a reason. What was it? Agnes drew her gaze away from the sky, scanning the beach for clues. A woman in a bikini sat back against a palm tree, her hands mimicking the glint of the sand, while her hair was as green as the fronds above her. A camouflager, it seemed. Lounging on the beach. Well, why shouldn't she? Enhanced humans must vacation, too, though Agnes had never personally known one who did.

Somehow, Agnes doubted that Wave planned to enter the resort business. So what was this place?

A goat leapt out of the foliage behind the camouflager,

followed by another. Babies, she thought, watching as the small animals frolicked along the beach. After a minute, a person darted out of the trees to chase the animals down the shore, disappearing and reappearing at intervals along the sand. A teleporter?

Fran tapped her cane on the dock, a signal Agnes was quickly learning to read as 'let's go.' The old woman led the way toward the beach, beelining for a narrow path into the jungle. The sun beamed hot, making Agnes regret her long-sleeved shirt and pants. She'd gone from underwater bubble to submarine to Yacht, to submarine *again*, before landing in the tropical heat. Such variation in secret hideouts made it difficult to gauge wardrobe choices.

The jungle path lasted only a few feet before depositing them in a neat little village. That was the only word Agnes could think of as she took in the clusters of wood-sided build-ings, nestled against each other like small houses. No fences, just shared stretches of lawn with porches and window boxes, and the occasional lawn toy warming in the sun. Goats bleated in the background, and she could hear someone hammering.

Agnes breathed in the scents of sawdust and earthy soil, greenery mixed with the trappings of a fledgling community. The breeze rustled the leaves above, sending wide-leafed fronds waving as if in greeting. "What is this? A vacation spot? A monastery?"

The old woman gazed almost fondly at the little village, though the crease between her eyebrows added a level of concern that made Agnes's heart squeeze. Fran cared about this place, clearly. Who were these people?

Fran had paused, as if to give Agnes a moment to take in her surroundings. She moved forward now, though more slowly. "More like a rehabilitation center. The people who live here at the moment were only recently returned to us. From LIO."

Agnes swallowed, her throat suddenly dry. "The prisoners."

"Nathan Pearce released them, and they returned to us. Every one." Fran tapped her fingers on the top of her cane, fingernails clacking against the wood. "But they did not return unharmed. Iron walls, clipped wings, solitary confinement... those traumas occurred even before the league took charge of them."

Agnes could follow the sequence of events easily enough. "And then LIO dosed them with Mange's power suppressant."

Fran drew in a long breath. "It was never tested for safety, you understand. I regret our part in that particular aspect. The Committee was too eager to expose LIO, and it made us short sighted."

Agnes had spent the better part of her life studying enhanced abilities. Where they came from, why they affected the body, and how to adapt them to create better technology. She'd gone to work for LIO in hopes of using that technology to create a better world.

Instead, she'd been working for an organization that had actively worked to imprison innocent people. Eloise might have better intentions than her mother, but she'd allowed the Wave prisoners to be dosed with Mange's power suppressant.

Wave had used the serum on Agnes, once. But they'd trusted her enough not to keep her plied with it, to tell her the truth, and to ask for her forgiveness. Eloise, in contrast, hardly seemed to realize LIO had done anything wrong.

Fran continued along the dirt path, nodding greetings to the people they passed. "You know now that the Committee runs Wave. Do you have any questions? About what you saw?"

Any questions? Agnes sincerely doubted that Fran would

be willing to discuss the political tensions between Committee members, or the process by which they'd been raised to leadership. The smell of a baking cake wafted out of a window, mixing with the salty air, the sweet aroma of flowers in the background. "Why are you bringing me here?" she asked. "Instead of Bradley?"

A pair of horses trotted around the corner in front of them, and Fran nudged Agnes out of the way with a friendly wave at the riders—who both looked far too young to have been imprisoned for over a decade. Either LIO had locked them up as children, or they had some kind of anti-aging powers. Agnes looked after them, aware that her jaw hung open and unable to do anything to change it.

"Bradley Archer is a good operative. Loyal. Smart. A bit impetuous, at times, but trustworthy. We need him elsewhere." Fran stepped back into the road, giving Agnes's sleeve a tug to pull her along. "However, the Committee has decided to take a personal interest in you."

"And my connection with LIO." The words burned in her mouth, like bile. But it was true, wasn't it?

Fran's lips twisted in a wry smile. "In your work, Ms. Foremost Expert on Enhanced Abilities. In the world."

Agnes felt heat rush into her cheeks. She wasn't used to thinking of herself that way, not really. And her reception in the underwater labs had been lukewarm at best. Not that she blamed her Wave colleagues for mistrusting a new operative that had joined them straight from the ranks of their gravest enemy. She just... wished they'd give her a chance.

Still, it made perfect sense that she'd jump to a few conclusions about what the Committee wanted with her. Namely, information on LIO.

Fran looked up, and Agnes's gaze followed hers as a person shot through the clearing overhead and into the tapestry of

jungle, wings jutting out from their powerful shoulders. *Wings.*
Incredible. "We may, with your permission, seek your advice
regarding the league," Fran said. "From time to time."

Foremost Expert. Yes, she was the foremost expert on
enhanced abilities, and on LIO, too. Well, it made some sense,
even if it didn't explain her exact mission here. Agnes dropped
her gaze back to the Committee member, who was watching
her with sharp, glittery eyes. "My opinion isn't likely to
change."

Fran inclined her head, acknowledging. "And we're likely
to remain in agreement." She started down the road again, her
cane sinking into the sandy dirt with a soft *shh.* The people
they passed waved to her, and Agnes too. No cold-eyed glares
met her here, only enthusiastic welcome.

"Do they know who I am?" Agnes asked.

"They do. They're excited about the prospect of you
working here."

Agnes scanned the street—if it could be called that—
looking for signs of unease at her presence. Of fear. Instead, she
was met with smiles from the people who swept their little
porches, knelt to tend gardens. "You told them I was coming?"

"We took a vote, child. They favored your presence. Unanimously."

A vote. Agnes tried to imagine how a vote would work in
LIO, and failed utterly. Eloise would never loosen her grip long
enough to allow that. And yet Wave clearly ran some parts of
the organization through democratic means. These people had
voted for Agnes's help? After the league had imprisoned them?
She wet her lips, uncertain. "Why?"

"Some of them have experienced difficulties in restoring
their powers, as well as other... side effects." They had reached
a long building at the end of the row, which Agnes had
assumed must be here to stable the horses. The idea of power-

related side effects made something inside her clench in anger. And no small amount of fear. "We'd like you to assess their abilities. See if you can help."

Agnes frowned, her brain already working up a list of the materials she would need to run tests like that. It was a long one, given the variety of abilities she'd noted just walking in here. And interview questions, of course, to gauge each person's ability levels before and after the long-term exposure.

Fran leaned on her cane. The woman stood eye-to-eye with Agnes, who was small herself. She had a slight stoop to her shoulders, and Agnes wondered how old she was. If she had any abilities herself. "Even setting their trauma aside, it's been a long time since anyone studied their powers," Fran said. "Science has progressed since they were first incarcerated, largely in thanks to you."

That, Agnes supposed, was true. Though she was hardly the only talented scientist who dealt with enhanced abilities.

"I hear you specialize in developing progressive technology based on these abilities. On your own, specifically."

Agnes's heart leapt, and she forced the hope back into her throat. This was why she'd joined Wave in the first place—the promise of making the world a better place. She realized she hadn't responded yet, hadn't agreed to come here, and that the old woman was still working to convince her. Was that a measure of anxiety in Fran's gaze? Did she really think Agnes would refuse to help?

Clearly, Wave had no plans to handcuff her to a table if she did. "I'll need a lab," she said.

Fran's answering grin gave her a childlike look, and Agnes wondered if she, too, was a science enthusiast.

When Fran opened the door to the rectangular block of a building where they'd paused, Agnes didn't bother to hide her shock. A blast of air conditioning hit her in the face as she stepped inside the most fully outfitted laboratory she'd ever seen. Glass cases lined the walls, the test tubes within labeled with every active ingredient she'd ever used to tease out abilities, identify them within cells, view them under a microscope.

And speaking of microscopes, there was a standing electron microscope attached to a desk and computer in the back of the room, plus a test area, with plastic barriers, mats, and targets. Glowing tubes pulsated light from cubed cases, and she didn't know their uses. But she wanted to. She wanted to know everything.

"My family," Agnes said, her voice sounding far away. "Can my family come?"

Fran sat down on a lab stool, inching her body back on the seat and clearly enjoying Agnes's assessment of the lab. "They're already on their way."

Agnes nodded. Lucy would enjoy the horses, she thought. And Tam would have space to play music. This seemed like the kind of place where people might even enjoy a concert.

"Just one thing." Fran adjusted in her seat, and Agnes turned to face her, already braced for the fall. The disappointment. Of course this couldn't belong to her, not without a price. They'd shown her the world, and now they planned to rip it away. What would it be? LIO betrayal? A promise to hurt them somehow? Agnes wasn't sure what she'd say to that.

Fran looked her straight in the eye. "I want to make sure you're considering the big picture, when it comes to... your former employers."

Agnes frowned. "I'm not sure what you—"

"Make sure you're not simply holding a grudge."

Agnes shook her head. After all LIO had done, who wouldn't hesitate to partner with them? On anything? Agnes had nothing against them personally, but their entire mission was skewed. Yes, Eloise was a different person than her mother, but she had still incarcerated innocents. She had allowed injustice to continue.

She also let them go, a part of Agnes reminded her. Oh, she knew it had been Nathan, but Eloise could have informed her government friends, could have sent the full force of the league to chase them all down. Fractured as it was, she might have succeeded. But she hadn't done that.

Still, Agnes couldn't advise Wave to trust LIO, or ally with them. She never would. "I'm not holding a grudge."

"Good." Fran slipped off the stool and adjusted her skirt. "Let's go find something to eat. I'm half starved."

THE HOTEL ROOM SEEMED NICE, at least by this world's standards. In her own travels, Sloane had seen rooming houses that ranged from 'sleep in a drawer for thirty galactic tokens' to the kind of sprawling resort that maintained its own hover-train transportation system. Her father gravitated toward the latter, whenever her family booked a vacation.

As this world didn't have hover trains—or hover *anything*, to its detriment—Sloane could only make guesses about the standards of her current accommodations based on how shiny everything seemed. Shininess seemed to be an important measure of fanciness on Earth. Good accommodations meant glittery light fixtures and highly polished floors and staff wearing uniforms with buttons that could blind you for an hour if you approached from the wrong angle.

Naturally, Sloane selected the hotel that gleamed most brightly. Alex and Hilda had pushed for less noticeable accommodations, but Sloane had no intention of bedding down with egg roaches, or whatever equivalent vermin made their homes in lower-level Earth hotels. What was the point of stealing, if you couldn't enjoy the benefits?

Most of the surfers—that was the name for the people rode the waves for hours with just a thin board standing between them and destruction, she'd learned—locked their personal effects up somewhere that Sloane had not been able to detect. By watching the beach for an hour, though, she'd finally caught sight of an unusually trusting soul. He'd tossed all his things under a towel on the sand, as if that would conceal them, before diving into the surf.

Which was how she was now sitting at a kitchenette with an ocean view and a fire in the fireplace, while Alex slept in the bedroom and Hilda made use of the jets in the sunken bathtub.

The translation app had recognized the paper in the surfer's wallet as currency. The papers looked different than what the app knew from whatever past it shared with this world, but were close enough for recognition. It was Alex who'd picked up on the fact that the slivers of plastic with raised numbers also functioned as currency.

They'd eaten. They'd found clothing that was Earth-like enough to make people stop asking for photo ops, though based on the narrow-eyed look of the hotel desk clerk, Sloane's selection hadn't quite hit the mark. She wasn't sure if it was the buttoned shirt bearing cartoon versions of the scraggly trees—they were everywhere, so she assumed Earth people loved them—the shell-like hat that buckled under her chin, or the red shoes held together by strings. Perhaps it was the combination of the three.

However strange her outfit might have been, it hadn't stopped the clerk from giving her another plastic card—this time to open the door to a suite, where they'd spent two blissful nights resting. Not hiding. Just resting.

Now, with the sliding window open to the sounds of the sea, Sloane sat on a stool and stared at the box that held the Blade of Starlight. She'd wiped Oliver's blood away, trying to adopt a clinical attitude toward the task and instead dissolving into a pool of unproductive tears. Nevertheless, the box was once again as white as the Blade itself, if not as shiny. Pearly, with swirled patterns carved into its sides like whirlpools. It didn't *look* that special. Certainly not worth dying for.

Sloane glanced down the little hall that led deeper into the room. Alex's door was still shut, as was the bathroom. She was alone.

Carefully, Sloane lifted a finger to the box's latch and flipped it open.

The gleam of the Blade made the box look like a child's toy. It was a moon compared to a boulder, a star compared to dirt. She stared, aware that her head was dipping toward it. If she listened through the rush of the waves outside, and the shuffle of the windblown curtains, she thought she could hear the Blade whispering. Calling to her.

Alex had said it was dangerous. Oliver had said so, too. And still, Sloane couldn't stop herself from reaching out a finger to caress its silken side.

As soon as she touched it, a pulse of energy burst from the Blade, launching her off the stool and into the counter behind her. Sloane's head cracked on the edge of the sink before she slid to the floor, dazed, her finger blazing red and smarting as if she'd burned it.

The treacherous thing. It had *called* to her. Baited her, more like. And now it was blinking. Either the damn thing was laughing at her, or it had an incoming call.

As the thought passed through her mind, a blob of mist thickened in the air beside the Blade, materializing in the shape of the man who'd killed Oliver. Or at least, she thought he had. Up close, his figure looked like a patch of smoke, white tinged with edges of blue and purple. He still had that cloak draped over his shoulders as if to ward off a chill. If he'd looked out of place on that sunny plaza, he was downright intrusive here amid the questionable hotel furniture and fading carpets. His fat curls dragged across his shoulders as he surveyed his surroundings.

When his gaze landed on Sloane, he tapped a finger against his lip. Assessing. "Interesting," he said.

Sloane popped to her feet, wondering how fast she could get away. And how this guy had appeared here without seeming to understand where he was. And whether he could kill her with a thought, as he had Oliver.

"You look confused, my dear," the ghostly figure said. "Allow me to introduce myself. My name is Morik."

Sloane swallowed, her throat dry with fear. "How did you find us?"

Morik's gaze drifted to the Blade of Starlight, a hungry gleam in his eyes. "The case allows us to trace the Blade's resonance."

But only as a hologram. He couldn't come here in person. At least, not yet. Sloane collected herself, putting on her best fighting face and hoping that Alex and Hilda would stay where they were.

Morik watched her, his lips twisted in an approximation of a smile. "Come now. You cannot believe me to be your enemy."

"Can't I?" Sloane said, before she could gather the sense to filter herself. Well, she was all in now. Might as well pull out the stopper. "You killed my friend."

Morik touched a gnarled finger to his bottom lip, contemplating her. "A rather harsh conclusion to jump to, don't you think? Although under the circumstances, I see how the scene might have appeared... rather damning."

Sloane huffed out a breath. "You think? You murdered him in cold blood."

"Oliver was a Fleet deserter. Did you know that?"

She did. He'd told her himself, though only after the Fleet had come after the *Moneymaker*. Not a mere deserter, either; he'd sold some of their secrets. Secrets, Sloane could now guess, that involved a certain iridescent Blade. She nodded, hesitant to give this man even that much information.

"The Fleet equips all their soldiers with a... let's call it a failsafe, shall we?" He pressed a finger to his cheek, indicating the back of his jaw. "A capsule of poison, in case of capture."

"Oliver wasn't captured."

Morik lifted his shoulders, dipping his chin in agreement. "Which begs the question of why he would have chosen that moment to take his own life." His gaze dropped to the Blade, and Sloane nearly dropped it. Was he implying that this trumped-up cheese knife had somehow been responsible for Oliver's death?

Well, why not? The thing *had* just tossed her across a room. Maybe it could also mess with people's minds, convince them to pop a pod of poison.

"We were trying to help him," Morik said softly. "We're trying to help everyone, by ridding the universe of that *thing*. You cannot begin to guess how dangerous it is."

Ridding the universe of it? She wasn't sure she could believe that. This thing was valuable. Powerful.

Sloane licked her lips, thinking. "What kind of poison does the Fleet use?"

Morik blinked, and Sloane had the sense she'd surprised him for the first time in this conversation. "Why should that matter?"

Because a promising young medical student—or at least, a halfway competent one—could pair the effects of such a poison with what had actually happened to Oliver. Seizing, blood, etcetera. Morik did not seem to know who Sloane was, not yet, and this might be her one opportunity to use his ignorance to her advantage.

Sloane allowed her lip to quiver. "I just... want to know how he died."

The elf steepled his fingers in front of his chest. "Consider allying with us." He smiled, and the wrinkles around his eyes deepened. "It could be beneficial to all, Ms. Tarnish."

Right. So he did know who she was. She gripped the counter behind her, trying to pull a coherent thought together. Yes, she'd advocated for handing the Blade over to these people, and she still wasn't sure it would be the wrong course of action. Morik might be telling the truth; the Blade might pose a serious threat to the universe, and his people—whoever they were—might be able to stop it.

On the other hand, Morik wouldn't name the poison. He might well have been the one who'd killed Oliver.

Worst of all, those truths were not mutually exclusive. What if Morik and his friends *had* killed Oliver, but also intended to save the worlds from the power of this Blade thing? What then?

"Who are you working with?" Sloane asked. He couldn't pretend to be alone, unless he was addicted to the royal 'we.'

Morik opened his mouth, hesitated.

A knock sounded on the door, and Morik's figure blinked out of sight as if it had never been. He couldn't truly fear being caught, not here. Unless this world had developed a way to grab fistfuls of light. Not likely.

Was he still watching? Could he see what she did, somehow? Sloane gave her head a shake. No point in obsessing about that right now. She slammed the box shut and gave herself a shake, then stuck her tongue out at the Blade—all of this, everything that had happened, was because of *it*—before opening the door.

A man stood in the hall, wearing a dark blue uniform and a hat with a little bill. Law enforcement, if she had to guess, based on the arrangement of shiny pins on his lapels and the stern expression on his face.

Earth, it seemed, used shininess to denote authority as well as fanciness. An interesting combination. Had they somehow heard her fall? Detected the pulse from the Blade? If so, she couldn't imagine how he'd arrived here so quickly. Maybe Earth had teleporters, after all. Or perhaps the military kept that tech to itself. She'd seen that before.

"I'm sorry for the disturbance," she said. She gave him her best smile, but flirting was difficult with her head aching, her hand smarting painfully. And the memory of Morik's smile. What did it mean? "I fell, but I'm OK."

The security officer blinked. "No, ma'am, that's not the problem. The hotel tried to run your credit card for incidentals, and it was declined. They called the card company, who checked with the owner, and it seems his wallet is missing."

That seemed like a lot of steps to go through. That clerk must have suspected her, after all. "So?" Sloane asked.

Hilda had appeared in the hall, a white towel wrapped around her body and another in her hair.

"So," the security officer said, drawing the syllable out, "you're under arrest and you'll need to come with me." He glanced behind her. "All of you."

Hilda swore and darted into the bedroom, emerging a few seconds later with a dress pulled halfway over her head, a duffle bag slung over her shoulder and a blinking Alex one step behind. Hilda had insisted on buying a bag, and it seemed that had been the right call.

"I think this might be a misunderstanding," Sloane said. They needed time to get their boots on; she was all too aware of the strange string-up shoes on her feet, and their lack of hov-tiles. And here she'd thought that drawstring shoes would be funny.

"Ma'am, I have probable cause to search this room if need be," the officer said. He glanced behind her. "If there's been a mistake, we'll sort it out at the station."

Or they'd throw her into a cell until the Blade of Starlight's owner tracked them down. Its Earth owner anyway, who may well have stolen it in the first place.

Sloane glanced behind her. Hilda and Alex had their boots on; time to go. She stepped back and tried to slam the door. It landed on the officer's boot, but she didn't stop, instead heading after the others as they dove for the open sliding door at the far end of the room. Sloane swept the Blade of Starlight's box off the counter, praying that Hilda had packed all her things—her hov-tiles, most importantly—as the officer burst into the room.

"Freeze!" he shouted, and the translation app scrambled to explain that he wasn't attacking them with a cryogenic weapon, but instead meant for them to stop moving. Apparently the app could handle some of this planet's idioms, after all.

As Sloane crashed onto the thin balcony, Hilda and Alex grabbed one arm each and took off, narrowly missing the wooden rail as they sailed toward the beach. Sloane hung between them, weighing down the hov-tiles meant to carry one at a time, and feeling a little idiotic as she dangled in midair by her armpits.

Together, they crashed to the beach, spraying sand in every direction. Hilda scrambled to her feet, throwing Sloane's boots at her. "I told you the currency would be trackable, like galactic tokens," she said. "I *told* you."

Sloane shoved her feet into the boots, all too aware of the people watching. There would be digital records floating around the feeds in minutes. If not seconds. The hov-tiles were too out of place in this trash heap of a world. "We had to sleep somewhere," she said, "and their currency is made of plastic. How was I supposed to know?"

Hilda rolled her eyes, but there wasn't time for a fight. As soon as Sloane's boots clamped around her feet, they took off down the beach.

ELOISE WOKE WITH A GASP, the Pearl Knife's voice singing into her mind with a desperate, keening cry. For a moment, she could only stare at the ceiling, unsure of where she was but positive she'd heard the Knife calling to her. Sure she could hear its echo in the beating of her own heart.

A dream. She sat up in bed, sweat beading her forehead though the AC cooled the Manhattan Beach safe house with perfect efficiency. She rubbed her eyes, trying to dispel the hopeless cry of the Knife as nausea churned through her stomach. She'd been asleep, damn it, not fighting or exerting herself. No zip lines, no poison-darted drones, and still she felt weak. If only she could chalk it up to an oncoming flu. If only it were that simple.

Eloise took her time getting dressed, willing her limbs to stop shaking. When she made her way into the kitchen, Dad was sitting at the table with a cup of coffee and a book. He smiled when she came in and marked his place in the book while she poured herself a cup of coffee. Of all the safe houses LIO possessed—and they possessed many—this was one of the more comfortable ones. Not a warehouse, a storage unit, or an underground tunnel. Just a normal apartment in a normal, beachside neighborhood. Expensive, but nice.

"What are you reading?" Eloise asked, sipping gratefully at the coffee. Dad always made good coffee. She wrapped her hands around the mug to hide their trembling, hoping her stomach would respond positively to the caffeine. She wasn't ready to share her weakness, even with her father. Not yet. What good would it do to worry him? And the others?

He ducked his head, sheepish. "Oh, just a novel."

As if he ever read anything else. Mom might have teased him about that, once upon a time, but Eloise certainly wouldn't. She, at least, understood the value of escapism. She slid the book toward her. "Jane Austen?"

Dad tipped his nose in the air. "I've always liked Mr. Darcy."

Eloise laughed. "I've never read Austen." She'd never had much time for reading, in general.

He pushed the book closer to her. "You have to, El. I insist."

"When you're finished rereading."

He pulled the book back, hugging it possessively. "Thank goodness. Sleep OK?"

She thought of the way the Knife had pulled at her mind. Had that truly been a dream? Or could it have been real? With the Knife, it was impossible to tell. "Fine," she said. "Just trying to decide on our next steps."

Steve and Ire had spent the night canvassing downtown L.A., meticulously retracing the steps of the fight with the aliens. Interviewing locals, looking for clues, and trying to catch a trail on the Knife-snatchers. They'd be back soon, and Eloise desperately hoped they'd bring new intel with them. Without further information she wasn't sure what her next step ought to be.

"I was thinking of splitting up to search along the beaches

for a few miles," Eloise said. "Maybe I could go south, and you could go north."

Dad frowned, pushing the book around in front of him on the table. "I'm not sure we should separate. What if they ambush us?"

"That is the risk."

"But?"

Eloise sighed. Even after two years away, he knew her well. She didn't want to bring up his powers, didn't want to initiate the conversation. Not when he'd endured so much. But she was also the head of the league. It was her job to make sure she knew what was happening with all the operatives. Even her father. "But with neither of us using our abilities, they could ambush us together, anyway."

Dad bobbed his head in agreement. He had to understand the unasked question, yet he didn't respond. Eloise wanted him to tell her about his powers, to volunteer the story without her having to ask outright whether they were somehow gone. But she more than suspected that he simply chose to lock them away, because of how Dolly had misused them. And if that was the case, the topic was a sensitive one. She had no desire to revive his trauma.

Eloise thought of Ire, of how Wave had used Mange's mind control potion to use his powers in ways he'd never have chosen. Was it as bad for him, knowing what he'd done? He hadn't hurt Mary freely; his brain had simply been obeying orders. Eloise hadn't thought to ask how he might be dealing with that.

They really needed to recruit a therapist to LIO.

Dad clearly didn't intend to respond to her hint, or delve into that conversation now. She might have to push him, if she wanted to know the truth. Later. There'd be time for that later.

Ire and Steve's voices echoed down the inside hallway of the apartment building, several levels too loud, and Eloise snapped her head up to stare at the door. So much for discretion. She heard them coming well before they pounded the agreed-upon knocking pattern, before the key turned in the lock. She heard them because they were arguing, their voices raised, and they didn't stop as they entered the apartment together.

Ire closed the door, locking it with care and pressing an eye to the peephole as if to check that they hadn't been followed, while Steve stormed into the room. She'd never seen such a sour expression on the man's face, and she tried to catch his eye, to smile at him, but he was beyond noticing. He slammed the refrigerator door open and scanned the interior. Like an angry teenager after a fight with his parents.

"We should have asked everyone we saw about the hologram," Steve said. "We should have told them about the hover boards, about everything, instead of beating around the bush with vague questions. 'Did you see anything strange? Was anything off?' It's L.A. Something is always off."

Apparently satisfied with what he saw in the hall, Ire stepped away from the peephole and strolled toward the kitchen, his huge arms crossed over his chest. His red hair came close to brushing the ceiling in here. "We hardly needed to draw more attention to ourselves."

Steve slammed the fridge door closed without removing anything. "The world knows about LIO now. Why do you insist on staying in the shadows?"

"Because we still have secrets to keep," Ire spat back. "A concept that seems lost on you."

Eloise glanced at Dad, who had his hands folded on the table as he watched the argument. The coffee wasn't sitting well in her stomach, the nausea returning in full force. She really didn't need another complication in all this madness. She needed people to get along. Was it truly too much to ask?

"I don't see why you refuse to just proclaim LIO business and do what you need to do." Steve paced across the tiny kitchen, clearly agitated. "Make badges or something. People would talk to you. This is my *whole* problem with the league, with the way you operate."

"Then maybe you should go," Ire said. "Seeing as you're not an official part of the league at all."

And then, beyond all reason, the two men turned to look at Eloise. As if she could solve this fight that they were clearly halfway through already. As if she could shore up Steve's trust in the league, and Ire's trust in Steve.

Except... except that usually, she wouldn't hesitate to attempt those things. To *do* those things. But the coffee was doing nothing to ease her murky thoughts, and she could feel a headache already starting to knock at the fringes of her skull. Right now, it was one challenge too many. Right now, she needed them to solve their own problems.

Eloise stood, still clutching her mug, and pushed past Ire to make her way back to the room where she'd slept. She refused to entertain this conversation until two grown men stopped acting like children. That was all; there was no other reason she needed to escape the room. She could hear their voices, still rising and falling out in the kitchen area, and she turned the lock. Heat crawled across her skin, her stomach protesting every move she made.

With her lungs constricting in her chest, Eloise breathed as easily as she could manage. On a good day, she'd knock the men's heads together.

Today was not a good day.

She opened her tablet, logged into the secure messaging system, and began composing a note.

She couldn't continue like this. How could she ever hope to claim the Knife back, if she couldn't even shut down a fight between two of her operatives? She knew she shouldn't reach out to Agnes—not when Agnes could expose Eloise's troubles to Wave. But if she worded the message correctly, vaguely, she might intrigue Agnes into helping her. She thought of calling Mary for advice on this—after her years in Hollywood, the woman was a master at handling tricky communications—but Mary was already worried enough. So instead, Eloise found herself typing out the barest, least-desperate message she could conceive of.

Agnes,

We may be at odds, but you studied Dolly's condition for years. Can you tell me anything you might have learned about how to counter the effects of the Knife's absence?

Your discretion is appreciated.

Eloise

Who was she even kidding with this? Wave probably read every incoming email on its servers. But it was as vague as she could get. And she needed help. Real, expert help.

After reading the message four times, Eloise took a deep breath and hit send, just in time for someone to knock on her door.

Eloise sat back in her chair, wondering how long she could pretend not to be here. Sighing, she got up and opened the bedroom door to find Steve standing in the hall with a sheepish grin plastered across his face. His annoying, too-handsome-to-punch face.

"Don't start," Eloise said. "I don't want to hear it."

"My apology?"

"Not particularly."

Steve gestured toward the room. "Can I come in?"

Eloise gripped the edge of the door. "Are you going to lobby me against Ire?"

"He won't even come up." Steve dragged his finger in a sloppy X across his chest, as if to seal the promise. She'd roll her eyes and call him a child again, except for the fact that he seemed sincere.

Eloise opened the door, stepping aside to let him enter. "Test me on this, and you're out." She returned to the desk chair and sank into it, swiping the tablet off the table as casually as she could while Steve took a seat on the edge of the bed. She'd just left the message center open, for anyone to see. For Steve to see. What if he'd read her note to Agnes? Eloise cringed inwardly, not wanting to picture that conversation. She really wasn't thinking straight.

Steve didn't seem to have noticed her haste to stow the tablet. He leaned his palms on the bed and looked at her. His shirt was rumpled from a night combing the city, his shoes scuffed.

"How many pairs of shoes do you wear through?" Eloise hadn't quite meant to ask the question out loud, but it was hard to imagine how regular shoes could withstand his super-speeding powers. And something about the man left her feeling frustratingly off-balance.

Steve grinned, wiping away the concerned expression he'd been wearing. Not her intention, but a nice side effect. "A lot."

"I'll have to see if the lab can cook up something for you."

She hoped the topic wasn't too league-centric, that it wouldn't bring them directly back to his altercation with Ire. For some reason, Steve was still helping the league, but he wasn't one of them. Eloise couldn't let herself forget it.

Steve didn't jump on the chance to start questioning their methods again. Instead, his expression flipped back to serious, as if he'd pushed a button. "How're you feeling?"

Like she didn't need anyone asking questions, or tempting her into confiding in them. That was how she was feeling. Everyone had enough to worry about, and besides, they'd have the Knife back soon. She could suffer a few headaches and chills in the meantime. "Strong enough to punch you for acting like a child."

"So I'm forbidden from discussing the argument back there, but you're not?"

"Exactly. Glad you understand the situation."

Not for the first time, Eloise wondered what his story was. What had he been doing in the years since he and his father had left LIO? Besides tailing Nathan, and working as a cop in Boston. What did he know about the league—or not know—that made him so antsy about the way they worked? And what made him cover his serious side with an exterior of well-dressed charm?

Steve just sat there on the edge of the bed, considering her, as if he could assess her health and wellbeing with that warm-eyed stare of his. "You want to change the way the league operates, distance yourself from your mother's cruelties. How do you expect to accomplish that if you don't deal honestly with the public?"

Eloise blinked. It wasn't what she'd expected from him,

though she wondered why not. He'd argued with Ire, sure, but that disagreement involved a mission they were both directly involved in. Now he wanted to challenge the way she ran the league?

"I don't know if you've noticed," she said carefully, "but I've barely been treading water since the fight with the retirees."

"But you've known about Dolly's crimes for months," he pushed.

And it was Nathan who'd released the prisoners, not Eloise. Steve didn't say it, but it was what he meant. With Mary gone, a new recruit program to handle, and swarming reporters—not to mention a new relationship with the government that needed managing—Eloise's plate had been well and truly full since the moment Jenna Carpenter had blown the league's cover.

Treading water? It was a wonder she hadn't drowned.

Eloise raised a hand, pleasantly surprised to find that it was steady. "I cannot have this conversation with you right now."

If he insisted, she'd kick him out. If she insisted, she might have to... What? Send him away?

Thankfully, Steve just gave his head a little shake, like he needed to reset his brain. "I'm... yeah, I'm sorry. I really just wanted to check in and make sure you're OK." Steve kept his attention laser-focused on her, and she half felt like he was interrogating her. "I know you weren't feeling well at HQ."

"Well, I'm fine now," Eloise said. "Thanks for checking."

Steve watched her, as if waiting for her to keel over any second and prove that she wasn't actually OK. If he stayed too long, that might actually happen.

Mercifully, Eloise's phone rang, saving her from the need to further defend her health. For the moment, anyway. She'd never been so happy to see Pete's face.

"Have you checked into social media today?" the surveillance expert asked, by way of greeting. Not uncommon for Pete, actually.

"I haven't," she said. "It's just past six here."

A pause. Eloise wasn't sure that up-with-the-dawn Pete would make the connection between 'six AM' and 'just woke up.'

"OK," he said. "Well, apparently there was a bit of a commotion up near Santa Monica Beach. Commotion involving strangely dressed people on flying boards."

Hope seized onto her chest, sending her heart pounding into her throat before she could tamp it down. Maybe she really *had* heard the Knife this morning. Maybe it had somehow managed to call her.

Maybe she would get to see it soon. "Send me the highlights," she said. "We're on our way."

AGNES STARED at her tablet screen for a full five minutes, reading Eloise's message again and again, trying to make sense of it. Agnes might not be privy to the ins and outs of LIO's current dramas, but she knew for a fact that Dolly no longer enjoyed the position she once had. Agnes had no idea whether the former Pearl Knife still lived at LIO HQ, but after the revelation of her crimes, Eloise certainly wouldn't hold her in the same esteem.

Had Dolly's condition worsened, leaving Eloise to ask for help on behalf of her mother—despite the woman's crimes—or... Agnes frowned at the screen, trying to sift through the too-formal email. Eloise knew how little Agnes had learned about Dolly's health, and its connection to the Pearl Knife. It was a situation that had stymied them both, for years.

To someone who didn't know Eloise, the message might have been a mere request for information. A stiff one, but polite enough. Businesslike.

And yet to Agnes, the fact that El had reached out at all after the fiasco in Las Vegas, and after Agnes's refusal to help in the fight against LIO's retired members... If El was reaching out anyway, it had to mean she needed help. Desperately.

With a quick glance around her lab to ensure her privacy—old habit, given that few people entered here without knocking—Agnes delved into her old LIO files. She'd saved everything; she always did. It wasn't as if the league classified things. The secrecy involved in every choice, every blood test, remained a given.

Not that Agnes had any intention of passing her inside knowledge on to Wave. Whatever she felt about the league, it wouldn't have been the ethical choice. She was just going to look. Refresh her memory. She had some distance from the research now; maybe she'd be able to see it with fresh eyes.

Diagrams, blood tests, cell samples. She remembered studying Dolly's deteriorating health, and trying to compare what she saw in the woman's ragged cells with characteristics of the Pearl Knife. But the Knife didn't like to be studied. It shorted out equipment, resisted material analysis, and gave unfriendly, electric-like zaps to anyone who tried to touch it. Except for Eloise, of course, not that El had had any more luck subjecting the thing to LIO's equipment.

Agnes pulled up her diagram of the Pearl Knife. Such a funny way to put it; it was a drawing, one she'd done as a last ditch resort, a way to look more closely. Like diagramming a plant for high school biology. The Knife's surface had almost seemed to be made of tiny pores, when she'd studied it through a magnifying glass—the one close-up the blade *would* allow. Bent over her Wave-provided desk, Agnes wracked her memory for some clue that would explain the Knife's properties. Any of them.

Agnes squinted at the screen. And then she pulled Eloise's email back up. She didn't know the answer, but maybe...

"Are you working with the Pearl Knife again?"

Lucy's voice startled Agnes, making her jump on her lab

stool. She shut off the tablet and swiveled around to find her daughter standing right beside her shoulder.

"You scared me," Agnes said, holding a hand to her chest. "I thought you were a ghost."

Her daughter's mouth pressed in a tight line, and she twisted a dark curl around one finger, a sure sign of anxiety. "Are you?"

Agnes glanced at the screen. "Just looking a few things up."

"You should be looking things up for our *friends*. Not people who lock them in jail and crash airplanes." She tugged on her curl, her upper lip trembling. The girl was one misplaced comment away from tears.

Agnes reached out a hand to beckon Lucy to her side, but the girl kept her feet firmly planted in place. "Eloise never crashed any planes," Agnes said.

As for the other charge, well, Agnes couldn't honestly defend Eloise on that account. *She* had kept their new friends behind bars, and it was impossible to expect that Lucy wouldn't have heard the truth about that. They'd been enveloped in Wave for months now, with Lucy and Tam welcomed in a way they'd never been welcomed to LIO. Dolly hadn't allowed outsiders at HQ. Neither had Eloise.

Of course Lucy would have heard about the league's crimes. Maybe Agnes should have explained it herself. Had she been protecting her daughter by neglecting to do so? Or had she been protecting herself? Thinking of all she'd done to bolster LIO's resources over the years, to hand them technology they could use to hurt or control others... It made her chest hot with shame.

Lucy's attention skipped to the screen and back to her mother's face, her eyes glistening. "Are you going back there? Are you leaving? Because we're safe here. *You're* safe. And you're helping people."

Agnes swallowed hard, now fighting her own tears at the thought of her daughter worrying for her safety. Working with LIO had meant time away from her family, and she'd always worried about how her absence affected Lucy. She hadn't ever considered that her daughter might have been afraid for her when she left. The distance was meant to keep Lucy and Tam safe, but clearly Lucy hadn't been convinced of that, either.

Agnes swiveled her stool and closed the window with the Pearl Knife specs. Eloise would need to find a way to leverage the league's glory, and its extensive resources, to solve her problem. Whatever it was. "I'm not going anywhere," she said.

Lucy's eyes narrowed—the girl was eight going on eighteen —but she dropped her hand away from her curls, and her shoulders relaxed. "Did you know Mama's planning a concert? She said I could play a song on my flute."

Agnes tucked her tablet under her arm and took her daughter by the hand, half expecting Lucy to pull away. Which, thankfully, she didn't. She still had some kid time left, after all. "I didn't," she said. "It sounds like a great idea. Let's go get some lunch, and you can tell me all about it."

MARY HADN'T REALIZED her brain needed a break—from engineering, from designing, from HQ in general—until Gail asked her to help Pete out with surveillance. He needed another pair of eyes, one that knew the top-secret news of the Knife's disappearance. Could Mary give him a hand?

Instead of leaping at the chance to watch cameras with him, to find out firsthand what was happening with El and the others, Mary heard herself offer to cover the desk in the public relations office up top so that Gail could come down to help Pete.

Judging by Gail's quick acceptance, she needed a change of pace, too. The poor woman spent her days dealing with the general public. Of course she could use a break.

LIO's public relations office was comprised of a small brochure-stuffed customer area and a wooden counter. Mary's place was behind it, sitting in an office chair before a computer, with a copy machine at her back. It felt so... normal, compared to the world it supposedly led to. Though Mary suspected Gail spent most of her days talking to curious tourists and booking press appointments for Eloise. Pretty normal stuff, really.

Today, the office was blissfully quiet. It was February in

Niagara Falls, after all, when most people fled wintery conditions in favor of Disney World. The room smelled like wood
and paper, and the vanilla candle Gail had set up on the desk.
Mary lit it, enjoying the simple pleasure of watching the flame
burst to life, and spun her chair around a few times.

She hadn't made any progress on a Knife-capturing appara-
tus, despite her best efforts. It had only been a few days, but
there was a deadline here. Sooner or later, the aliens would
figure out how to zip back to their own world. They'd take the
Knife with them.

Mary couldn't let that be an option. But she knew too little
to think of a workable solution.

When the door opened with a little chime—like this was a
gift shop or something—Mary stopped spinning her chair and
sat up, trying to look professional.

The man who entered did an actual double take at the sight
of her there. She supposed she ought to have anticipated that.
Famous face, drudge of a job. It was a weird enough combo.
The man regained his composure fairly quickly, though,
reaching for his neck as if to adjust a tie before realizing it was
under his overcoat. He was young, with white-blond hair
peeking out from under a black knitted cap.

"I have an appointment with Eloise Reyna," he said, like he
was showing up for a job interview with the CFO or something. He set a briefcase at his feet and rested his elbows on the
counter.

"Eloise isn't here," Mary said. "You must have gotten the
date wrong."

The man frowned at her, like he was about to ask to speak
to her manager or something. "Check her appointment log," he
said, his tone just this side of condescending. "I'm sure you
must be mistaken."

Mary grinned at him. It wasn't that she'd been itching for a fight since she came to HQ, not exactly, but she also wasn't sorry to come face-to-face with someone who might potentially deserve a good tongue lashing.

But OK, yes, she ought to try and be nice to start with. Gail certainly would. Mary kept up the smile, trying to tamp down the part of her that was eager to start a fight. So entitled guy felt entitled. She'd spend years in Hollywood; she was hardly a stranger to that attitude. "You know who I am?" she asked.

The man swallowed. "I know who you are."

She kept her tone even. The very best in customer service. "So you're aware I'm not just the receptionist. And that I probably know a thing or two about where Eloise might be."

He glanced around, taking in the copier and the shelves full of office supplies. "You look like you're the receptionist."

The door opened again, and Mary decided that Gail was a very patient woman to put up with that cheerful little bell.

When it was Nathan who entered, she thought she might actually call Gail. Who would not be impressed that the independent operative couldn't handle a few hours sitting at her desk. Or a few minutes. Right. So she'd stick it out, then.

Mary ignored Nathan and pulled up the calendar on the computer. "No appointments for Eloise today," she said sweetly. "As I said."

The man took off his gloves. "Where is she?"

Nathan leaned back against the wall by the door, a favorite spot of his in any room. Not that she'd noticed. He watched the interaction with that slanted smile Mary had loved, once upon a time. He wasn't going to help her out here? Fine.

"I'm not at liberty to tell you," Mary said.

The man actually sputtered at her. As in, his lips got all tangled up, and spit flew around his mouth. "I am your liaison to the United States government. I'm meant to know exactly what you're doing, and when."

Nathan raised his eyebrows. Mary pretended not to see him. "Oh," she said, "you're the kid."

The kid's face turned bright red. As a person with pale skin, Mary was aware of the dangers of a rogue blush. This guy —Travis, Eloise had said—apparently didn't. Or couldn't control it. And he turned much, much redder than she hoped she ever had. Apple red.

"I am not a *kid*," he said. She half expected steam to pipe out of his ears like a cartoon character. "I am a government employee with a *significant* position and resources that would wipe that smile off your face."

Unlikely, given that LIO's own resources included submarine cars and an underground compound that was probably bigger than the White House, though she'd never made a study of the square footage. But this guy was staring at her like he meant what he said. He really thought he was entitled to LIO's secrets.

Mary just blinked at him, trying for innocent. She wanted to unleash her sarcasm, but she wouldn't give Nathan the satisfaction of witnessing that. "Eloise isn't here, and I can't answer your question because it's classified."

"You can't classify things. The government classifies things."

Mary shrugged. "Not my problem, Senator."

Travis shoved his hands into his gloves and whirled around, startling when he saw Nathan watching from the wall. Without another word, the aspiring bureaucrat swiped up his briefcase and stormed out the door, slamming it behind him.

It was probably too much to hope that Nathan would go, too. He pushed away from his station and approached the counter, leaning against it with one elbow. Mary glared up at him, her satisfaction at angering the government kid draining away at the sight of Nathan's face, at his casual amusement.

And the memory of the rainbow-haired woman with her hand on his shoulder.

Well, Mary wouldn't speak first. She refused.

Nathan, though, didn't seem to have the same hesitation. "That went well," he said. "Maybe in your next career, you'll be a diplomat."

NATHAN FULLY EXPECTED Mary to kick him out of the public relations office. By words, by force, by whatever means necessary. Or to refuse to acknowledge his presence, as she'd been doing since she arrived.

It was her prerogative. Nathan actually hadn't come here to bug her; he'd come looking for Gail. But the chance to witness Mary dealing with Eloise's cocky government friend? So very much better.

The last time Nathan had stood in this office, it was because Jeff Hayes had come to see him. To beg him to go after Mary, to stop her in her crusade against the LIO retirees. It had been unexpected to say the least, given how much the man enjoyed taunting Nathan whenever they crossed paths. Honest though the movie star's intentions had turned out to be, Nathan vastly preferred Mary's company.

But maybe that wasn't saying much. As long as she wasn't trying to punch him in the face, Nathan still preferred her company to anyone else's.

She didn't kick him out. And to his surprise, she didn't ignore him, either. She sat back in her chair, arms folded, and regarded him with cool composure. Her golden curls were tied back in a ponytail, her green eyes as sharp and unyielding as they'd ever been. Even sitting behind a desk, she looked ready to strike, muscles coiled for action.

Nathan had been expecting a reckoning ever since Mary's return to HQ. He'd been braced for the showdown, ready to endure whatever tirade, whatever accusations she launched at him. He hadn't pictured it happening among the office supplies and the smell of copy toner, but the setting hardly mattered. He deserved it. He'd accept it. Though he did glance behind him, to make sure the shades were drawn.

"So I hear you were injured," Mary said finally. She might have been asking about a new pair of shoes, or a pencil. Something inconsequential, rather than a moment that had nearly killed him. The sting of the dart in his neck had been bad enough; when he'd felt himself tumble over the side of the boat, his consciousness receding as he fell, he'd certainly expected death.

A stranger might have assumed that Mary didn't care about what had happened, or almost happened. But he thought he knew her as well as a few months together could allow, and he was certain that if Mary didn't care, she wouldn't ask. No matter what she might pretend.

"I'm fine," Nathan said, trying to sound as casual as she did. Not easy, with his heart doing its best to hammer its way out of his chest. So what if she didn't want him dead? That was hardly a stellar recommendation. "The recruits were on it."

"Well, as long as the *recruits* were on it."

She could have acted with the best of her colleagues in Hollywood; her casual, wide-eyed expression didn't change. But something in her tone... Nathan blinked, trying to interpret the truth behind the performance. She almost seemed... jealous?

His heart certainly thought so. It flipped joyously into his stomach, even while his brain counseled him not to read into anything Mary said. Games were her specialty.

Nathan cleared his throat, still leaning on the counter. It was as close as she'd ever let him get. He wanted to pace away from her, to expend the nervous energy in his own muscles. He wanted to lean in closer. "Without the recruits, we'd have been shorthanded."

Her eyes flashed with something like anger, there and gone as quickly as a bolt of lightning. "If you're implying I should have been there, I didn't know about it until the fight was done."

And wouldn't have come even if she had, based on her choice to stay behind at HQ rather than search for the Knife with the other operatives. He still didn't understand that, but he certainly knew better than to ask. A minefield of a conversation between them was better than no conversation at all.

But he hadn't been thinking of her when he considered how shorthanded they were. He'd been thinking of Dr. Gordon and the other Wave operatives, and Eloise's refusal to let him reach out to them. How helpful would it have been, to have had them there on the boat?

Nathan raised his palms off the counter in surrender. Every move felt like a trap. Was it weird that he missed this? Probably. "I'm implying nothing. Although you'd have enjoyed smashing the drones."

"I don't enjoy smashing tech." There was finally a bite in her words, a sharpness she couldn't hide. "Especially tech that's shooting darts at you."

Nathan lifted a hand to his chest. "You wound me."

"Well, I'm sure Rainbow Brite will patch it up for you."

Rainbow... "What, you mean Tally?"

Mary lifted a shoulder, and a dozen responses crowded into his head. Implications, insinuations, and *Why, would that bother you?* If she truly was jealous, Nathan could fuel the fire.

He forced himself to take a step back from the counter. "There's nothing going on between Tally and me."

The shoulder again, an eye roll. "If you say so."

He should leave now. Pull his gloves on, say something polite, and leave her to her day. She might be jealous, but that didn't mean anything. He couldn't let it mean anything.

Instead of leaving, he hesitated. Yes, Mary was his ex. That much was clear in every biting interaction between them. But she was also a longtime member of LIO. With Ire and Steve away, he could use some advice. Gail surely would have helped where she could—he'd come up here to ask about putting together some kind of HQ orientation for the new recruits—but her experience tended toward the administrative rather than the political.

Maybe it was wrong to seek advice from Mary, or use it as a subject change. An excuse to keep talking. Still, they had to at least learn to act as colleagues. At some point.

She'd dropped her gaze to the computer screen, a clear dismissal. She was done with him for the day. Maybe forever.

"I've been thinking about the Wave operatives," Nathan said. "I wondered... I thought you might have an opinion."

Mary didn't look up. "You mean the criminals you released?"

"Prisoners, yes. Criminals? They weren't."

He hoped she wouldn't argue, wouldn't take Dolly's side. That any barb she tossed out on this subject would be about Nathan, and not about the people Eloise's mother had falsely imprisoned. He couldn't truly picture her siding with the former Pearl Knife, not after what the woman had done to Mary's parents. When she nodded, he let out a breath of relief.

"I know they're not criminals," she said. "And they helped in L.A. So?"

Nathan relaxed his hands, tried to mirror her casual attitude. "So I wondered if it wouldn't be wise to keep a line of communication open to them. There are a couple dozen, all people who want to make Wave a better organization."

Just like Eloise wanted to make LIO better. She might not know them the way he did, but he still didn't understand how she could dismiss their attributes so swiftly. Yes, LIO and Wave had a long history of enmity. But two such powerful organizations could do so much good in the world, if only they'd join forces. Or at least agree to form a let's-not-kill-each-other alliance.

"No coincidence there, I'm sure," Mary muttered. "Sounds like Dolly made a point to root out Wave's best."

Nathan blinked. He hadn't put that together before. "Right," he said. "You're right."

Mary looked up from the computer, the screen's light reflecting on her face. "I think we're up against more than we know. After L.A., it feels like... It feels like the populated universe is an iceberg, and Earth is the tip." She shook her head, freeing a few of her curls from their tie. "When I chased after the aliens, I saw this... figure. Like a ghost, communicating with them."

A ghost? Like these aliens could somehow summon the dead on their behalf? Because that really would be a problem.

"Probably a hologram of some kind." She tapped her fingers on the desk, and he could tell she'd steal the tech's secret in an instant, if she could. She'd twist it into something even better. "But I don't know how, and it disappeared too fast for me to get a good look. I just get the sense we might be in over our heads. Maybe staying in touch with your friends would be wise."

He should be focusing on what she'd said, on the threat of

these newcomers, on the mysterious hologram. Another threat. All he could think was that she'd said something to him, something real. No threats, no passive aggressive comments. At this point, Nathan half expected Mary to disagree with any idea he presented, simply out of spite. Maybe their romantic relationship couldn't be reconciled—he didn't dare hope for it, however his treacherous heart might stutter—but a friendship? A working partnership, even? Could be salvageable.

"Eloise said no," he said.

Mary's thoughtful expression shifted to a glare, and she clutched the edge of the desk like she might pick it up and throw it at him. If she had super strength, she might just. "Then why ask me?" she said. "If it's no, then it's no. Don't use me as your excuse to break orders."

Or maybe they'd hover in this space forever, where she barely tolerated him. Where he tried to pretend it didn't matter. He could protest. Probably should. He would never use her as an excuse, and she should know it.

But Mary had gone back to whatever fascinating thing was on the computer screen, and Nathan doubted she'd be enticed to look up again. He left without saying goodbye.

"I DON'T KNOW what to tell you, son," Senator Jones said, his irritation plain even through the phone. "Sounds like someone messed up."

He meant that *Travis* had messed up, though even the senator didn't dare say so. No matter how powerful Travis's family was, though, or how generous with their donations, it didn't stop the senator from ending the call. And probably the chance of any additional travel funds.

A mistake. A grave mistake. Travis gripped his phone in a gloved hand, trembling with cold and no small amount of rage. Launching his phone into the falls would do him no good.

In kicking Travis out of that scummy little office of theirs, the League of Independent Operatives was declaring war on the United States government. Senator Jones might not see it, the liaison committee might not see it, but Travis Bertram certainly did.

These people were making a mockery of everything he stood for.

Travis didn't know why Mary O'Sullivan of all people— Coral, as she'd once been—was staffing a lowly desk. He didn't much care. He wasn't one to get starstruck over anyone less than a world leader; certainly not over a slutty page-six regular.

She'd kicked him out. That was the only thing that mattered. And she was going to pay for it.

Tourists moved around him, their parkas like splatters of paint on a miserably icy canvas. They, too, ignored him in favor of the snow-capped falls. A trio of giggling teenagers bumped into him as they passed, phones already poised to capture the icy falls that hid the league's impenetrable headquarters. The teenagers didn't bother to apologize for jostling him, didn't even turn. He might have been invisible.

No one even knew who he was. No one cared.

They would. Everyone would. With a deep breath, Travis lifted his phone and steadied his fingers enough to make a call.

He should have listened to the EAEA from the moment they'd started showing up in his office. Late was better than never, and if no one else would take action, at least he had an ally.

The senator would be thanking him on bended knee before this was over. They all would.

"It's time," Travis said, as soon as Chloe picked up the call. "Go ahead and send your people in."

Sloane was getting tired of racing down beaches.

They'd evaded the law enforcement officer, who'd clearly not expected them to go flying out of the window. The hov-tiles had carried them down the beach faster than he could have possibly anticipated, given the limited transportation options in this world. And even though Alex's had given out about a mile from the hotel, the sound of sirens—the officer's backup, Sloane assumed—had been distant by the time the three of them slipped down a side street to hunker in an alley that smelled like cats and week-old ale.

Impressive escapes aside, Sloane wasn't meant to be a thief. Not really. And she was beginning to suspect—though perhaps it ought to have crossed her mind before—that none of them were. Hilda was a pilot; a little too skilled in evasive maneuvers to claim a completely clean record, but still a pilot. Not a criminal mastermind. And Alex? Just a scientist.

After what seemed like an age, they emerged from the alley and back into the daylight. When no law enforcement officers pounced on them, they set about solving the first of their mounting problems: the dying hov-tiles. Their ability to fly was their one leg-up in this world, as far as Sloane was concerned. If they failed to maintain it, they'd be caught.

Which was why they were now crouching together on the curb beside a bank of stick-like consoles in a beachside parking lot. Alex had an inkling that the bright white mini towers that were stationed here could provide some kind of an electric charge, and as Sloane's ankles were sore from so much hover-escaping, she didn't object to the idea of a rest. Besides, she wanted to give the translation app a break. The poor thing had been trying to install updates practically since they'd arrived. Sloane still didn't understand how that could be possible, or where the app might be connecting with a datapoint. Maybe it was just glitching out.

All the more reason to rest it. So they'd set up camp here, first watching from a bench while several electric vehicles pulled up and connected the console wires to charge. Now, as the sun cast molten hues across the sea behind them, Alex sat fiddling with the charging wires, trying to find a way to apply them to the hov-tiles, while Sloane stretched her feet off the curb and into the parking lot. Beside her, Hilda chewed on some sticky Earth candy that came, inexplicably in the form of neon-colored worms.

It wasn't unpleasant here. The air was warm and scented with sweet-smelling flowers, or maybe fruit. If they ever got out of this mess—if Sloane ever extricated herself from her uncle's not-so-criminal crew—she might suggest this planet to her father as a vacation spot. Assuming he'd be willing to speak to her again, after her brief foray into the world of crime. Or what-ever this was.

"You're a decent pilot," Sloane said, the words leaving her mouth before she'd quite realized she meant to say anything. That seemed to happen to her a lot.

Hilda glanced at her, still chewing her candy. "If you call

the woman who holds the Parse record for the fastest Tri-Orbit circuit 'decent,' then yes."

Sloane frowned. Her father obsessed over the Tri-Orbit race every year. He'd even attended in person a few times, watching from a viewing schooner that followed the fastest part of the track—the gravity sling between Elter's two moons—though Sloane had never paid much attention to the stories he told about it. "Really?"

Hilda surveyed a blue and green worm, giving it an experimental tug. "I'll save you the trouble of asking why I took a job flying the *Moneymaker*. Because the champion's life isn't nearly as lucrative as you'd think, and card games are a thing."

It took Sloane a moment to understand what she meant. "What, you've got gambling debts?"

Hilda shrugged, scraping a toe across the pavement. "Here and there."

"I've never seen you play cards."

Hilda scowled at her. "That's because I learn from my mistakes, girl. Do you?"

Sloane wanted to say that Hilda would need to narrow it down, given how many mistakes she tended to make. But she hesitated, still feeling a tug of conscience that insisted she was responsible for this crew. They might not think much of her, but she should still be working to reassure them. She needed to drum up some confidence, somehow.

Before she could think of a way to do that, Alex looked up from her tinkering. "It's not going to work," she said calmly, standing to return the wires to their proper spot. She gave her hov-boots a little kick, as if hoping she could restart the battery out of pure annoyance. It was one of the few marks of frustration Sloane had ever seen from her. Someone needed a snack.

Sloane bent to rub her ankle. She should enroll in a course

to review her hov-tile stance, because clearly she was leaning too hard or something.

Sore ankles. A magical, palm-stinging Blade. Sandy underwear. Maybe this world wasn't so vacation-worthy, after all. "What do you mean?" she asked. "You created a wormhole. You're a brilliant scientist. Surely you can make it work."

Alex huffed a strand of red hair out of her eyes, ignoring the compliment. "I can't create an adaptor out of nothing. We're going to need a new trick."

Or a new heist. The thought twisted in Sloane's gut. She wasn't exactly eager to try stealing more things. So far, their criminal activity on Earth had not been smoothly accomplished —and the limited criminal activity they'd actually managed to achieve in the Parse Galaxy had all been Oliver's doing. "Surely there's a store here that has the parts you need," she said.

Alex glanced around. "With this world's primitive technology? Doubtful."

Hilda, who'd been so quiet that Sloane had thought she might have fallen asleep with her mouth full of worms, said, "Maybe something you could strip to raw parts and reassemble?"

Brushing her hands off on the flower-print pants she'd purchased with the stolen currency, Alex started back toward the beach. Not a fan of the raw-part plan, then. Or maybe going off in search of some, though Sloane hardly expected to find anything useful in the water. Sighing, she got up to follow, with Hilda right behind her.

Her feet had barely hit the sand when Alex stopped, pointing back in the direction of the hotel they'd escaped from —and the pair of figures striding toward them along the beach. "I think we're going to need the adaptor sooner than that."

For a moment, Sloane thought one of people was small—

very small—but as they came closer, she realized it was because his companion loomed beside him like something out of a Forgeian myth, where stones came alive and statues crushed the enemies that had frozen them in place for centuries. A patch of red hair burst up from the man's scalp like a flame, as orange as the setting sun.

He was clearly coming for them.

Sloane grabbed Alex's arm, and Hilda followed suit. They'd managed to drag Sloane out of the hotel room that way; they could do the same for Alex, since Hilda had thankfully stashed Sloane's boots in the duffel bag before their flight from the hotel. Sloane didn't know how she felt about their apparently mutual mind reading, but her closeness with this crew was something to unpack later. When they weren't about to be attacked by a rock-muscled giant.

Their feet had hardly left the sand before the giant's companion moved—an insufficient word for what he did. He *pulsed*, blurring into a line across the sand as if someone had taken a time-lapsed vid of his movement the way they sometimes did to demonstrate planetary orbits.

"Hurry," Sloane said, but it was too late; the blurred line melted into a blurred circle, the man moving so quickly that he penned them in. Sand spit around their legs as he ran, and Sloane wondered if, when he stopped, he'd leave a trench behind.

It didn't matter. What mattered was that if they tried to escape the tight cage-circle, the runner would slam into them, and Sloane *really* didn't want to know what that would feel like. Usually, the hov-tiles would be able to lift them over and above, but with Alex's weight distributed between Sloane's and Hilda's, they'd never get enough lift to fly above his trap.

Sloane wondered how long the runner could sustain this.

She'd dismissed him as soon as she'd seen the big man beside him, but that had clearly been a mistake.

She seemed to be making a lot of those lately.

"These Earth people have strange powers," Hilda said, deactivating her hov-tiles and dropping back to the sand. Alex just gazed at the giant in silence, expressionless. Or maybe Sloane simply didn't know her well enough to understand the expression. *Did* these people have powers? Or was it technology that kept one running, the other puffed up with muscle?

She could see the giant approaching them through the blurred view, like looking through wavery glass in an ancient Govrin City ruin. He stopped, the wind from his friend's movement stirring his hair slightly. "Give us the Knife," he said, his deep voice resonating easily through the wind, through the stir of sand that bit at her legs through her cheap Earth pants.

The Knife. A paltry word for the Blade of Starlight, if she understood anything about it. If it really had originated in the Parse Galaxy, it might be the greatest piece of technology on this backwater planet, and yet these people discussed it like cutlery.

"Pick another prize," Sloane shouted. "Your friend will tire eventually. And then we'll escape."

"Takes me a while to tire." Judging by his voice, the running guy wasn't even breathing hard. It felt like talking to a circle, the sound echoing around them like an announcement in a virtual reality entertainment experience.

Even though the circle guy was on his side, the giant scowled at that. "You're going to start a tornado."

"Surely if that happens you'll just bench press it into submission."

Before Sloane could contemplate the relationship between these two, or the vitriol in their tone as they spoke to each other, the giant bent his knees. And then, he leapt right over the human cage that was his friend. Or, if not his friend, at least his... partner?

The giant landed within the circle, shooting up another significant spray of sand. Alex and Hilda pressed close to her on either side—a motion Sloane noted with distant surprise—but a united front meant nothing to this man. The runner's cage forced him close to them, and there was nowhere to go; half a step, and he held Sloane's collar in his fist, the cartoon trees on her shirt bunching under his massive fingers. He lifted her off the ground, separating her from her friends, and she kicked her feet instinctively—uselessly—against him.

It didn't hurt, but it certainly wasn't comfortable. Her heart beat wildly in her chest, and she struggled to maintain some shred of dignity. "You're going to rip my shirt," she said.

"The Knife doesn't belong to you," he said, as if she hadn't spoken. His voice was a deep growl in the back of his throat.

Sloane coughed. "It doesn't belong to you, either." Probably.

The giant grinned. Somehow, she didn't think it was because he wanted to make peace. "You're right," he said. "It belongs to her."

The circle guy kept circling, but even with her neck tipped back at an angle and the frosted view of the beach beyond the cage, Sloane could see the woman she'd stolen the Blade from, heading toward them down the beach. She had a large-ish man with her, too, though the giant still dwarfed him.

"We're so screwed," Alex said.

Sloane didn't disagree. She imagined the Blade, locked in its time-out box in the bag she had slung over her shoulder. She imagined it trying to call to the woman, trying to escape.

What would happen if it did?

No bounty, she decided, was worth getting gutted by such an artifact. If the Blade was even half as dangerous as Morik suggested, Sloane wouldn't risk angering anyone who yielded it. Politics be damned.

She actually opened her mouth to surrender.

A second blur flashed out of nowhere, knocking the cage-making blur toward the waves. The two figures struggled together, and as best she could see, it was like watching two balls of vaguely colored light try to pummel one another into the sand.

Hilda activated her hov-tile, Alex's arm clutched in hers. But the giant still held Sloane, and she didn't doubt he'd be able to hold her back if she attempted to fly. She didn't doubt it at all. She thought about kicking him, but she had a feeling his muscles were too rock-like for it to make any difference. She'd probably just stub her toe.

Hilda hesitated, apparently unwilling to leave Sloane behind. Sloane wasn't at all sure she'd have made the same call, not with the Blade's Earth-based owner moving toward them across the beach. The person at her side wore a helmet over his head, with a tinted visor covering his face. The woman darted a glance at the wrestling balls of light, clearly trying to determine if the one on her side needed help.

If she even could help him, without her Blade-Knife-what-ever-it-was.

And all of a sudden, there was an army on the beach. Sloane supposed it wasn't really sudden; the giant was still dangling her from his huge paws like a doll, which did limit her vision. The second blur had to have come from somewhere, though, and now she could see where: a dozen or more people approached from the south, led by a woman with red hair and freckles scattered across her cheeks. Sloane didn't know any of these players, their names, their roles. She wasn't sure she wanted to.

But these people, it seemed, weren't here to help Sloane's

enemies. Which could only be a good thing. Not that she had any desire to end up stuck in the middle of a battle between the two groups, but battles meant chaos. And chaos could mean escape.

"Is there an surplus of redheads on this planet?" Sloane said. "Seems unnatural."

"I hope you're not counting me," Alex said.

"Right. Definitely not."

The giant lowered Sloane just enough for her toes to brush the sand, surprise registering across his features as he faced the oncoming army. "Aren't you Pearce's sister?"

Sloane didn't know who the cursed stars Pearce was, and she didn't much care. The giant was distracted, which meant that eventually, he'd make a mistake. When he did, Sloane would make her move.

She could lead them out of this mess. She had to.

"I am." The army-leader redhead's voice rang with authority. And distaste, apparently at the mention of her sibling, though who could say? More importantly, what part of this information could Sloane use to her advantage? "And I'm authorized to place you under arrest."

THE SUNSET CAST the scene in fiery hues, the sand appearing almost molten beneath their feet as shades of purple and gold soaked into the waves like shards of stained glass. Normally, Eloise might have found it beautiful. At the moment, it only felt ominous.

Nathan Pearce's sister stood not fifty yards down the beach, a flock of her followers arranged behind her. She was authorized to place people under arrest? Since when? The way she was dressed, in that prim pantsuit, it would be like getting arrested by an accountant.

Those followers, however, gave Eloise pause. They looked more like a S.W.A.T. team. How many of them were enhanced? Steve was still scuffling with his speed twin at the edge of the water, while Ire was clutching the brunette alien woman by the collar. The alien's two companions were watching the scene with darting glances, like cats considering an escape through a closing door. Eloise wondered how long they'd stay, and whether they'd leave the brunette behind. They looked ready to do exactly that.

Next to Eloise, Dad stood tense. Ready.

Where was the Knife? She couldn't feel its presence,

couldn't hear its voice. But these people had it. They must. She could dart forward, try to steal it. If she did, Chloe's team would intercept Eloise, and then everyone would know that she'd lost the Knife. She wouldn't be able to fake that. She couldn't afford that. Not with the way her body felt, aching and trembling, as if succumbing to a nasty flu.

The aliens would have to wait. Chloe Pearce was a much bigger—and more immediate—threat. Eloise stayed where she was, focusing on Chloe. "I thought you hated enhanced abilities. How is it your friend there can run almost as fast as mine?"

At least, Eloise hoped it was 'almost.'

Chloe brushed a strand of hair out of her face. Her followers hadn't moved. "You should know by now that we have the capacity to create time-limited enhanced abilities."

Oh, Eloise knew. She remembered the thieves that had wrecked that hotel in Las Vegas, the ones she'd captured with Wave's help. Their enhanced abilities had faded mere hours after their arrival at LIO HQ. They were still on the prison level, as it happened.

"You mean that you control the abilities, so it's OK." Eloise had to force herself to keep her hands loose at her sides. She might be able to distract Chloe long enough to take control of the situation. She wasn't sure how, exactly; she needed time. "Isn't that a bit hypocritical?"

Chloe just smiled. Smug. The woman was smug as hell. "While we're on that subject, why did your strongman just demand the Pearl Knife from this woman?"

There was a long list of people who shouldn't know about the Knife's disappearance, and Chloe Pearce topped that list. The EAEA would leap on any chance to undermine LIO's already tenuous status with the U.S. government. If the league lost that foothold, if they instead became enemies of the state...

She wasn't sure how she could possibly go about repairing such a rift.

Eloise could feel the tension radiating from Dad, standing stock still beside her. Chloe couldn't know he was alive, either.

And she couldn't know that Eloise's knees felt like they might give out at any moment, that a headache drilled at her temples. That, with the Pearl Knife meters away, she felt as weak as she'd ever been. She hadn't heard back from Agnes, either. Not a word.

Eloise ripped her thoughts away from Agnes, from her physical distress. She could out-stare Mary O'Sullivan. Chloe Pearce should pose no challenge whatsoever.

But Chloe stood there, smiling, as if she could wait forever. Before Eloise could collect her thoughts enough to form a response, the dark-haired alien woman—who was still dangling from Irè's hand—said, "We stole the Knife. Want to buy it? I'll give you a discount. Full disclosure, though, the thing's more trouble than it's worth." She tapped Ire on the arm with a free hand. "My neck's falling asleep. You want to let me go?"

Ire just stared down at her like he couldn't believe what he was hearing. Eloise didn't want to, either—at least, the part where the woman admitted to stealing the Knife right in front of the EAEA—but she'd always been one to deal with reality as it happened.

"Stolen," Chloe repeated. Eloise found herself looking for a hint of Nathan in the woman, but aside from their matching accents, they might have been strangers. "Isn't that a breach of trust? My friend Travis Bertram didn't mention that the Knife had gone missing. How curious."

Her *friend* Travis? Well, that explained how she'd managed the authority to bring them in. Eloise had been picturing Travis's position as a fairly empty one. A figurehead. A symbol.

Maybe she'd been wrong about that. And now he was

working with Chloe, and the EAEA? How long had that been going on?

What else had she missed? Not just since the loss of the Knife, but—as Steve had hinted—since the league's public debut? She thought of the entitled reporter she'd sent away from HQ mere weeks ago, the recruits she hadn't spent enough time with. Where else had she erred?

Eloise reeled, trying to steady herself against the questions that crowded into her thoughts, replaying every dismissive, condescending thing Travis Bertram had ever said to her. She couldn't put a finger on it, not with the EAEA facing her down. Not with her people in danger.

If she didn't think Chloe's army would leap on her, she'd call Travis right now. She'd unleash every unwise diatribe she'd ever wanted to level at the self-entitled puppy of a bureaucrat.

Not that it mattered either way. The next move had been inevitable, from the moment Eloise stepped onto the beach. A breath, a nod from Chloe—who clearly thought they were past words—and her little army was moving. Fast.

The EAEA operative next to Chloe sprang into a high jump, landing inches from Ire. Before the strongman could react, the operative wrenched the alien out of his grasp while a trio of Chloe's minions rushed him from the other side. They might not be as coordinated as the league, but their abilities gave them the kind of speed that Eloise simply couldn't match without the Pearl Knife's assistance. Dad was already running to meet another attacker, to keep him from joining Steve's fight near the waves. With fists, she assumed, rather than with fire.

The jumper, clearly strong enough to handle Ire, penned him in place from the back, while one of the trio aimed for his face. When he tried to dodge, a second hit caught him in the stomach, and he actually doubled over in pain.

She'd never seen Ire doubled over in pain. Or reacting to a

punch of any kind, really. She wasn't used to standing on the fringes of a fight. With her body still feeling weak and sluggish, she didn't know where to jump in. How to help.

The aliens didn't wait. Two of them activated those damn flying shoes, catching the third between them, and Eloise felt herself running toward them as they jetted away from the scene, dragging the redhead a few inches off the ground. Eloise was aware of Ire resuming his fight, but he was surrounded, EAEA assholes grabbing him on every side. She'd lost track of Steve, and Dad.

Eloise pumped her legs harder, willing her Knife-sick body to work, to catch up with the escaping thieves. If she could just catch hold of the dangling woman's legs, she thought she could drag all three of them to the sand. What she'd do next, she wasn't sure.

Someone caught hold of Eloise from behind, and she staggered, spinning to try and take them out with a solid kick to the knees. But her foot met with air as the guy anticipated her move—whether by enhanced abilities, or because he simply knew how to fight—and she lost her balance.

She fell to the sand, vaguely aware of Dad fighting off a group in the distance, of Steve locked in his epic battle in the waves, of Ire overcome. The aliens had disappeared, their flying shoes having carried them too far down the beach—or down a side street—for her to see. There were civilians here, too, lingering at the borders of the fight. Watching. Recording, probably. She couldn't do anything to protect them; she could only will them to run.

She crawled forward, the laughter of her enemies ringing in her ears. But she didn't need to escape. There were too many enemies to hope for that.

She just needed to make a call.

Eloise wrenched her phone out of her pocket and barked a voice command, watching the screen until Mary picked up.

"We're about to be taken in," Eloise said, her breath heavy between her words. She hoped Mary could understand. She hoped Mary would act. "You have to get the Knife back."

A boot crunched down on her phone, and Eloise cringed as the metal and glass came apart under the operative's grinding foot.

"All right," she said, speaking loud enough that she hoped the others would hear even above the melee, even though she faced the sand. "Enough. We surrender."

THE FIRST BAR Mary could find after the call with Eloise cut off was a cheesy tourist restaurant with a garish tiki theme, where the staff scrambled around in circles when she entered— apparently thinking she was there for their pineapple pork chops or whatever—until she pointed to the bar, handed the bartender a hundred dollar bill, and instructed her not to water down the drinks.

After that, they left her alone. All but the bartender, who kept her supplied with a steady stream of gin and tonics.

Someone had thought it was a great idea to decorate this place like a combination luau-slash-Disney-World attraction. They had canoes hanging from the ceiling, all painted in brightly colored flowers, and surfboards attached to the walls. Fake palm trees graced every corner, their leaves several shades too green. And there was fake grass. Everywhere. Skirts on the servers, fringes on above the bar. There was even grass bordering the doors to the restroom.

It was a ridiculous theme for anywhere, but in winter Niagara? It was like a sick joke.

Didn't matter. The place had alcohol, so they had Mary. Lucky them.

Eloise's call left her with a vise clasped around her chest, one she couldn't break with all the engineering know-how in the world. Eloise didn't understand what she was asking for. No matter how dire the situation—and Mary had known it would turn dire, had tried to convince Eloise to stay—Mary couldn't save her sister, or retrieve the Knife. Mary would only make things worse. Why couldn't El see that?

She was on her third drink when Nathan slid onto the stool beside hers. He glanced up at the grass-fringed bartop, and she couldn't help thinking of the first time they'd met in a Boston dive not all that long ago. Could not have been more different than this tiki-vomit wonderland.

She'd expected someone to find her, eventually. She just hadn't expected it to be him.

"You're like the plague," she said.

Nathan turned his body stubbornly away from the bar, swinging his legs around so he faced her. "I was in Eloise's office with Pete and Gail. I'd tell you why they called me in to help with this particular surveillance issue, but we saw Eloise make the call, so I think you know."

Mary tossed back her drink and signaled the bartender for another. "Drew the short straw, did you?"

"Believe it or not, I actually volunteered to come get you. Risky, I know."

How long did it take to make a gin and tonic? Maybe Mary could start ordering them in taller glasses. A thermos would be good. She made a point not to turn to Nathan, or meet his eyes. "If you saw El make the call, then you already know she wasted her time. I can't go. How'd you even find me?"

"Like I said, I was in surveillance." He leaned over and slid his phone out of his pocket. "Also, you're all over social media."

He tapped an icon and shoved the phone in front of her face. A series of photos popped up on the screen, some of them angled from the other side of the bar. She met the bartender's eye. "Thanks for nothing."

The bartender just shrugged and passed her another drink. Even though the restaurant was fairly empty, Mary suddenly imagined she could hear people whispering over the Beach Boys soundtrack, that she could see the reflections of the colored tiki lights as they lifted their phones to record her every move. With her luck, the social media posts would be drawing a crowd soon. Great.

"I don't know why you're surprised by this," Nathan said.

"The part where Eloise needs me to join the mission after all, or the part where I'm fodder for the public's insatiable voyeur?"

"Pick a card, any card."

What would it be like to go out in public and not be a spectacle? They were all spectacles now, but the publicity circus was new to the others. An oddity, maybe even a source of amusement. Mary had lived with this reality her entire life, and she could feel the fatigue leaking through her body, soaking into her bones. She wanted to storm through the restaurant, to stop the whispers by shoving someone's face in the frozen margarita machine behind the bar. Which only made things worse, because she was clearly tired enough—and emotional enough—to consider hurting people, essentially for looking at her the wrong way. Like she'd hurt Goldi.

No, Mary definitely could not be trusted.

As for Eloise, well. Mary was only surprised that she'd chosen to call Mary, of all people. Surely Nathan could scrape up a team without her. She glared at him. "The only thing that surprises me is the fact that you've got a FaceGram account."

"I like cat photos as much as the next guy." He leaned an elbow on the bar and looked at her with those stupid gray eyes.

He smelled like pine and cedar. It took everything she had not to lean into the comfort of it.

"Why did they have to send you?" Mary muttered.

"Like I said, I sent myself. Because I'm the only one left."

El and Will, detained. With Ire and Steve. Agnes still hanging with the Wave crowd. He wasn't wrong. Still, she couldn't tamp down the instinct to be petulant with him. "Gail's left."

"Gail's busy with *her* job. Her multiple jobs, really." He leaned toward her, propping the heel of his hand on his knee. She hoped he'd fall off the stool. "I'm going to L.A. to look for the Knife, at least until Eloise gets away from my sister."

And, apparently, the government cronies that Mary had angered. Unwisely. But what else was new? "Why not rescue them?"

"Because that's not what Eloise asked for."

And Eloise was the boss. Hadn't Mary emphasized that herself, the last time they'd talked? She was done with reckless decisions that got people hurt. Like contacting Wave operatives against El's orders. Who did he think he was, to suggest something like that? Yeah, it might be good to have a few more allies. And maybe Eloise was being stubborn about it. But she usually saw moving parts Mary didn't, and she certainly understood the politics better than either of them. Nathan had only been a part of this world for a few months. It was Eloise's *life*.

Nathan was still watching her, as if he expected some kind of a response. What did he need, her blessing? "Fine," Mary said, twisting her drink around on its parrot-themed coaster. "Good luck. Try not to die."

Nathan tapped his fingers on the bar. "Oh, didn't I mention? You're coming with me."

A few months ago, he'd have been running a hand through his hair. Nervous around her, or frustrated by one of their arguments. He was becoming someone she didn't recognize. More confident. She liked it, and she didn't want to admit she liked it.

Mary squeezed her lime into her drink. She could knock this one back, too, but she was already feeling the warmth of the gin, trying to pull her toward him. At least, it felt less dangerous to blame the gin. "Nope. Take your rainbow girlfriend."

"Tally isn't my girlfriend, and the recruits aren't ready to handle their powers on a mission like this."

"The way I hear it, they handled their powers on that boat just fine."

They'd saved his life, in fact. So why was she so bitter about it? She could hear the petulance in her tone, and the irrational reasoning. She didn't care.

Nathan shook his head. "They haven't been oriented to LIO procedures. A Niagara-based mission is one thing, but they need more time. They're a last resort."

He talked as if he'd been here for years rather than months, as if he knew this place so well himself. Well, maybe he did. Maybe he knew it better than she did, in some ways.

Nathan leaned toward her, sliding his hand so close to where hers rested on the bar that she thought he might touch her. He didn't. He said, "Eloise called you, Mary. Not Tally. Not Rajni. Not even me. She needs *you*."

Mary decided to drain the drink, after all. She needed to get beyond pleasantly tipsy. She needed to get so drunk she forgot this conversation altogether. And yet somehow, she couldn't keep herself from continuing to talk to him. "You know what I hear when I think about heading out on a mission? When I think about suiting up and going after the bad guys?"

He just watched her, his expression calm. Open. She had the sudden, nearly irrepressible urge to run her fingers through the hair above his ears. She wrenched her gaze away to stare at the bar instead. "I hear Goldi. I hear her screaming, because I shot her in the back with a grapple hook."

"By accident," he said softly. "It was an accident."

"And that makes it OK? Makes me more capable of handling a mission?" She couldn't keep the tremble out of her voice. The gin. It had to be the gin. "Every decision I make ends up hurting someone. I protected my identity at Jeff's party, and Andrew died because of it. You said so yourself."

She remembered their argument after the party, the streaks of blurred red bleeding through his soaked white shirt, the way he'd propped his palms on her kitchen island in Malibu and looked at her with eyes full of disappointment. Betrayal. She'd been so angry with him, so betrayed herself. Maybe she'd only felt that way because he'd had a point.

Nathan ran a hand through his hair, his nerves finally fraying enough to let it show. "Mary, the person who said that to you didn't understand the intricacies of this life. The demands of the job, the split-second decisions... I was wrong, and I'm sorry."

"You weren't completely wrong."

He was just a breath away. Too close. Way too close. If she turned her head, if she leaned forward an inch, she'd be kissing him. She wanted to. She didn't want to.

"I get it," he said, his voice low and resonant against her ear. "You don't trust your instincts."

With an effort, Mary leaned back, holding her empty glass up in a mock toast. "And here I thought you'd never catch on."

He nodded. As if he'd never expected any better of her. Good. He shouldn't. He should accept who she was now.

Instead, he held her gaze. "This time, your instinct is telling you to stay behind," he said. "Maybe you should consider what that means."

Mary opened her mouth, but no words came out. She had no defense for that, no counterargument.

Because it was true. Her decision to stay behind... Eloise hadn't fought her on it, but she'd hadn't agreed with the idea, either. If Mary couldn't trust her own instincts, then she should be following Eloise's. And her sister had called her first.

Nathan slid off the stool, as if he knew he'd won. "Eloise has no one else. We need to get the Knife back for her, before it's no longer an option. The van leaves for the airport in half an hour."

THE HOLDING facility looked like a cinderblock, both inside and out. It certainly wasn't an aesthetic that would have comforted Eloise under any circumstances, with its guarded gates, metal detectors, and barred windows—particularly as she currently found herself on the wrong side of them. But it was the location of the place, tucked out of sight in a mountainous area with enough trees to qualify as a national park, that raised her hackles. They'd driven several hours to get here, and she couldn't say precisely where they'd landed. Somewhere secret, clearly. And that made her stomach tumble with unease.

Secret government facilities were not something she tended to view as a positive. If that was a bit hypocritical coming from someone who made her home in a secret facility of her own, well, at least she didn't use taxpayer dollars to run it.

When they reached the secret cinderblock holding place, whatever it was, Chloe's minions handed Eloise and the others off to guards, who separated them into two different rooms. Eloise waited with Dad, who still wore his helmet. Ire and Steve waited together in another room, god help them all. She only hoped they could keep from acting like fools for a few hours. It wouldn't improve the situation if those two starting punching each other now.

She wasn't sure what they were waiting *for*, or whom. Only that whoever it was, they were taking their sweet time getting there. During which Eloise could only sit and worry. Would Ire snap his zip ties and try to escape? And if he did, would he leave Steve behind? Did the EAEA have the power suppressing serum? Did the government? What part of the government was holding them? She expected to see Travis Bertram at some point, given what Chloe had said, but did he have the power to be doing any of this?

Most importantly: Dad had entered the building masked, and still wore his tinted helmet. So far, no one had even commented, but she couldn't imagine they'd allow him to stay that way. What would they do, when they found the Inferno here alive?

Worries piled upon worries, and there was nothing Eloise could do about any of it. Not with the door shut fast, and likely not once it opened, either. She'd worked her already fatigued body to extremes, and it was affecting her ability to think. To plan. She could be kind to herself and admit that it was difficult to plan without knowing one's precise situation, but that wouldn't solve anything. She had to last, just a little longer. It was her fault that her people had gone after the Knife, and that she'd underestimated Travis Bertram—and the EAEA—so disastrously.

She had to get them out of this situation. If only she could *think*. But the concrete room felt small, and suffocating, and Eloise was all too aware of how long it had been since she'd slept, of night trickling into morning. The fluorescent lights flickered unpleasantly, and the black-eyed cameras in each corner made conversation impossible. So they sat in silence. And they waited. And Eloise worried.

Would Mary go after the Knife like Eloise had asked? Would they ever get it back?

At least the uncomfortable physical sensations she'd been associating with the Knife's absence had calmed, for the moment. The nausea had dissipated, the dizziness melted away, though she still felt tired enough to be grateful for the uncomfortable metal chair.

Eloise had no reliable way to gauge how much time had passed before the steel door opened with a loud clank, and Travis Bertram entered the room flanked by Chloe and another white woman, a blonde, who looked vaguely familiar. Two more guards followed, one in a simple uniform, the other with EAEA lettering emblazoned on his sleeves.

"I don't want them here." Eloise kept her voice calm as she nodded to Chloe and her friend. "They have nothing to do with this, and I can't imagine they're authorized."

Travis had his hands clenched in fists at his sides, his lips pulled so tight they were turning white. Whatever was going on with this kid, he'd clearly decided to take it personally. "They have everything to do with it, and I've authorized them. They're a part of this now."

"Ask your boss about that."

Travis pulled out the metal chair across from her, scraping the legs along the concrete with an unpleasant ring before seating himself. He didn't look smug, or bored, or pleased with his accomplishment. He looked pissed. "After the incident in Santa Monica, Senator Jones agrees with me. At least, he wants you investigated, and the liaison committee wants to contract the EAEA to assist."

"Because they're so neutral?" Dad said, his voice muffled from behind the helmet.

Travis's eyes flickered in his direction. "Yes, actually. They are. New laws will be forthcoming. You'll see."

New laws. Just what they needed. Eloise didn't know how much of this was fact, and how much was Travis reading his own truths between the lines of what his superiors told him to do. Given the existence of a super-secret government holding facility like the one they were currently in, she wasn't certain she wanted to know the answer.

"And I suppose those laws won't apply to the temporary powers these clowns have managed to put together," Dad said.

A part of Eloise wanted to will him to silence, but he was right to speak up, to question the hypocrisy. The bigotry, really, the outright fear of people simply because of their enhanced abilities. According to Nathan, his sister had wanted to imprison every enhanced human who refused to operate under LIO's umbrella. What would they do now that the EAEA—and Travis, apparently—no longer trusted the league? To enhanced humans like Mary's people-tracking reporter friend, who had no wish to work as an independent operative? To the league itself?

History told Eloise exactly what they'd do, and the thought was enough to cloud her mind with panic. It was why she needed to escape from this place, as soon as possible.

Travis leaned forward, his hands trembling. In rage, Eloise realized. Pure, unadulterated rage. She found herself drawing back, angling her body away from his. Who here would stop him, if his rage went too far? He pointed a quivering finger at Dad. "And you. Who *are* you?" He glanced back over his shoulder and hitched his chin at the gray-clad facility guard. "Remove his mask."

Dad sat up straight in his chair. "I can do it myself."

Travis actually sneered at that. "As if I'd let them release your restraints. The mask."

The guard hesitated for a brief instant, then stepped

forward. Eloise's heart beat hot fear through her veins, but there was nothing she could do about it now. Not when she was restrained herself.

The league's secrets had been blown before, and they'd survived. The thought did nothing to calm her worry on behalf of her father. The man wasn't a wanted criminal. He was a beloved hero.

One whose reappearance would prompt questions. A lot of them. And one whose powers absolutely couldn't be denied. Eloise hadn't seen him use them since his return, but she had no doubt that Travis would see an immediate threat. Everything about this situation screamed danger, and there was nothing she could do about it. Nothing she could do to save any of them. She dug her fingernails into her palms, trying to unclench her jaw.

She had to stay present. She had to *last*, damn it.

"Gotta undo the chinstrap first," Dad said. The guard did, his fingers fumbling with the ties. Finally, he unclipped the strap, and there was nothing Eloise could do to stop him as he eased the helmet from Dad's head.

Under different circumstances, Eloise would have enjoyed the shock on Travis Bertram's baby face, the way his face drained of all color, his eyes practically popping out of his head. But she couldn't, because everything this entitled kid did felt dangerous.

"The Inferno," Travis breathed. "You're alive."

Eloise just looked at him, and Dad remained motionless, too. Waiting.

Travis's gaze hardened, and he turned to Eloise. "The Pearl Knife is missing. The Inferno is alive. How many more secrets is the league keeping?"

Eloise had always prided herself on her ability to handle

the diplomacy her position required. She was good at working with the authorities, and with bureaucrats like Travis. Or at least, she had been. For the first time, she didn't know how to spin this. She didn't know what to say. With Chloe standing at the door smiling like a pleased cat, the familiar blonde woman looking equally smug, Eloise had no idea how to extract her team from the situation.

She wanted to drop her head to the table and weep in frustration, but she refused to give these people the satisfaction of breaking her. She wouldn't do it.

The door clanked open, and Travis twisted around. "Keep it closed," he barked. "We're not finished."

But another facility guard entered anyway, followed by a silver-haired man in a suit. He looked out of place in this stark room, the colorfully paisley handkerchief in his pocket standing out like something from another world. He carried a briefcase, and a thin gold chain glimmered under his collar.

"Who is this?" Travis said. "Get him out of here."

The guard cleared his throat. "He says he's their lawyer."

"If you'll have me," the silver-haired man said. He stepped up beside Travis and slid a card across the table for Eloise to read. *Holland Gold, esq.* With offices in Los Angeles. "Jeff Hayes sent me to help. Said you might need a hand here."

Eloise nodded, her lips numb with shock. Jeff Hayes. Mary must have called him. Did that mean Mary would go after the Knife? Or was it her way of saying it was all she could do to help?

More importantly, how had Jeff Hayes's lawyer—if he really was—known where to find them? Perhaps the team had managed to track the van here. Their phones had been confiscated, but they were still on the premises, and as far as she knew only hers was broken.

"Excellent," Holland said, scraping out the chair beside Travis's and settling into it as though it were the most comfortable seat he'd ever experienced. "Catch me up here. What are the charges, and how long do you intend to hold my clients in this hellhole?"

THE WOMAN SEATED on Agnes's examination table was leaning back with her palms propped on the surface, and everything about her posture said she was trying to look as if the outcome of this appointment meant nothing to her. Gigi's body language said she was calm. Casual. But the way the woman watched Agnes's every move as she lounged with her wings extended to either side, she was plainly anything but disinterested.

Agnes had hidden the fancy lab behind a curtain, as she'd done for the last few days while meeting individually with each ex-prisoner. It had taken some maneuvering to configure the space for Gigi's twelve-foot wingspan, but the lab was nothing if not spacious. She'd done her best to make the room pleasant, adding fresh flowers to the corners, and Lucy was working on a few drawings to liven up the blank walls, too. She hadn't mentioned the Pearl Knife again, and Agnes could only hope her daughter believed that they were here to stay.

The majority of the Wave operatives living on the island had lined up at Agnes's door to make appointments, eager to assess their powers—and to understand any issues they'd been facing. A handful had avoided her, but Agnes refused to force anyone. They'd come when they were ready, or they wouldn't. Fran had said they'd invited her unanimously, but Agnes could understand their hesitation to endure more poking and prodding.

Gigi, the winged woman Agnes had noticed on her first day here, had a petite, wiry stature, her skin pale and freckled. Agnes knew from reading her file that Gigi had been incarcerated for more than a decade after Dolly had caught her working with Wave, first in a federal facility and later with the league. Her enhanced abilities didn't come from her cells or her blood; she simply had wings.

According to Wave's files, she'd merely been a scout and a messenger for the organization. That Dolly had managed to convince a court of criminal proclivities on Gigi's part was evidence of the former Pearl Knife's influence. And her ruthlessness. Gigi was unique among the powered humans Agnes had studied; with the others, Agnes could almost understand the need to keep them under careful guard, to suppress their powers. She disagreed with it vehemently—particularly since LIO's cells had been well-equipped to contain them, powers or not—but she could see the reasoning when it concerned the ability to set other people on fire, for example.

Gigi was different. Her wings couldn't have helped her to break out of a cell or overpower guards, yet over the years she'd been subjected to sedatives, Mange's power suppressing serum, and other cocktails that proved authorities feared those with enhanced abilities. *Any* enhanced ability. It made Agnes grind her teeth with anger and frustration, at the pure ignorance of it. The cruelty.

The lasting effects from Gigi's imprisonment, however, were apparent in the wings themselves. The woman had been stretching them out for five minutes, no more, and already her whole body trembled from the effort. Her muscles were atrophied, the tendons stiff from lack of use. Someone had clearly restrained her for a long period of time, clipping her wings to limit her mobility. Though LIO had discontinued the practice, allowing her wings to grow again, they'd still kept her in a space far too small for any sort of recuperation. Gigi faced a long road of recovery.

"I used to be able to cross oceans," Gigi said, voice strained from the effort of holding out her wings. "Provided I kept a snack in my pocket."

Agnes smiled, but it felt false. How could she find humor, faced with these poor deteriorated wings? Any facility doctor should have noticed the same thing.

They probably had. They just hadn't cared.

Gigi sighed. "Now I can hardly cross the island."

"You will." Agnes leaned in to get a closer look at one of the wing joints. They were incredible creations—not creations; they were natural, somehow—the downy brown feathers flecked with specks of white. "You've been doing all the right things."

Exercising, working the wings each day. It had to be so fatiguing. Agnes's anger spiked, like a nail between her ribs, and she tamped it down. She didn't want Gigi to see anything but her calm. Her ability to handle the situation, to help.

Gigi's smile looked as forced as Agnes's had felt, thin and trembling. A breath away from tears. "It'll be better now you're here."

"I'm not a medical doctor," Agnes said. She had taken some courses, endured an internship or two, but this was far outside her area of expertise. "Dr. Gordon has been advising you well.

"He can't heal me, though."

"Because what you need is time. Keep exercising, and keep showing up for your appointments. You'll cross oceans again."

It was a more optimistic answer than she had to give many

of the island's other occupants. Gigi's physical issue was a matter of muscle mass. Dr. Gordon could soothe her aches, and Agnes could help bolster her mental state.

As for the others, though, the doctor's healing powers only worked on some. The teleporter she'd seen chasing goats on the first day could only leap as far as he could see, where once he'd been able to hop from place to place without restraint, and Dr. Gordon hadn't been able to heal him—even though he'd restored the lounging camouflager to her full capacity.

Agnes didn't have enough data yet to know if Dr. Gordon's powers simply didn't work on all types of enhanced abilities, or if there was something wrong with him, too.

Nevertheless, he *was* a true doctor. One Agnes already respected deeply. Anyone with healing powers who made that kind of effort to understand his field, spending years in medical school, was a hero in her book.

She'd only been here a few days, but she hoped that studying how the islanders' abilities transformed their cellular structure could help her to repair their powers. It was a starting point, anyway.

But with Gigi, the problem was entirely physical. "Your powers are a bit different than the ones I usually study," she said.

Gigi met her eyes, a spark of amusement in her brown eyes. "You're going to need to ask our origin stories eventually. If you're hoping to learn more."

Agnes returned her gaze to the wings. "They can be traumatic. I don't like to push."

Gigi stretched her arms behind her head and lay back, keeping her wings extended. "Mine's not. It's just hereditary."

"They had to come from somewhere."

Gigi shrugged. "Mom didn't know why. Grandma didn't know why. According to them, Great-Grandma only ever said they should be thankful for their blessings. They're pretty sure *she* knew why."

Interesting. Had Gigi's Great-Grandma had the wings, too? Agnes would have to ask more about that, later. "You can rest now," she said, and Gigi folded her wings behind her back with a relieved sigh. "Keep seeing Dr. Gordon, and sign up for a slot with me next week. I want to keep an eye on things."

Not that Dr. Gordon couldn't do so just as easily, but Agnes wanted everyone on the island to feel they had another source of support when they needed it.

Gigi slid off the metal table, her bare feet hitting the tiles with a soft smack. "Thanks, doc. Can't wait til we're having air races."

At that, Agnes really did grin. "I don't think I've ever raced with another flyer before."

Gigi winked. "Oh, you will."

The woman ducked through the curtain and headed back out through the lab. For a moment, all Agnes could do was stand there and breathe out her anger. If she didn't allow it to surface between patients, she'd explode during their visits. And her poor wife, Tam, who'd come with Lucy the day after Agnes's arrival, had to hear the worst of it. Agnes couldn't help it. The cruelty of it made her want to weep. It made her want to throw things, and she was not by nature a violent woman.

Whatever the world wanted to believe, there'd always been an anti-abilities sentiment hanging around, a thread of lawmakers who voted against the community. They were a small group, their concerns ignored by the majority. Sidelined as LIO played the heroes. Now, though, Agnes couldn't help wondering whether enhanced-ability-motivated fear played a stronger role in the running of the country than she'd thought.

The league might be seen as heroes, but Agnes didn't know how long that could last.

With anger still tilting her vision, she moved out of the clinic area and over to the sink, where a few beakers waited for a second round of washing. Wave had given her the works; even the sink was deluxe, with double stainless steel bowls and plenty of counter space for drying. The water ran over her hands, warm and soothing, and she let the suds build up as she scrubbed.

How could they do this to Gigi, to all of these people? How could Eloise have perpetuated this cruelty after the Wave operatives transferred to league HQ? It had taken Nathan Pearce's rogue action to free them. Agnes didn't know him, not really; they'd crossed paths only a couple of times. But she knew what little the ex-prisoners had told her, and how Mary had felt about him.

She wouldn't have minded having those two back on her side. Working with Wave.

"You're going to crush that beaker if you're not careful."

Agnes looked up to see Dr. Gordon standing a few paces away, a small smile on his face. He had bifocals propped on his nose, and his loose clothing gave him a slightly rumpled look.

"So you thought startling me would be a good idea?" Agnes smiled back to show she was joking. She certainly wasn't angry with *him*.

Dr. Gordon shrugged. "I know I'm early for my appointment, doc. Sorry."

Agnes set down the beaker and dried her hands, waving him back toward the clinic. "It's no problem."

"What's got you twisted in knots today, Dr. Jenson?"

"Please, it's just Agnes."

"You're the foremost expert on enhanced abilities in the world. It's never 'just.'"

"I see you took your charm pills this morning."

Dr. Gordon hopped up on the table. He was in his mid-sixties, and he'd worked to maintain his physical fitness during confinement. Agnes was monitoring his cells by drawing blood every few days, trying to understand if his abilities were stable or changing at all, in either direction. She'd get to field tests in the next few weeks, but she couldn't develop hands-on assessments for anyone until she understood their abilities enough to develop relevant tests.

She'd need to ask Fran about getting some assistants in here. Soon.

Dr. Gordon watched while she prepped her blood draw kit. "All seriousness. Doctor to doctor. What's wrong?"

Agnes shook her head. Doctor to doctor, but he was her patient, too. How was it fair, to burden him with her worries? She secured a rubber band around his left arm, and he closed his fingers into a fist without being asked. "We all support each other here, Dr. Agnes," he said, as if reading her hesitation.

It really seemed to be true. "How can you stand it?" she asked. "They let your powers dwindle. They dosed you continuously with an untested drug. If they didn't consider the consequences of that, they were negligent. If they did..." She shook her head again. "That's even worse."

"Careful with that needle, doc," he said, eyes shining. "They're trying to do better. Just like we are."

"You believe that?"

"I do."

"Then you're more forgiving than I would be."

Before he could respond, the lab door opened to admit Agnes's wife, Tam. Dr. Gordon slid off the table and brushed his hands together. "Looking forward to the concert tonight," he told Tam. "I hear there's going to be a dance party at the end."

"Someone's been leaking our secrets," Tam replied, but she

was beaming. The island sun had brushed her skin with freckles in what had felt like mere hours in the sun, and her auburn hair sported new streaks of gold. Tam had jumped into island life with enthusiasm; when her guitar practice garnered interest from the other residents, she'd started teaching music lessons to anyone who wanted them. Fran had seen to the delivery of more instruments, and Dr. Gordon felt it was excellent for morale.

And tonight, Tam was going to perform. Something she hadn't been able to do since Agnes had whisked them all to Wave's underwater hideout.

"Shouldn't you be getting ready?" Agnes asked as Dr. Gordon made his way out of the lab.

Tam raised her eyebrows and cast a glance at her outfit, a bright red sundress that would put the tropical flowers on the island to shame. "What? I don't look ready to you?"

Agnes laughed and pulled her wife in for a kiss, then twined their fingers together as they started for the door. "Trust me, I'd like nothing more than to make you half an hour late for your own concert. I meant I thought you might need to warm up."

"I'm ready. Besides, some of the students decided they wanted to play. I figured we should keep it casual."

They stepped out of the lab and into the humid evening, electric torches already lighting the center path through the village. Tam had planned the concert for the beach, and people were making their way toward the shore, some carrying instruments or plates piled high with cookies.

Tam walked in silence, smiling and returning waves, but her fingers were tense in Agnes's. They'd been married for almost fifteen years, and Agnes knew when there was something on her wife's mind. She waited.

"I found a packed bag under Lucy's bed this afternoon,"

Tam said finally. "It was full of food, comic books, and Mr. Buns."

Agnes frowned. Lucy never moved the stuffed rabbit from his spot on her bed. She might not admit it anymore, but misplacing Mr. Buns at bedtime meant she had trouble going to sleep.

"When I asked her about it, she said she wanted to be ready to evacuate."

"Evacuate from what?" Agnes asked, though she had a feeling she already knew.

Tam hesitated. The sound of tuning guitars drifted through the night, a pleasing kind of dissonance. Agnes thought she could hear Lucy's flute trilling among them, along with another wind instrument she couldn't place. "The Pearl Knife," Tam said.

Agnes had told Tam about Eloise's message, and about Lucy's reaction to seeing the diagram on her computer. And though she'd thought of Eloise more than once over the past few days, sometimes with a twinge of guilt, she hadn't been able to bring herself to respond, to reenter LIO's orbit.

The idea that her daughter felt the need to be ready to run because of Agnes... She could hardly bear the thought of it. "She's still worried," Agnes said.

Tam didn't need to answer. "I think she packed the bag for another reason, too." She sighed. "If you did decide to go back to LIO, I suspect you'd find a stowaway under your seat."

"But Lucy's afraid of the Pearl Knife."

Tam squeezed her hand. "She's more afraid of losing her mom. We always understood the need for you to be away. You know that. But the past few months have been amazing, having you around for more than half the time. I think Lucy wants to keep an eye on you."

"What about you?" Agnes asked softly. "Are you afraid, too?"

"Honestly? It's hard not to be. Every time you left us, I always thought... I always treated it like the last time."

Because Agnes's work with LIO had involved as many high-risk missions as hours in a lab. How had she never realized how deep Tam's worry ran?

They reached the edge of the trees, where the forest opened into a wide stretch of sandy beach. Someone had arranged a cluster of lawn chairs opposite the semi-circle of guitarists, and several others were working on lighting a camp-fire. Closer to the water, Gigi leapt to catch a frisbee, her wings lifting her a few feet off the ground. She was laughing. Agnes tried to imagine a scene like this at LIO headquarters, but the image was too ridiculous. Wave felt right, and this place? This place felt like home.

More importantly, it felt *safe*. Agnes wrapped an arm around her wife's waist. "Don't worry," she said. "I'm not going anywhere."

WITH LIO SURVEILLANCE picking out boxy, government-like cars stationed at every airport within a reasonable radius of Los Angeles, watching—for what, they could only guess—Nathan and Mary flew into Las Vegas, instead. A four-hour drive? Not unreasonable at all.

This Travis guy clearly expected some attempt to rescue Eloise and the others, and he clearly underestimated the league. Nathan suspected his spies were EAEA, rather than government, but he couldn't be sure. And he couldn't help glancing at his passenger side mirror every few minutes, scanning for a tail. They'd picked up the silver Camaro in the airport garage, and Nathan had offered to drive, but Mary had just laughed at him. Somehow, despite the number of drinks he'd watched her consume a few hours ago, she was completely sober.

He still wasn't quite sure how to categorize the conversation they'd had in that kitschy Niagara bar. Every time he thought he was making some kind of progress in breaking down the barrier between them, Mary seemed to realize it. And her first reaction was to sever any connection they might be making.

Now they were cruising across the desert, engine humming joyously beneath their feet, dusty hills rising in every direction. In all his frenetic travels across this country during the past half year, Nathan felt like he'd hardly seen any of it. He lived behind one of the continent's most recognized landmarks, which was still coated in layers of frost and snow, and yet a few hours on a plane carried him to sand and cacti and hills that shifted from amber to blue with the passing light. It was still amazing to him, the way America's physical landscape contained so many dramatic differences.

Mary had her window cracked open, a breath of wind stirring her curls into wispy tangles around her face. She navigated the road as if she knew it well, her foot heavy on the gas, though he guessed that was more habit than her desire to actually reach L.A.

She'd spent the entire plane ride in silence. When she spoke now, he nearly jumped in surprise.

"Stop looking at me like I'm a bomb about to explode," she said.

He tried to picture working beside her in the league for another year, another five years. Another ten. Would she keep up this vitriol? Would she drive him out? "Oh, pardon me," he said. "How wrong that was."

Mary gripped the wheel. "You think I'm overreacting. You think I'm refusing to act because I'm stubborn, not because I've been compromised. Which I *have,* in case your memory is that sporadic." She was looking at the road so intently he thought it was lucky she didn't have laser sight. They'd probably crash, or disappear into a Mary-made sinkhole.

Nathan wasn't sure exactly what kind of conversation he'd expected to have during this trip. Not license plate bingo, maybe, but 'oh isn't that cactus pretty' and 'maybe we'll play some slots on the way back.' Or 'how should we go about busting the aliens with flying technology so we can get the Knife back?' Perhaps a fair bit of silence...

Apparently, they were going to skip past the small talk and the shop talk. Straight to the point. He chose his words carefully, lest she pull the Camaro to the side of the road and boot him out of the car, leaving him to walk to L.A. amid the snakes and scorpions. "I'm in no position to judge your decisions," he said.

Mary snorted. "That's just another way of saying yes. You think I'm stubborn."

Not exactly. What *did* he think? That her decisions had saved more lives than they'd cost, by far. That this life was messy, that the heat of the moment never allowed a person the time to think through every ramification, or count the potential victims, or see three chess moves ahead.

He thought... He thought that whatever had happened to her over the past few months, that it had broken her. Not that he would ever dare say that. Again, the snakes. The scorpions. Probably bandits, too, if the movies had taught him anything. Just because it was beautiful didn't mean he wanted to be abandoned here.

"I don't know what you went through," he said.

"Because you left." She said it like it had been on the tip of her tongue for months. Matter of fact, no acid, no malice. Just a fact. Because the sky is blue. Because the grass is green. Because you left.

He had to wrench his eyes away from her to stare out at the hills. "I left," he acknowledged. "It was the wrong call."

"For you? Or for the league?"

For us. And he couldn't escape the sudden, inescapable need to run again, to get as far away from her as he could. But even if he were to leave her a second time, he knew the truth now. He couldn't have her—he knew better than to try—but he'd never stop loving her, either. No amount of distance would ever change that.

Nathan cleared his throat. "I was wrong to leave you. I'm sorry."

When she didn't respond, he risked a glance back at her. She was staring down the road like it had insulted her personally, green eyes narrow with focus. He could see that little tic in her jaw, the one that said she was grinding her teeth.

"The retirees," she said finally. "They're murderers, and torturers, and they'd steal the whole league out from El's feet if they could. But what I did to them, locking them up? It wasn't any better. At the very least, Flick was innocent."

Subject change. Well, fair enough. It wasn't like he had any right to expect absolution from her. At the moment, he could help her most by listening. And maybe that was a form of absolution, her willingness to trust him enough to have this conversation. So he just watched her, unsure of how to answer, unsure of whether she had more to say. She bit her bottom lip, and he wondered if she could even see the road for all the memories crowding into her mind.

"They burned down my house," she said. "You never saw it, but it was... a haven, I guess. They burned it to the ground, they killed the version of the System that was my friend. And the only thing I can think is that I deserved it."

She didn't deserve it. She didn't deserve the torture she'd endured at the hands of the Trap. Her parents certainly hadn't deserved to be murdered, and nor had the System.

Before he could formulate a response, she said, "Did you call your Wave friends?"

Nathan blinked, trying to understand the second change of subject. Talking to her was like being passed between currents. One might lead you gently across the sea, while another could pull you under and watch you drown. It was disorienting as hell. Had it always been that way?

"I haven't contacted them, no," he said. "I still think we should. But two very intelligent colleagues of mine feel I shouldn't, and that's enough."

Mary stared hard at the road. "I didn't say I think you shouldn't. I said El vetoed it."

And that was enough for her now. Because Mary had made so many mistakes, she no longer believed that anyone else could make them, too? Eloise was smart to be cautious, but Nathan knew the league could benefit from partnering with Wave. Even a passing affiliation. Or at the very least, a meeting to air their grievances.

After getting to know Dr. Gordon and Jo, and the others, Nathan was sure the two organizations could patch up their differences and move on.

"Have you thought of calling your sister?" Mary asked. "You know, to get Eloise and the others released?"

He'd seen the videos of his sister there on the beach, dressed for the board room, as always. Though Nathan hadn't seen her clearly enough to make out her expression, her stance had been pure determination. How she'd ingratiated herself with the federal government to the point that they'd allow her to assist like this, he didn't know. Though he could see how LIO's position with the government could have already set up a precedent for... whatever this was. Some form of privatized law enforcement, clearly. He didn't know whether the EAEA had signed any official contracts, however, or if they were simply working under sanctioning. Just as the league did. Or had.

In any case, Chloe had obviously moved on from trying to recruit Nathan, and the league along with him. And he'd helped her along. Worse, the EAEA was bigger than he'd thought. Talk about mistakes.

"That door is closed," he said.

Mary gave a brusque nod. "Good."

Nathan frowned. Not the response he'd expected. Mary's lips tipped up at the corners. Almost a smile, if he squinted. "I don't know why you're surprised," she said. "You wanted your family back, but I'm not particularly startled to learn they're the villains they always accused you of being."

He wondered how long she'd believed that, if she'd privately judged them when she'd first heard the story. How they'd ostracized him, driven him away. Blamed him for something he'd been tricked into doing as a child. By an organization he now wanted to partner with.

Villains. Maybe so, on Chloe's end. And Mary had suspected it all along, even if she couldn't have predicted the whole EAEA mess. She made it sound like Chloe was a villain purely because of the way she'd treated Nathan. Maybe his father, too.

If he wasn't careful, he might convince himself that she cared.

"I understand mistakes," he said. Dangerous territory, veering the conversation back to Mary's fears. But he didn't think she'd spoken them merely to air her feelings and move on, whatever she might tell herself. He had to say *something*. "I understand the weight of blood on your hands. But Goldi didn't die. None of the retirees did. Maybe it was a mistake to track them down yourself. Maybe you stopped an even greater tragedy. Nothing says it can't be both."

He had more to say, more thoughts to collect, but Mary punched the radio on, filling the car suddenly and violently with staticky strains of classic rock. Whatever he said next would be drowned beneath electric guitars and smoke-rasped voices.

She'd obviously run out of words—or tolerance for his.

Nathan settled down in his seat, staring out the window as the landscape rushed by faster than ever. As if Mary could do no better than to reach L.A. as quickly as physics would allow, escape this car, and finish the job—and her partnership with Nathan. The conversation was over, and so were they.

AFTER THE SMUG redhead arrested the massive redhead who'd held Sloane by the collar—Sloane was firmly on the smug redhead's side, though she'd had no idea what was happening between those two groups—she and Hilda had dragged their own redhead as far as they could manage, dipping inland on the hov-tiles and dropping to the pavement as soon as they dared.

They'd spent the night flitting from bar to bar, hiding in dimly lit clubs until closing time and wandering the streets until morning finally rolled around. Back in the harsh light of day, everything about them felt like a giveaway. In any Parse planetary system, their descriptions would be circulating the feeds, and maybe photographs, too. Anyone with a tablet—which was everyone—could turn them in. If law enforcement thought they were worth setting a bounty, they'd become the target of professional hunters.

Despite her fears, no one troubled them as they hurried along the sidewalks, past rows of beachfront hotels that gave way to outdoor shopping centers, ever framed by rows of those rag-headed trees. Earth people really liked those trees.

"We need to change clothes," Alex said as they paused to

catch breath, all three of them squeezed onto a single bench outside a row of boutiques. "They'll be looking for us in these."

Sloane wasn't sure who was left to search for them, but she wasn't looking to take any chances. "I'm not stealing another one of those 'credit cards.'" No matter how much she wanted to check out the flower-print halter dress in the window of the store across the way. "They can track us with those."

She didn't know how, but they definitely had. Maybe it was similar to the way galactic currency could be tracked. Digital. That had to be it.

"There's paper currency, too," Alex said.

That could be an option. The surfer hadn't carried much of it, but perhaps they'd been an anomaly.

"Or," Hilda said, "we could wear our own clothes. From home."

Sloane looked up to see if the pilot was trying to make some sort of joke. No one here wore armored suits like theirs. But Hilda was pointing at a procession of people dressed in costumes, like the ones they'd seen on the kids who'd been so fascinated by their Parse Galaxy outfits when they'd first arrived. Though Earth's versions seemed to involve a lot more aluminum foil and plastic fabrics, cone-like hats, capes, wigs, and boots. More than one of these people had swords shoved into cardboard belts.

None of it would last a single second in actual space. But that didn't seem to be the point.

After a quick stop in a convenience store bathroom, Sloane was back in her gray, flared-leg jumpsuit, tool belt secured around her waist. Hilda wore her black pilot's uniform with a *Moneymaker* patch tacked onto the left breast, while Alex had on a dark green smock, goggles perched on her head.

All three of them had armored panels sewn across their chests, flexible plates that allowed for easy movement and, apparently, an excellent space look—because the moment they joined the parade, people began stopping them, and *specifically* them, to ask for a 'selfie.' Which turned out to be another term for photograph. Sloane wondered what the difference was, but her translation app maintained what felt like a bemused silence.

"The space paraders like us," she said, smiling for the millionth handheld camera-tablet. Her cheeks hurt from how often she'd had to do it.

"They said they were going to the Take Flight Comic Con," Alex whispered.

Hilda shook her head, her long braid swinging behind her. "Whatever that means."

"Let's ask," Sloane said, but Hilda and Alex both looked at her like she'd lost her mind.

"Why would we be going there if we didn't know what it was?" Alex asked.

OK, true. But that was no reason for the rolled eyes and the 'obviously' expressions. So Sloane didn't always think her ideas through before voicing them. She could read between the lines, between the other women's shared glances. It was so clear they might as well say it out loud: why had their captain left the care of his ship, and his crew, to someone so clueless?

Whatever. It wasn't like she wanted to be here, either. Still, she was surprised to find that she actually cared about what Hilda and Alex thought of her, if only a little. And so far, what they thought? Not great.

The procession wound through the streets, eventually slowing into a long queue. Airplanes swept over their heads regularly, so close that Sloane almost felt as if she could reach up and touch them, the roar of engines drowning all conversation every few minutes. The Take Flight Comic Con. Take Flight, because the event was happening in the airport. Clever.

She still didn't quite know what the event *was*, but she could still make a connection every now and then.

Eavesdropping revealed the meaning of 'con'—convention —and waiting revealed the location. Not the airport, but in a nearby hotel, one that Sloane doubted could actually squeeze in all of the space paraders. Conventioners? Whatever they were.

"We need tickets," Hilda said, leaning close to Sloane's ear as they neared the doors.

It was Alex who pressed plastic cards into their hands. Larger than the 'credit card,' these were attached to red cotton lanyards, with big red spaceship decals plastered across the front.

"What?" Alex said, when Sloane and Hilda both stared at her. "I can steal stuff."

Sure, she could. She just never had, at least not that Sloane had seen. If anything, Alex always seemed vaguely contemptuous of the crew's less lawful doings. Clearly desperate situations called for some degree of moral departure.

Security guards scanned their stolen badges at the doors, and then they were part of it, hidden within a sea of furry aliens and stuffed tentacles and, most importantly, fake space outfits. Just like theirs. Kind of.

Sloane doubted even Morik would be able to find them in this crowd.

A pair of women with antennae headbands and tentacles sprouting from their backs paused to snap a picture of Sloane. "Are you *Expanse* or *Stargate*?" one of them asked.

"It's obviously *Guardians of the Galaxy*," the other girl said. "Look at her pants."

Sloane made a point of not looking down at her pants to see what might be wrong with them. "Parse Galaxy, actually."

The girls shrugged, and one of them tugged a small notebook out of a pocket to scribble something down. "Don't know that one. We'll look it up."

And then they were gone, swallowed into a crowd of strangeness. "Expanse of what?" Sloane asked, staring into the crowd after the women as if they might return to offer some explanation.

"I didn't think anyone had star gates," Alex said, no doubt thinking of her wormhole machine. Not to mention the backwards technology of this planet.

Hilda caught them each by an arm and ushered them further inside. "Come on. Let's see what we can learn while we're here."

The crowd moved forward at a crawl, though for the most part they all seemed to be aiming for the same place. There were so many people that Sloane had to force herself to breathe slowly. It was no different than a spaceport, she told herself. Except for the smell of plastic fibers and popcorn. Banners fluttered above their heads with pictures of books and vid shows and collector's items. Strange, to have ads on fabric rather than screens, though there were plenty of those, too, from the small, common ones attached to people's hands to a few larger ones indicating what appeared to be schedules.

A few times, Sloane caught sight of someone wearing golden curls that reminded her eerily of the woman who'd chased her down after Oliver had procured the Blade of Starlight. Each time, a band of nerves tightened around her chest, until she realized that some of the people here were *pretending* to be that woman. After each initial shock, she could see that the person imitating her was too short, or too wide, their curls tacked clumsily on their heads. Some wore masks, too.

Once, Sloane tapped a fellow attendee—a man dressed as a turtle—and pointed. "Who's that supposed to be?"

He blinked at her, and for a moment she thought he might be too dedicated to his turtle persona to speak. But then he said, "She's dressed as Coral. Mary O'Sullivan? No one knows how to cosplay her anymore, now her ID's out. Surprised you didn't notice, she's got the white lining on the sleeves."

His friend, who wasn't pretending to be a turtle, nudged him. "It's mother of pearl."

Sloane frowned, and the turtle grinned as if he might ask to buy her a drink, or maybe a hot pretzel in the shape of a space person or something. She didn't quite understand the theme to this convention, but she was beginning to understand that these were all *fans* of something. Or different things. But there appeared to be no specific theme. According to her app, the name 'comic' suggested something funny, or a flimsy paper book with more pictures than words. Was that what *Expanse* meant? A flimsy storybook?

Holding tightly to Hilda and Alex, Sloane thanked the turtle for his help and navigated them away through the crowd. She didn't need to understand this place. She just needed to hide in it. Preferably without wanting to jump every time she saw one of those... cosplayers pretending to be the woman who'd chased them down. And offered them help that Sloane couldn't trust.

Coral. Mary. Sloane didn't understand that, either, but at least she had a name. Two names. For all the good that would do her. Hiding in the convention crowd was all well and good, but what would they do when it ended? Whoever Mary-slash-Coral might be, Sloane doubted she could help them return to their ship.

After a frustratingly slow beginning, the crowd finally began to disperse to different areas. The majority, though, headed up a pair of staircases and into a huge open space that was full of... stuff. Row after row of tables and displays were piled high with books, leather-based outfits, plastic swords, dragon models, and spaceships of various shapes and sizes.

Sloane exchanged a glance with Alex, who shrugged, but Hilda was already tugging them toward the middle of the room as if she'd seen something she liked.

"I'm not stealing a hat for you," Sloane said.

Hilda rolled her eyes and stopped in the middle of the aisle, which had been widened for the sake of an enormous glass display case. Inside, a collection of action figures stood in fighting positions, some elevated on little boxes to make it easier to see everything.

And several of the figurines looked familiar. One was definitely Coral—or Mary, whatever—with her mask on, hair pulled back, frozen in a fighting stance. Beside her, the orange-haired muscle man who'd dangled Sloane over the beach. And next to *him*, a figure wearing a mask that covered her full face, the Blade of Starlight clutched in her hand.

"The League of Independent Operatives," a guy said, and Sloane looked up. But he wasn't talking to her; he was pointing to a sign above the vendor stand that accompanied the display of figurines. "What'd you do, pull all your independent operative inventory from last year under one banner when it turned out they were working together?"

The man running the table folded his arms across his ample chest. He wore a wig that looked suspiciously like the muscle man's hair. "It's all new. Like the sign says."

"I bought that remote-control Pearl Knife last year," the would-be customer argued.

Sloane's eyes drifted to the selection on the table. It was covered in models of the Blade of Starlight. There was other stuff, too—costumes, grapple hooks, various vehicles—but iterations of the Blade took up more than half the table. So it was well known here. Popular, even.

"If you're not buying, move on." The vendor scowled at the guy before turning a more hopeful smile on Sloane and her friends.

Sloane started to pull Alex and Hilda away, but another flash of golden curls caught the corner of her eye. She couldn't help it; she whipped her head around to face the latest Coral-Mary O'Sullivan costume.

Except this time, it wasn't a costume.

"If you want to stay hidden," the real Coral said, "you really shouldn't let people post your picture on social media. Every few steps, from what it looks like."

"Coral," Sloane said.

"She's not wearing her mask," the customer who'd been arguing with the vendor said. "Probably should call her Mary."

Sloane glanced at him. "I thought they were the same person."

He shrugged, then sidled toward the vendor table, clearly sensing trouble as Mary took a step forward. She had a friend with her, Sloane realized, a man with closely cut hair and gray eyes. He wasn't dressed as a vigilante, or whatever this Mary person was supposed to be. He just had on jeans and a T-shirt.

"Look," Mary said to him, jutting her chin toward the case beside Sloane. "LIO figurines. I don't see you, Nathan."

Her companion frowned. "Maybe I'm sold out."

Mary raised an eyebrow. "Before me?"

"Point taken. But I'm new. They'll add me. Right?" His accent didn't match hers, and Sloane found herself wondering whether he hailed from another continent, or even another planet. She hadn't seen any space-bound ships, true, but maybe they were all concentrated somewhere. She'd have to try to wring more information out of her app. Later.

The orange-wigged vendor, who'd backed away a bit,

shrugged. "You don't have a signature look. But sure, yeah. I mean, we'll find a way."

"Cheers. Just don't make it a cop thing, right? I'm not a cop anymore."

Sloane couldn't tell if this guy was serious. The convention goers were keeping their distance, but everyone in Sloane's peripheral vision had cameras raised. 'Social media.' Was that something like the community feeds she knew from home?

Hilda nudged Sloane in the ribs. "Let's get out of here while they're negotiating with merchandisers."

Somehow Sloane doubted these two were actually distracted by the figurines, but she checked the batteries in her hov-tiles anyway. Low. Extremely low. Like, make-it-to-the-end-of-the-room-then-run kind of low.

But it was better than nothing. She activated the boots, and Hilda followed suit. They could get Alex out of here like they had before, no problem. People around them gasped and ducked out of the way as she and Hilda rose up from the floor. Close quarters. But they could do this.

They made it four feet into the air before the boots just... stopped. The lights sputtered out, and Sloane dropped to her knees, hands hitting the grimy showroom carpet hard as Hilda and Alex crumpled beside her. She cringed at the jolt to her knees. At least they hadn't been soaring high.

Mary stepped up to them, showing off a boxy black device in her hand. "Jammed your tech. Game's over, friends."

And it seemed like it really, truly was. They'd done their best, but this was where they failed. Hilda and Alex were looking at Sloane, and as much as she'd wanted them to show some faith in her as a leader, she was hardly equipped to come up with a solution here. What was she supposed to do, punch this woman in the face and somehow secure safe passage out of the hotel? None of them were fighters, and Mary-Coral most certainly was.

She had the merchandise to prove it.

As Sloane stood on the point of surrendering, a stream of golden light sliced through a table at the end of the row with a loud crackle, tearing piles of metallic dragon masks into pieces. The vendor shouted, leaping out of the way, and the crowd grew even thinner as the golden threads widened into a full-on portal.

As soon as it did, an army streamed through the gap.

OK, maybe not a full army. But in their battle helmets and black body armor, crimson capes swirling behind their backs, the half-dozen soldiers might as well have been one. They poured out of the portal and formed a line before it.

For a breath, no one moved. Sloane scanned the soldiers for any sign of Morik. Someone had made it to the *Moneymaker*, or the soldiers wouldn't be here—and if they weren't with Morik, she'd eat her own boots. The curly-haired elf might be inside some of that armor, though she highly doubted it. He was probably sitting back in her break room, brushing his hair while eating her favorite snacks and watching what was sure to be her humiliation. And, unless this Mary person's outfit was a lot stronger than it looked, probably all of their deaths, too.

The soldier standing in the middle raised an arm, pointing directly at Sloane. "We're here to claim our master's property. Hand it over, and we will suffer you to live."

Someone was buying into the whole epic elf vid genre. Before Sloane could open her mouth, Mary said, "And who is your master?"

"Sever forged the Blade of Starlight," said the soldier. "He demands its return."

At that name, Sloane actually stuck a finger in her ear to

clear out the dust. Because there was no way the soldier could have said Sever.

Except... except that Oliver had said the name, hadn't he? She'd thought he was using it as a verb, but... but what if he'd meant the *person*? If Sever could even be called that.

At her side, Alex whimpered softly. Sloane nearly joined her. Even she, a sheltered medical student from an out-of-the-way corner of the Parse Galaxy, knew about Sever. A godlike entity with a planet-crisping tendency, he disappeared for decades at a time—until everyone assumed he'd finally died, or left them alone for good—and then resurfaced, suddenly. And usually violently.

No. No matter Oliver's last words, the soldier *couldn't* have said Sever. Sloane glanced at Hilda, whose face had gone paper white; Alex's lips were twisted, as if she might throw up. No denying it, then. Even in Sloane's panic, the memory of Oliver's last moments crystalized in her mind, and she could easily imagine him asking Morik the identity of his employer. Remembering the horror on Oliver's face as he'd tried to flee, she knew—she'd always known—that he hadn't chosen any poison capsule. He'd tried to run, and Sever's people had killed him.

But Sever's reputation, like everything in the Parse Galaxy, clearly hadn't made it as far as Earth, because Mary frowned. "Who's Sever?"

Sloane licked her lips, trying to form a response, but her tongue had gone numb. Morik was one of Sever's minions. She'd said no to helping *Sever*. Not that she'd willingly have helped a mass murderer—even she had her limits—but she might have been a little more polite about refusing him.

"He's no one good." Alex's voice was hardly audible. "And he's here. Which means he found our ship."

To MARY, Eloise's portals looked like moonlight. Or at least, the single portal she'd seen Eloise make had looked that way, strands of silver light parting the air. Somewhat alarming, yes. But pretty. In line with the little Mary knew about the Pearl Knife.

The portal that now cut through the comic convention sales floor might have been forged out of blazing sunlight, a violent rending rather than a delicate parting. It seared Mary's eyelids with every blink, reminding her painfully of the arrival of the aliens and the fight that had lost them the Knife. What had that been, a week ago? More? It felt like an eternity.

And the people who now guarded the portal were a *bit* more intimidating than the original Earth-crashing thieves, who were currently cowering at Mary's feet. Whoever this Sever guy was, he scared them. A lot.

His soldiers didn't exactly give Mary warm fuzzy feelings, either. They were huge, for starters, as if they'd all been recruited because of their same towering height, and they wore plated black armor. Helmets. Capes, too, which was weirder, but she wasn't about to write them off because of a little pomp.

With the head soldier's speech complete, his employer's

demands revealed, Mary doubted he intended to enter into a lengthy negotiation. She reached down to drag the dark-haired alien thief behind a nearby table as the soldiers started toward them, no doubt intent on capturing the Knife. The woman's friends scrambled along behind them as Nathan crawled up from the other direction, eyes wide.

Yeah. It was a lot to take in.

The comic con crowd was dispersing in earnest now, wigs flying off of panicked heads, ill-fitting shoes coming loose, cheesy swords and masks and pistols scattering in the con-goers' wakes as they ran away. Good. The fewer civilians present, the better. Thankfully, the armored intruders weren't shooting at anyone. So far.

Mary took cover behind a table covered in stage makeup and wigs. "I take it these guys aren't with you," she said.

The brunette Knife-stealer shook her head, her olive-toned skin drained pale. She glanced at her friends, who stared back at her like they knew what she was thinking. Mary didn't, so she decided to assume the woman might double cross her any moment. She took hold of the woman's arm, resisting the urge to give it a shake. "They're *not* with you," she repeated. "Right?"

The woman shook her head again, more adamantly this time. "No. Nope. They're not."

"Right. Then we're on the same side now. I'm Mary. This is Nathan."

Who, to his credit, simply nodded. Not the time for long introductions. She'd enjoyed their banter by the LIO figurine case, ill-timed though it might have been. She'd enjoyed it more than she should have.

The woman swallowed hard. "Sloane. This is Alex and Hilda."

Mary wasn't sure which was which, but they could sort that

out later. She glanced over a pile of glittery makeup kits. The soldier people were organizing into a formation, clearly getting ready to sweep the room. They didn't look like they were in any particular hurry. Confident in their mission, she supposed. And those armored plates across their chests. Mary wouldn't have minded adding one of those to her closet. "Any idea how to beat these guys, Sloane?"

Sloane coughed. "Yeah. Give them the Blade of Starlight, or let them take it off our bodies."

"Not liking those options."

Was it possible that Sloane had the Knife on her now? She must; where would she hide it on Earth? Unless she knew the planet better than Mary thought she did. If only Mary could wield the damn thing. But there was no use wasting time on the impossible. Right now, she and Nathan seemed like the only two people in the group capable of throwing a decent punch, and she needed to focus.

Sloane's redheaded companion, who looked even less like a fighter than Sloane, leaned across her friend's body to talk to Mary. "How did you interfere with our hov-tiles?"

"Your flying shoes?"

Alex-or-Hilda nodded.

"Bit of tech, bit of luck," Mary said.

"I might be able to use the tech to stop them."

Mary wasn't sure it was the best idea to hand over the only method she had for stopping these three from bolting, but there was no time for suspicion. Besides, she thought she could catch this one if she tried to bound away. She tossed her the device, and the redhead turned it over in her hand before prying open the console with a fingernail. Mary would have objected, only it seemed this space woman might know what she was doing.

"I can use this to block the wormhole's frequency," the woman said. "To close it. Temporarily."

"Are you sure, Alex?" Sloane asked.

Alex gave her friend—leader? Boss?—a sharp look, brows drawn together. "Yes, I'm sure."

Crashes echoed across the mostly empty floor as the soldiers began their sweep, obliterating tables and scattering merchandise as they started across the room. Mary wondered if she'd ever be able to fight a world-saving battle without destroying other people's property.

She wasn't completely sure this *was* a world-saving battle, but if these guys wanted the Pearl Knife, it seemed like a strong possibility. She doubted they planned to use it as a night light.

Crouched on Mary's other side, Nathan said, "If you close the portal, the soldiers will be stuck here. How does that help?"

Alex was already digging into the tech. She rose up onto her knees to grab a laptop from the vendor stand, plugged the jammer in, and started typing. How she knew what was what, when she clearly came from other worlds, Mary had no idea. Alex frowned at the screen. "It's not a portal, it's a wormhole."

"Whatever it is, we'll close it slowly," the older alien woman said. "Maybe Sever's minions will jump back through."

Alex pressed her lips together. "It's hard enough to close the wormhole with rudimentary technology like this. I don't know that I'll be able to control the speed."

Mary decided not to take offense at the term 'rudimentary,' and its application to her work.

The older woman, who had to be Hilda, patted Alex on the arm, earning herself an even deeper scowl. Which she ignored. "I believe in you, kid," she said.

The soldiers were getting closer, their boots pounding on the carpet. They needed to act. "You think they'll jump back through if the portal starts to close?"

"Wormhole," Alex corrected.

"Maybe?" Sloane squeaked.

Mary sighed. The soldiers turned down their row, shattering table after table. Why did they have to break everything? Why couldn't they simply *look*? "We'll hold them off."

"We? How?" Sloane's voice somehow squeaked even higher. Who was she, and how had she gotten herself tangled up in... whatever this was? Yes, she had flying boots, and yes, she'd crashed the hotel fight after-party with the intention of stealing the Knife. But her friend had done that part, betraying her in the process. As far as Mary could tell, Sloane didn't seem capable of swiping so much as a pack of gum.

Later. Mary would get the details later. She looked at Nathan. "Did you see those models of the Pearl Knife?"

Nathan smiled his sideways smile, as if he could read her mind, and Mary's heart performed an ill-timed flip. "I did."

Mary grabbed Sloane's arm. "Let's go."

She thought she might have to drag Sloane back across the showroom, but apparently the oncoming soldiers were enough to convince the woman that staying put was no longer an option. If they moved, they could buy Alex some time to do her thing.

After which Mary intended to have a long conversation with the alien scientist. With all of them.

Mary didn't bother to duck as she ran, the better to draw attention away from Alex's hiding spot. One of the soldiers shouted in a language Mary couldn't understand—no translation software activated, clearly. Rude. She ran harder, with Nathan on one side and Sloane on the other, hoping the older woman had gotten out of harm's way. Or that she was deadlier than she looked.

They reached the LIO merchandise display—none of which, Mary suspected, was licensed—and Mary grabbed one of the Pearl Knife models before darting down the wide corridor to meet the soldiers halfway. Damn, but they were doing their best to look scary, heads covered in pointy helmets, boots stomping heavily along the floor. They wore all black, except for those bright red half-capes.

Mary held up her hands, the fake Knife tucked under her thumb. It wasn't a bad imitation. She couldn't say anything about how closely the weight matched, though it was probably much lighter than the real thing. Whoever designed it had illuminated it with some kind of a bulb, coming close to duplicating the blade's unearthly glow. The hilt was right, too. Whoever had made this, they were clearly a true fan.

Smiling, Mary held the Pearl Knife out, dangling it where the soldiers would see. "Looking for this?"

One of the soldiers lunged—no banter here, apparently—and Mary pulled a quick-draw, removing the remote from her tool belt and sending the Knife toy flying for the ceiling.

Nathan must have filled Sloane in on the plan, because three more Knives joined Mary's, pulling toward the ceiling beams in an arrow-like formation before scattering in different directions. The soldiers moved fluidly, without hesitation. Four of them chased after the fake Knives.

Two stayed put. No mindless henchmen, these. They were well trained, not easily tricked. And they worked together as a team.

Even if Alex managed to herd them through a closing portal here, these people would return. Mary could feel it.

One of the remaining soldiers advanced, and Mary threw her body into a roundhouse kick, landing a foot in the middle of the soldier's chest plates. The intruder didn't even pause. She could practically feel the hit reverberating through the armor as it absorbed the blow. The soldier grabbed for her, but she whipped her leg out of the way, using her momentum to dodge. With the soldier's face hidden, the neck protected, the hands covered—where was she even supposed to aim? She couldn't pick out a single vulnerability.

But this was a study in patience, not a battle she was supposed to win. All she had to do was hold them off. The soldier punched, and Mary ducked, rolling under the case of LIO figurines. Her opponent crashed a fist through the glass, and she rolled again, leaping to her feet as the LIO figures went flying.

She decided not to take that as some kind of ill omen.

Behind her opponent, Nathan and Sloane had engaged the other soldier. In her peripheral vision, she could see the rest of them leaping for the soaring Knives, jumping much higher than gravity should allow. Flying boots were apparently all the rage where these people came from.

The soldier fighting Nathan and Sloane shouted, and Mary's opponent looked back, giving Mary an opportunity to see what had called their attention.

The portal was sliding closed. Slowly, the ends drifted together like an elastic band straining not to snap. Alex was obviously smoother than she thought. For a beat, the soldiers watched it—or at least, their helmets focused on it—and Mary held her breath, the battle paused. Would they take their chance to flee? Or risk getting stuck here? She could imagine a conversation happening within their helmets, orders being given.

A heartbeat, two, and the Knife-chasers abandoned their quests. Half flying, half running, they dove through the portal in single file. Mary's soldier joined them.

Nathan's didn't. Sloane lay crumpled on the floor, unconscious—or so it seemed—and as the other soldiers leapt out of the showroom, the last one stayed put. On orders, or because they'd gone rogue? It didn't matter. With one brutal swipe of a gloved hand, the soldier lifted Nathan off his feet as if he were nothing more than a kitten. The sides of the portal drifted ever closer as Nathan fought back, flailing to reach the soldier's throat.

Mary could easily picture the soldier grinning beneath that helmet as they held Nathan halfway over the portal. He struggled, kicking at the soldier's legs, but it did no good. The hands that held him might have been made of metal. Perhaps they were.

Mary stopped breathing. The portal had cut the dragon-mask stand in half when it had appeared here, obliterating everything. What would it do to a person? She realized she'd frozen in place, fear lancing through her body, and she gave herself a shake. Mary O'Sullivan didn't freeze. *Coral* didn't freeze.

Still halfway across the showroom, Mary moved. Nathan's foot grazed the edge of the contracting portal, and he grimaced in pain.

And all Mary could think was that she couldn't lose him now. Everything that stood between them faded into the background as she ran, her legs working as if fighting through molasses, the portal's blinding gap closing too quickly. She wasn't going to make it.

So she did the only thing she could think of. She unhooked the grapple hook from her belt, and she shot it at Nathan's captor. The weapon that wasn't a weapon, the cluster of metal hooks that had injured Goldi so grievously, tumbled out of her grip as if in slow motion until the grapple met the soldier's head, knocking them ever so slightly off balance.

Mary lunged, throwing her arms around Nathan to wrench him out of the soldier's barely loosened grip. Tilting sideways from the pull of Nathan's weight as he dropped to the floor, she kicked again.

The soldier tripped through the portal, and Mary whipped

her foot back a split second before the rubber-band threads snapped together with a sizzle.

Mary dropped to her knees beside Nathan, who was already pulling himself up to sit. Treacherous relief tore across her chest, making the effort of holding back tears physically painful. She wanted to hit him for scaring her like that. She wanted to pull him close.

Instead, she avoided meeting his eyes and focused her attention on his foot instead. The sole of his boot was shorn in half. She peeled it away, feeling his gaze on her, but the sock was fully intact.

"The way you were pulling faces up there, I thought that portal was about to cut you open," Mary said.

He leaned over, examining the obliterated boot. "I could feel the heat. It felt like..." He gave his head a shake, like he wanted to forget it, and Mary wasn't sure she wanted to know what he'd been intending to say. "No blood?"

"No blood," she said. "Just you acting like a baby."

Alex joined them, balancing the laptop and jammer in her arms, while the older woman knelt beside Sloane. "She's alive. Just knocked out."

Mary grimaced. For a moment, she'd actually forgotten about Sloane. This was the problem with having Nathan around. Even when they weren't a couple, the man was distracting as hell. "I'm guessing that won't hold our friends for long," she said.

Alex shook her head, and Mary helped Nathan to his feet, grateful against her will for his weight against her shoulder.

"The wormhole follows the Blade of Starlight," Alex said, helping her friend to lift the still-unconscious Sloane off the floor. "Or perhaps the case that holds it. I didn't design it—the wormhole, that is—to do that, but there appears to be some kind of a resonance."

That made sense. But they couldn't exactly put the Knife in a storage locker, could they? And they certainly couldn't bring the thing back to HQ, not with it acting as a certified space-soldier magnet. "Is there a way to jam the frequency from this end?" Mary asked. "Stop the resonance or something?"

Alex nodded slowly, her expression far away. "Maybe. I'll have to work on it."

Mary let go of Nathan, who seemed perfectly capable of walking on his own. In one boot, but still. "Then I guess we'd better get out of here, before they come back for another round."

FOR A BRIEF INTERLUDE, Holland Gold's mere presence seemed to ward Travis Bertram away. The kid had more backbone than Eloise had originally assumed, so she couldn't decide if he was affronted by the appearance of a lawyer—a big, important lawyer, apparently—or if he was off trying to cause them more trouble.

At least Holland's appearance had vanished the EAEA representatives. So much for Travis's claims of getting them official clearance. Eloise couldn't object to that, though she couldn't imagine it was the last she'd seen of Chloe and her friends.

After a restless few hours of sleep in a concrete-walled box of a room that was furnished with a cot, a sink, and a toilet, Eloise found herself wedged behind the same charming table in the same charming interrogation room as the night before. No handcuffs, at least. A black-eyed security camera watched from the corner as a guard escorted Dad to sit beside her.

As the guard headed for the door, Holland entered, stepping aside with a tilt of his head to let the man pass. The lawyer looked as polished as ever, his cufflinks shining in the poor light of the interrogation room. Eloise wondered where the man could have gone while they were sleeping. Somewhere civilized, judging by his creaseless appearance.

The guard narrowed his eyes, but said nothing. The lawyer, it seemed, was expected. And unwelcome.

"Hoping to have you out of this black hole by the end of the day," Holland said, settling into the chair on the other side of the table. "Sorry they wouldn't let me bring coffee."

Coffee would have been nice. Or bourbon. She'd lost track of the time and suspected they'd slept through the morning. Despite the hours of containment, though—and despite the fact that she hadn't bathed or changed the clothes she'd worn for the fight on the beach—Eloise felt more robust, at least physically, than she had in days. Since the disappearance of the Knife, really. It almost felt like she was recovering from a stomach bug, rather than the mental hold of an artifact no one understood.

She shouldn't have the mental capacity to consider it at all, but the fact that she did? That gave her hope. Yesterday, she hadn't been able to think straight. Today, she might be able to figure out how to extract them from this situation.

Was it progress, a benefit of having dissolved the Knife from her consciousness? Or would the effects return in force as they had with Dolly? Eloise sometimes suspected that the Knife had taken some amount of revenge on Dolly, punishing her for the things she'd forced it to do. With Dolly no longer in close proximity, would she heal, too? As Eloise and Dad waited with Holland, she couldn't help but wonder if the situation might give them a new angle to study. Along with a suite of new problems.

And she couldn't help but wish that Agnes had responded to her message. Holland made small talk while they waited, chatting about the weather and the trees and nothing in particular as Eloise's mind wandered through history, trying to piece the Knife's secrets together.

At length, the door clicked open, admitting Travis Bertram in a fresh suit and goldenrod-yellow tie. The kid was the definition of 'trying too hard,' but what did Eloise have to say about it? He was the one who had her wedged behind a table.

And he looked far too cheerful. Eloise watched with trepidation as he pulled out the chair next to Holland's, half expecting him to spin it around and sit backwards. Instead, he plopped down with a self-satisfied smirk. "Happy to report you'll be staying with me for a time," he said.

Holland raised a silver eyebrow. "Oh? On what charges?"

Travis leaned his forearms on the table. "Plenty of options. Physical assault. Disturbing the peace. But none of them are necessary. I have the clearance I need to hold you here."

Holland didn't even twitch. "Meaning?"

"Meaning," Travis said, grinning, "I can keep them here indefinitely, simply because I believe them to be dangerous. You're welcome to stay, by all means. I wouldn't deny you the pleasure."

"Unconstitutional." Holland gave away no sign of nerves, no shift in his expression. The man worked in Hollywood? He could have excelled on the screen. Eloise felt like her teeth might crack from the tension in her jaw.

"But precedented." Travis was practically beaming. Like someone had promised the kid a lollipop or something. "Terrorists can be held without charges."

"Also unconstitutional," Dad murmured.

Certainly. Yet if Holland were forced to leave this place—she made herself think of *if*, rather than *when*—precedent allowed for much worse things than imprisonment. If they didn't extract themselves, she could too easily envision such a future for all enhanced humans. It was what the EAEA wanted, wasn't it?

It was enough to coat the inside of her mouth with bitter fear.

Holland nodded. And, to Eloise's dismay, he scraped his chair back from the table. "Well, in this case, I've got some people I need to talk to."

Travis practically wiggled in his seat, clearly ecstatic with joy. He thought he'd gotten rid of the lawyer, but Eloise's had a feeling the fight had just begun. Still, it took time for issues like this to work their way through the system. A lot of time, during which a lot of bad things could happen. To her. To her friends. To the entire population of enhanced humans. A fractured population, certainly, but a community nonetheless.

She couldn't stay here. She needed to get the Knife, to return to HQ. She needed to be able to fight this. Panic clawed at her throat, and she wasn't sure she'd be able to contain it.

Holland picked up his briefcase, pausing when he reached the door. "It's funny," he said. "The government passed off its enhanced criminals to the league for safe keeping, didn't it? I wonder you're not concerned about being able to hold them here."

Holland was looking straight at Travis, who was grinning back at him, yet Eloise had the distinct impression that the lawyer was talking to her. As the thought crossed her mind, Holland's steel gaze met hers. "Ms. Reyna. Mr. Reyna. Jeff Hayes sends his regards. He regrets that he's currently out of the country, but he hopes to see you at his home when he returns. Another pool party, perhaps."

Travis snorted. "Not likely, unless he plans to be gone a very long time."

Eloise didn't share his mirth. She watched Holland, trying to read his expression. Another pool party, after the disastrous one Jeff had hosted last fall? Not a likely invitation. With

Travis's attention locked on the door, she risked glancing at Dad. Was Holland trying to tell them to escape?

Reading the question in her eyes—or so she hoped—Dad gave her a single nod.

With the door still swinging closed behind Holland, Eloise leapt to her feet, knocking her chair to the floor with a clang. The guard whipped around, hand halfway to his belt, but Eloise was already rounding the table. She grabbed onto Travis, who raised his hands to protect his face. But much though she wanted to, Eloise didn't hit him. She seized him by the shoulders and shoved him into the guard, knocking both men into the wall.

The element of surprise. It was almost as good as having a superpower.

With Dad on her heels, Eloise bolted out of the room and slammed the door shut, locking it behind her and calling Ire's name as a trio of guards hurried toward them, guns drawn.

"Any idea if they're even down here?" Dad asked.

The sound of wrenching metal screeched out of the interrogation room beside theirs, and the door burst off its hinges as Ire stormed into the hall, Steve by his side. Ire launched the door down the corridor, forcing the guards to duck as it ricocheted off one wall and crashed into the other, sending chips of stone spraying toward the ceiling.

Eloise didn't stop to see whether the door had hit the guards or merely delayed them. She followed Steve's lead, running away from them and toward what she could hold only hope Steve had scouted as an entrance.

Where was Holland? How had he disappeared so quickly? And what kind of lawyer encouraged their clients to bust out of jail?

Jeff Hayes's lawyer, apparently. And if Eloise understood correctly, the movie star had invited them to hide out in his home. It wouldn't take Travis long to figure that out, but it might buy them some time.

Steve careened around the corner, blurring ahead to scout as the rest of them kept running. "Two guards at the exit," he said.

Ire grunted. "On it."

"I could be on it," Steve said.

"I said I'll handle it."

Clearly, these two had not bonded over their shared adventures. Eloise could yell at them later. For now, she bolted for the door, a step behind her father.

Someone grabbed her shoulders from behind, and suddenly Eloise found herself in a position she'd witnessed probably dozens of times in her life: a guard yanked her toward him until she stood with her back flush against him, a gun pointed at her head.

For the first time in her life, *she* was the hostage. The leverage. She didn't know if the guard would shoot her, but these people seemed to have little regard for trivial matters like laws and personal rights. All she could do was breathe. The others would get her out of this. She had to believe it.

Dad must have sensed her absence, because he slowed before the guard even called for him to freeze, Steve and Ire pausing just beyond the double doors. So close. They were so close to freedom. So close to the open air.

Dad's eyes burned with rage, his brows pulled together. He looked dangerous. He *was* dangerous. One lick of flame from his fingertips—to singe the guard's uniform, maybe, or his toes; she wouldn't have objected to toes—and Eloise would be able to pull free. He controlled fire with the same finesse that Dolly, and now Eloise, could control the Pearl Knife. Or he could do much, much more.

Dad raised his hands, and Eloise braced for the fire. Whatever was holding him back, whatever qualms he had about his powers, he'd surely use them now, to save her. If he could.

But the fire didn't come. Was Dad... He couldn't possibly be surrendering, could he?

Steve burst past Dad, blurring to Eloise's side in the matter of a second. He seized her by the arm, somehow sending the guard's weapon flying—Eloise couldn't make out his individual movements—before whipping her past Dad and out the door. When he paused on the sidewalk outside the compound to make sure Ire and Dad were following, he touched her cheek, concern wrinkling between his eyebrows. His arms were still wrapped around her, and she had to fight the urge to lean into the embrace. It was purely utilitarian, a way to get her out of the prison. That was all.

"Why didn't he use his abilities?" Steve asked.

Eloise swallowed, her throat dry. "Maybe he can't."

Steve gave his head a little shake, as if he didn't believe it. Eloise didn't quite believe it, either.

Dad and Ire rounded the fence, and they were off.

"Where are we headed?" Ire grunted, keeping pace with Steve at the front of the group as if his life depended on how fast he could run a mile. She would definitely need to address this little rivalry. And soon.

"First we need a ride," Eloise said, pulling Holland Gold's business card out of her pocket. She had a feeling the lawyer hadn't gone far. Maybe they wouldn't have to steal a vehicle to get to Malibu. Better to avoid actual crimes; they were going to need to call upon the public's good will, and soon. "Based on what Holland said, I'd guess we're heading to Jeff Hayes's."

SETTLING the aliens into a dubiously three-star motel near LAX was something of an experience. Mary showed them the limited amenities, and while they understood the refrigerator and the sinks, the shower confused them thoroughly. When she turned on the TV, they all started to laugh. At the same time. After twenty minutes in their room, she still didn't understand why.

While scientist Alex braved the shower and pilot Hilda flipped through the TV channels, still giggling under her breath, Mary sat on the edge of one of the two double beds beside Sloane. The woman's dark hair hung limp around her shoulders, tangles trailing down her back. She wore a T-shirt with a 'Take Flight Comic Con' logo and a pair of shorts Mary had picked up on the way over here.

She might be wearing Earth clothing now, but Mary had a feeling she wasn't any happier to be here. Still, Mary had been sitting with her for a good two minutes, and the other woman hadn't done anything but stare at her hands.

"OK," Mary said finally, "you have got to tell me what the deal is here."

Sloane shook her head, like she wasn't completely sure

herself. They all needed sleep, but Mary needed answers even more. "The Blade of Starlight," Sloane said. "The Pearl Knife? Whatever it is. This guy Sever has had a bounty out on it for decades. If we'd realized it was his bounty, we'd never have tried to steal it for him. Even Oliver didn't know who he was working for." She sighed. "I guess you don't know who Sever is."

"Not a clue."

Sloane twisted her lips, like she didn't want to say it. "He's like this legendary king who destroyed his entire court about a century ago, then locked himself away. Like a hermit. He surfaces occasionally to punish a planet for something or other, so we know he's alive, but..." She swallowed, picking at her nails. "Let's put it this way: all the galaxy flight paths skirt around his space station. Extra time, extra fuel, and no one ever complains."

OK, that sounded... weird. "So he's a scary dude." And, apparently, thriving at over a hundred years old.

Sloane frowned, eyes skimming the bedspread as if she were trying to read something. "That didn't fully translate. But yes, he's scary. And you stole the Blade from him."

Mary leaned back on her hands, watching the other woman. Nothing about her countenance made Mary think she was lying. She'd taken a bounty of some kind, and now this Sever guy had his sights set on Earth. "I don't know how we could have stolen the Knife from space. We don't have a way to get to your neck of the woods. We didn't know you guys existed."

Sloane lifted a shoulder. She still hadn't looked at Mary. "Someone must have. My app understands and translates your language. The other information is out of date, by a lot, but *someone* from the Parse Galaxy has to have been on Earth. At some point. There are maps."

"Can I see?"

Sloane nodded and reached across the bed for her tablet. It was just a strip of metal, actually, but when she pushed a button, it extended into a tablet-looking kind of thing.

"Are there settings?" Mary asked, leaning over her shoulder. "Something that tells you the last time Earth was updated?"

Sloane tapped through various screens, the language impenetrable to Mary. It looked like her finger was tapping in midair, too, like she'd push right through the blue-green data display. But it seemed solid enough.

Mary really wanted to play with it. Maybe if she made friends with these people, and if she asked really nicely, they'd let her take one apart.

"Here," Sloane said, pointing to a series of markings that Mary couldn't make out at all. "It says the information was last updated in 1930, Earth time."

Mary couldn't keep her jaw from falling open.

"What?" Sloane said. "Is that a long time ago?"

Mary resisted the urge to snatch the tablet away from her, to verify for herself. It wouldn't help. She couldn't read it. "About a hundred years ago. We hadn't even been to our moon yet."

Mysteries upon mysteries. At some point, someone—an alien, apparently—had shown up on Earth, catalogued some data, and taken off again. Around the same time, someone had stolen the Pearl Knife from this Sever guy. Maybe. Mary wasn't quite sure she believed that, though the Knife's origins were so mysterious themselves that it might as well be the answer.

What mattered was that Sever believed the Knife belonged to him. Mary wanted to believe that Sloane's understanding of his powers had to be exaggerated, but even if that were true, his access to robot armies was reason enough for concern. And what if he was some kind of extra-powerful enhanced creature? It was possible, wasn't it?

Sloane stored the tab, and Mary stood. They weren't going to figure out any answers tonight, and everyone was exhausted. "Get some sleep," she said. "We'll make a game plan tomorrow."

The alien woman lay back on the bed, and Mary thought she might not answer. As Mary reached the door, though, Sloane said, "You're going to need more than a strongman and a fast runner for this."

Mary paused with the door half open. "Yeah, I know," she said. "Get some sleep."

She had a feeling that Sloane, at least, would be passed out in the next few minutes.

And Mary should sleep, too. As she stepped into the evening air, a breath of wind stirring a chill through the warm L.A. evening, she felt wide awake. Sloane's door opened onto an exterior second-floor balcony that faced a gated swimming pool. Beyond that, streetlights beamed onto the parking lot as if to bathe the thing in orange-aid. Not pretty, but it worked as a hideout for now.

Mary wished she could contact Eloise, tell her what Sloane had said, but she hadn't heard a word from El since the EAEA had hauled her away. They'd have to solve that problem, too, and soon. At least Jeff had promised to send some lawyer over to help. Mary wished there were a way to track Dolly down, to force some answers out of her, but the Knife had taken precedence over finding her. LIO's resources, which felt like they were ever dwindling, couldn't handle everything at once.

Mary sighed and headed for her room. They'd managed to secure three in a row, and she had to pass Nathan's door to get to hers. She slowed, wondering if she ought to check on him.

Make sure he was OK after nearly getting sliced in half by a gateway to another galaxy.

He'd seemed fine after the fight, though. If anything, he ought to be the one stopping to see her. To thank her for saving his life. She passed her own door, pausing by the ice machine, and glanced back along the railed walkway. It wasn't like Nathan to avoid her after a fight. It wasn't like him to stay away. After their talk in the car, and the tiki bar, she'd thought he might try to give her more unwanted advice. Or commentary, like 'see, your grapple hook did some good after all.' But he hadn't said much at all after she'd saved him from getting sliced in half by that portal.

Before she quite realized what was happening, Mary was stalking back toward his room. She knocked on the door and stepped back toward the railing, waiting with her arms crossed.

Nathan answered the door wearing a T-shirt and jeans, as usual, his hair damp from the shower. She hated the way his T-shirts showed off his shoulders, and the fact that he always seemed ready to head out on a mission at a moment's notice. She never managed to catch him off guard, in an ugly bathrobe or something. He always had to look... well, like this. *Good.* It made her want to punch him just to get a bruise back on his cheek.

He took in her expression, then leaned on the doorframe, resigned, as if he knew she was getting ready to yell at him.

Well, good. He knew what to expect.

"I saved your life today," Mary said.

Nathan glanced along the balcony-slash-hallway, but there were no other guests around, no hotel staff to save him. "I know. I was there." He seemed like he was caught between confusion and sarcasm, like he couldn't decide whether he needed to prepare for more banter or prepare to defend himself.

Mary wasn't sure, either. "You look fine. You're not limping. No after effects."

Nathan quirked a smile at her. "And you look... disappointed?"

Mary gripped her elbows, keeping her arms firmly crossed. "If you're fine, you could have come to thank me." She hadn't been in her room, but he didn't know that. Unless he *had* stopped by and she'd missed him. She felt heat rising to her cheeks, but it was too late to stop yelling at him now. "You were grateful enough to Rainbow Brite after she saved your life. And also, you need more training so we don't have to save your life every time there's a fight."

Nathan waited a beat, as if to make sure she was done yelling at him. Which she was. For now.

"First off," he said, "Tally came to see me, not the other way around. Second, yes, I'm still in the midst of training. It's been paused due to extenuating circumstances I believe you're familiar with. Third..."

He hesitated, tugged his fingers through his hair. So he was nervous, then. Good. "Third, you've been clear in setting a pretty firm boundary between us. You've every right to do so, and I respect it. I'd be an ass not to. And part of respecting it is, I don't know, refraining from showing up at the door to your hotel room without an explicit invitation."

So he'd thought about coming, then. Wanted to, even, if she understood what he was saying. Only Nathan was a decent person who wouldn't pretend she'd done anything but push him away since she'd been back.

She was still angry with him. Yes, he'd apologized for his black-and-white, good-versus-evil take on the party at Jeff Hayes's home, where protecting her identity had gotten a friend killed. Truth be told, she still wasn't convinced he'd been entirely wrong about that. His choice to leave her in favor of

LIO had nearly torn her apart, but he'd apologized for that, too. He'd said it was the wrong call.

He'd also made a point to tell her that Will was alive, at the earliest opportunity, even though she'd been intent on fighting him at the time. And she knew he'd stayed in L.A. after that, after Diana had tortured her with her acid poison. She knew he'd searched for her.

She was still angry with him... Why, exactly? She couldn't articulate it, even to herself.

Mary didn't quite realize she was moving toward him until she was just inches away, close enough to smell his familiar hint of pine mixed with soap from the shower. Close enough to tilt her head back, ever so slightly, to look him in the eye. If she pushed to the balls of her feet, their lips would be touching. And still, he didn't reach for her. Her boundaries again? Or other concerns?

He *had* been the one to leave. Maybe he couldn't see past that. She thought of how she'd pictured him with Rainbow Tally, and how he knew she'd spent time with Jeff during her LIO hiatus. Could he have similar... fears? Would that hold him back?

"I didn't sleep with Jeff," she said.

Nathan blinked. "What?"

It was too late to step away, to pretend she'd closed the space between them for any reason other than her feelings for him. If Nathan wanted her...

"Jeff Hayes," she said. "He helped me, before I came back to LIO. But I didn't... We weren't together."

"How would it be my business if you had been?"

She reached up to touch his cheek, running her hand along his jaw. It wasn't his business, but she wanted it to be. He swallowed, looking at her so intently that she wondered if he meant to question her further on that topic.

She didn't intend to give him the chance.

When she kissed him, he drew in a sharp breath as if in surprise, and Mary nearly pulled away. He'd respected her boundaries; maybe she really had crossed over his. But as she started to draw back, he tugged her in closer, and she relaxed against his body, her palm still touching his cheek, his chin, his ear. She'd missed everything about him, the feeling of his arms around her, his breath mingling with hers.

Nathan pulled her into his room, allowing the door to slam shut behind them, hands on her waist as he pressed her back into the wall, kissing her like she planned to leave in the next ten minutes. Like he might not have another chance.

"Tell me this what I think it is," he said, murmuring into her neck, her collarbone, her lips.

Mary tipped her head back, trying her best to think straight without truly wanting to. "What do you think it is?"

"Just tell me it's not goodbye."

The defensive part of her wanted her to quip that she should be asking him that question, but she knew how he felt about her. She'd known since she'd come back to HQ to find him waiting, known that though he'd been the one to leave, he'd regretted it for months. No, Nathan was on her side now. And he wasn't going anywhere.

Mary kissed him again, gripping his hair in her hands. "I never want to say goodbye again."

SLOANE WAITED for a near-agonizing twenty minutes after Mary left her room before opening the door to her room. She peered out, startling a woman in a beige dress who was carrying a stack of towels. A car door slammed in the parking lot, but no one else appeared along the railed walkway. Mary, at least, had made it back to her room.

"What are you doing?" Hilda asked. "I'd keep that door locked."

As if a locked door could stop their enemies when Sloane was carrying around a direct route to their location. The box, the Blade, what did it matter? Sever's friends would find them. Sloane swiped one of the card-slash-keys from the desk and tucked it into her pocket. "Just wanted some air. I'll be back."

Hilda snorted, though Sloane wasn't sure if it was the fresh air part or the promise to return that amused her so much. Hilda's eyes were still focused on the vids she kept flipping through relentlessly. Sloane wasn't sure what the pilot was hoping to find, but she doubted they had Parse Galaxy soap operas here. Still, Hilda didn't protest as Sloane slipped outside.

Sloane let the door close behind her, taking another

moment to survey her surroundings. She had every intention of going back, just like she'd said. Or maybe ninety-percent intention. Part of her wanted to take the bag she'd slung over her shoulder and drown it in the pool, Blade of Starlight and all. Not that a little water would stop the Blade. Might slow it down, though.

Sever. The Blade of Starlight belonged to him, and even though he'd obviously been aware of Alex's wormholes and the possibility of tracking it—he'd sent Oliver to work with them— Sloane's actions, and her determination to collect the bounty, had smoothed his path to Earth. What *would* Sever do with the Blade?

Instead of heading for the pool, Sloane made her way to the vending machines at the end of the floor by the stairs. They were tucked into a concrete-walled alcove beside the ice machine, and she pretended to survey her choices—as if she understood what any of them were—while breathing in the heavy night air.

And somehow—maybe because of her restlessness, or because she hadn't quite recovered from the sight of those armored soldiers pouring through the portal—Sloane wasn't surprised when Morik's voice spoke up from behind her.

"We'd hoped you might decide to assist us today," he said, his ghostly glow reflected in the glass of the vending machine.

She didn't have the box open. It didn't seem to matter. "Why not open a portal right now?" she said without turning to look at him. She could feel the glow of his hologram, the energy of it. She didn't want to look at him. "You could come through and kill us all."

"Sever is now concerned."

Sloane found that doubtful. They'd won that fight by pure luck, and a little bit of trickery. "What, he's concerned about his own hide? I hardly think these people are a match for him."

The stories might not all be true, but she'd seen footage of the splintered remains of planet Callia after the last time he'd resurfaced. That was true enough.

Morik paused, and Sloane risked a glance in his direction, wondering if someone else was feeding him lines. "Sever has no reason to worry about his own safety," Morik said. "He's concerned about this planet you've found, about their apparent lawlessness. He's concerned that this unknown corner of the universe might have developed certain... pretensions."

Pretensions? Like trying not to die kind of pretensions? They should really just hand the Blade over and be done with it. But that idea was no longer alluring; it was only ribcage-tingling fear that made her think it at all. Sever caused damage enough without the Blade. Trying to organize her thoughts, Sloane studied the too-bright food wrappers in the machine, her brain drifting so far as to wonder what a Dor-it-o might be, and why it appeared to be orange.

"You can still help us," Morik said. "Sever is known for the brutality of his justice, but he rewards loyalty."

Loyalty? To Sever? The thought sent bile churning up into her throat. Sloane abandoned the Doritos and turned to face Morik's hologram. He looked the same as he had before, his cloak hanging regally off his shoulders, his curls untouched. Morik certainly hadn't participated personally in that battle. Sloane couldn't help but wonder what benefit he truly offered Sever. Surely a godlike being didn't need a spokesman.

Maybe Morik was simply an illusion. Maybe she was speaking directly to Sever himself. That would at least explain how he could show up like this with no projectors around to reflect his image. Sloane might not be a tech genius like Alex, but even she understood that this capability made no sense at all. It felt more like magic than technology—not unlike the Blade, actually—and that made her uneasy.

Whoever the guy was, he was clearly waiting for her answer. She licked her lips. "I can't help you," she said.

Morik sighed, giving his head a little shake of disappointment. "Despite his reputation, Sever so hates to approach negotiations with threats."

Sloane stayed still. He had to be bluffing; she had no chip installed in her body, as Oliver had. The threat was no greater in this moment than it had been on the comic-con floor, except perhaps that Mary wasn't here to defend her.

But Morik didn't open a portal. He withdrew a button from the depths of his robes and pressed it, revealing a projection within his own projection. Sloane's eyes blurred, trying to focus on the stacked images.

When the picture sharpened, she had to suppress a scream. It showed her family's home on Elter, a bird's-eye view that looked as if it had been captured from a camera in the ceiling. Her mother and father sat on the edge of their couch, hands clasped between them, while her six-year-old sister played on the floor at their feet. But young as she was, even Lissie kept glancing up at the caped soldiers. Two by the door. Two more by the windows.

The angle was strange, making it difficult to see her parents' expressions, but the threat was plain enough. Morik didn't even have to voice it.

Sloane swallowed back a wad of frustration, forcing her gaze back to Morik. "What do you want?"

Sever might not like approaching negotiations this way, but his spokesman obviously had no such qualms. There was a gleam of triumph in his eyes. Of certainty. "Gather your Earthly allies. When you've done that, we'll find you. We might as well extinguish them all at once."

Travis almost wished the rogue operatives had hit him on their way out the door, given him a fat lip or some blood to wipe away. Something tangible that he could point to that would underscore their villainy, and his own status as a victim.

Never mind. The situation was bad enough, the league's reputation shattered by lies, secrets, and now a jailbreak.

He'd been nursing a damaged ego in the interrogation room for hours, while pretending not to—and waiting for the phone to ring. All evening he sat there, staring at his phone while the guards avoided him. Maybe they were filing official reports, though somehow Travis doubted it. They seemed the types to put off paperwork as long as they could. He tried not to imagine them laughing at him. Or worse, degrading his reputation. They'd been the ones who couldn't maintain control in their own facility. He could get them all fired. No, he could get them all locked up themselves. They'd stop laughing, then.

Just when he was thinking he should visit a couple of them in the infirmary, make sure they'd survived—and that they were saying the right things—the door to the interrogation room swung open. Travis leapt to his feet, nearly knocking over his chair as fear struck through his upper body.

They were back. And this time, they'd kill him.

Instead, Senator Jones clomped heavily into the room. He had on khaki pants and a green polo shirt, as if he'd come straight from the golf course, his gray hair combed carefully over the balding patch on top of his head. Travis had seen the man scowl before—he was famous for that scowl, in fact; cartoonists loved the way his eyebrows practically formed curtains when he did it—but rarely had the expression been leveled at him.

So Travis had told Eloise Reyna a few lies when he'd claimed Senator Jones already agreed with him, and that new laws would be forthcoming. He didn't like to think of them as lies, really, though bending the truth was an occupational hazard when it came to working in Washington. It would have been naive to believe otherwise. And in a way, Travis had merely been sharing his hopes: that Senator Jones would agree the league had betrayed them, that they were a danger, that they needed proper oversight. How could the country's leaders do otherwise? They had the videos, the proof that their beloved, sanctioned superheroes were more than they seemed. Or less, at least in Travis's opinion.

Now, with Senator Jones scowling at him, Travis wasn't entirely sure this conversation would go his way.

"You're lucky I was in Nevada today, kid," Senator Jones said.

It took an effort not to scowl back at the man. Travis wanted to apologize for having interrupted the man's gambling —surely he hadn't been traveling on official state business—but he schooled his expression to neutrality. With a slight pinch to the corners of his eyes, as if to say 'I'm trying to be neutral, and yet I am in pain.'

Travis probably should have taken a few theater classes in school, instead of giving the drama nerds a hard time. Oh, well.

"You haven't been keeping me informed," Senator Jones said, pulling out one of the metal chairs. He sat, glaring at Travis from under those canopy-like eyebrows. If anything, the cartoonists didn't take their caricatures far enough.

There were moments to play the 'yes man,' to bow and scrape and flatter your way up the ladder. But eventually, a good politician had to break out. Take a risk, go out on a limb. If Senator Jones disowned Travis for telling the truth, he'd simply find another patron. His father might be irritated, but Dad had connections enough for an army of sons.

Travis tipped his chin up and cleared his throat. "With respect, Senator, you didn't want to be bothered."

The senator tapped his fingertips together, and Travis made a concerted effort not to hold his breath. "You're telling me the league kept a few secrets. What government agency hasn't?"

"I'm saying they lied to us outright," Travis said. His voice would not shake. He wouldn't allow it. "The Pearl Knife went missing, and they hid that. I'm more concerned about the fact that the Inferno is alive."

Travis pulled a second chair out, taking his time as he sat down. He held the senator's gaze, hoping to god he looked more confident than he felt. "These people have powers we barely understand. So far, they've done a good job pretending to use those powers to help the rest of us. But what if they have other plans?"

"Such as?"

Travis took a deep breath, let it out. Sometimes the difference between a future in politics and a forgotten cubicle came down to a single conspiracy theory, voiced out loud. "What if they want to take over?"

Senator Jones blinked, as though that wasn't what he'd expected to hear.

"They're powerful," Travis went on. "Powerful enough to escape from this prison."

The senator considered him for a long moment. This was a man whose poker face was unmatched, and Travis desperately wanted to find a place under his wing. A mentor, a champion. Someone who appreciated him for his own merits, rather than his father's reputation.

It took a concerted effort not to hold his breath.

"All right," the senator said finally, "you've got my attention. What is it you propose?"

AGNES HAD ALWAYS BEEN an early riser. As light crested the horizon ahead of the sun, she was often the first out of bed, never wanting to miss out on a single part of the day. It'd driven her poor parents to distraction when she was a kid, always up with the dawn.

Now, she began her day with a quiet walk. She liked to make her way to the lab by way of a winding sort of loop, breathing in the sweet flowers and citrus of the island as she walked. It rained most afternoons, leaving the soil fragrantly damp. Warm, but not too humid yet, the sun still dozing as Agnes stepped onto the beach to bid the water good morning. She walked along the shore, taking her time and trying to empty her mind.

A difficult task, under the circumstances. Her patients were recovering from their ordeal, though at this point she suspected only a small handful would decide to continue as Wave operatives. A couple of them even seemed to resent their presence here, though they also seemed to know they needed to continue under her charge—and Dr. Gordon's—for a bit longer.

Musing on how to let them go sooner than later—so much

for not thinking—Agnes made her way back into the jungle, following the path to her lab.

Where the lights were already on.

In all her morning jaunts, she had yet to see another person before six, at the earliest. Most people emerged around seven or eight.

Cautiously, Agnes approached the door, ready to snap into invisibility at the slightest sign of danger. Who would break into her lab first thing in the morning? One of the recovering operatives, looking for drugs? Or had someone else found them?

Whoever they were, they'd entered the lab without breaking the lock. Agnes's heart kicked into high gear; it couldn't mean that someone had broken into her home for the spare key. Tam would have pummeled them with her guitar.

If Tam had even heard them enter. Agnes's wife slept deeply.

Agnes lay a hand on the door, listening. When silence answered, she shoved the door open.

Lucy stood at one of the lab tables, staring at data Agnes had compiled—and put away—last night. Data that pertained to the enhanced humans who lived here, their blood test results, and Agnes's observations. Lucy jumped when Agnes banged the door open, stumbling backward into another table and nearly upsetting the microscope.

"Mom!" How Lucy managed that insulted indignation when she was the one who was breaking and entering, Agnes couldn't begin to say. On her way to preteen-dom, clearly. "You scared me!"

Agnes folded her arms across her chest. "You cannot be serious. Try again."

Lucy sighed, her shoulders sagging. "OK, sorry."

Agnes waited, arms still folded. When Lucy offered no

further explanation, she had to restrain an eye roll that would have definitely undermined her angry-mother exterior. "What are you doing in here?"

Lucy licked her lips, a guilty expression if Agnes had ever seen one. Agnes crossed the room to stand beside her daughter, looking down at the reports Lucy—who already showed night-owl tendencies and frequently had to be dragged out of bed in the morning—had risen early to peruse. "You're reading through my notes on how everyone here got their enhanced abilities."

"I just thought..." The girl trailed off, licked her lips again. Agnes had the urge to smooth back her daughter's curls, to cuddle her close. She'd handled so much upheaval in the past few months. Agnes thought of the packed bag beneath her bed, her fear that the island would fall under attack. And suddenly, she understood.

"You thought maybe you could figure out how to give yourself abilities?" Agnes asked gently.

Lucy's eyes lit up, and she smiled. Was that hope? She did not seriously think Agnes was going to give her any enhanced abilities. Did she? "Isn't that what you do?" Lucy said. "Try to figure out how to make accidental abilities... not accidents?"

Agnes flipped a page, glancing at Gigi's stats. She wasn't the type of scientist to try and grow wings on people, even if she knew how. "Mostly I try to use enhanced abilities to better technology in other areas. Testing on humans... It's not my thing."

"Unless you're testing yourself."

Astute observation. Agnes nodded reluctantly. "Sometimes."

Lucy whipped her phone out of her pocket and tapped eagerly on the screen. The device was mostly useless here, much to the girl's chagrin, but she still managed to watch an occasional video and post the occasional social media nonsense that took twenty minutes to upload because it had to pass Wave's approval processes.

Lucy found what she was looking for. She shoved the phone across the table as a shaky video started playing.

Agnes had seen this video earlier, on the news. In it, a company of armored soldiers leapt through some kind of a portal to destroy a comic convention. She'd have thought the thing was doctored, only she'd watched the same scene unfold from several angles—including the one that showed Mary ripping Nathan out of harm's way.

"Are you worried about this?" Agnes asked. "Those guys, whoever they are? They're not coming for us. We're surrounded by enhanced humans. We're safe here."

Lucy frowned. "Except that they're blaming us." She stopped the video and scrolled down, then handed the phone to Agnes. The caption on the video pushed the theory that the soldiers belonged to Wave, and the comments... As a rule, Agnes avoided reading comments online. She avoided reading most things online, unless they involved scientific findings or vetted news sources.

And this was exactly why. The comments on this video seemed, in large part, to agree with the caption's theory. And even if they didn't, no one protested Wave's innocence. No one said 'Wave would never do that.' Because everyone believed they would.

"It wasn't us," Lucy said. "Was it?"

"No," Agnes said, putting as much firm certainty into her tone as she could. "Absolutely not."

"But some people think it was. Which means the league might come for us."

Great. Lucy hardly needed another reason to fear the

league. "Trust me, Eloise knows we wouldn't do something like this."

But did she? And if her government friends disagreed, would El do anything to stop them from hunting down Wave? Oh, Agnes doubted they knew about the island specifically, but they could do plenty of damage elsewhere. And LIO might help, if it meant keeping their own secrets.

The league had treated innocent enhanced humans like animals, and not particularly well cared-for ones. Not the old league. Not Dolly's league. Their incarceration, and their exposure to Mange's serum, had happened under Eloise's watch. And it had happened to Agnes's friends. The fact that Nathan had released them only made Agnes want to recruit *him*, not to trust Eloise. Not ever again.

Lucy opened her mouth, clearly willing to challenge her mother's assertion, but Agnes put an arm around her shoulders and pulled her away from the lab table. "What would you have done, if I'd been a few minutes later?"

Lucy shrugged. "Nothing today. But I thought... Having enhanced abilities would make me safer. And you, and Mama."

Agnes guided her daughter toward the door, her heart hurting. If nothing else, it was the league's fault that the world felt this way about Wave, and Lucy felt unsafe because of it. Was that LIO's fault? Or was it Agnes's?

"Let's go home and get some breakfast," Agnes said, her head throbbing with the need for coffee. And answers. Because no matter what she told herself about that video, it was real, and she did want to know. Who were those people? And where were they coming from? No matter how curious Agnes was, though, she wouldn't reinstate contact with LIO. "And I think it's time we discussed how to monitor your internet access."

ELOISE HADN'T QUITE figured out what Holland Gold's deal was, but he'd apparently been telling the truth when he'd said Jeff Hayes was out of the country. Or at least, that he wasn't in Malibu.

Whether or not Jeff's whereabouts were a direct consequence of his visitors, Eloise couldn't have guessed. They'd arrived in the middle of the night, each collapsing in the first available guest room. Despite her weariness, Eloise found herself waking often, expecting to hear sirens or doors slamming open as law enforcement tracked them down.

Maybe Travis hadn't figured out where they'd headed. Maybe no one wanted to piss off Jeff Hayes by kicking his doors in. Maybe—she could only hope—Travis didn't actually have the power to chase after them. Whatever the reason, they'd made it through the night without incident, though Eloise hardly felt rested.

Now, with the morning sun sparkling through the window, Eloise eased out of bed, her eyes dry and stinging. No stranger to unexpected company, Jeff kept yoga pants and a rainbow selection of T-shirts stacked neatly in the drawers of the bureau, all still bearing their tags. Eloise wondered if the movie star had always maintained that practice, or if he'd started it during his close association with Mary in the last few months.

It didn't matter. What did was that she could shed her three-day-old outfit, shower, and change into something brand new. The soft fabric felt delicious against her skin, the fancy soaps and lotions bringing her back to reality through gentle scents of rose and jasmine.

Jeff Hayes. He could end up being a very important ally. Eloise made a mental note to contact him personally to express her gratitude.

When she ventured downstairs into the kitchen, she found freshly brewed coffee on the counter and Holland Gold seated at the island, wearing a crisp suit and reading the news on his phone.

"You stayed the night?" Eloise asked, surprised.

He glanced up, pushing the phone aside. His eyes were so blue, they practically looked silver. It was disconcerting to hold his gaze for too long. "Someone needs to protect your constitutional rights. Coffee mugs are in the cabinet next to the sink."

Eloise took the excuse to break eye contact, making her way around the counter to pour coffee into one of Jeff's identical ivory-colored mugs. No kitschy cartoon characters here. "Headed into the office?"

Holland tilted his head, bemused. "No. I'm at your disposal for the day."

Eloise considered asking why the lawyer was wearing a suit, in that case, but decided to refrain. "So how do you know Jeff Hayes?"

Holland blinked at her. "I'm his lawyer."

She somehow doubted that Jeff Hayes had Googled 'lawyers for move stars' and called up the best-rated attorney on Yelp, but she decided to let it go. She fumbled for another point of conversation, but Holland pointed to a set of carpeted stairs back by the entrance. "Your father's awake. He's downstairs in the recreation room."

Eloise thanked him and headed gratefully for the stairs. She appreciated Holland's help, confusing though it was, but it certainly wasn't easy to make small talk with the man. Though when she thought about it, maybe it wasn't so easy to make conversation with her, either.

She followed the sound of clicking billiard balls down to a large basement room where Dad stood bent in concentration, lining his pool cue up with the last few balls on the table. With a huge flat screen television on the far wall—but no seating area —and an arcade game stuffed into the back corner, the place looked more like a sports bar than a rec room. A movie star's rec room, she supposed.

Dad tapped the cue ball, sending the others spinning off against the side of the table. Two sank into diagonal pockets, while the third ricocheted an inch from its pocket and rocketed back across the table.

"Good shot," Eloise said, though she really had no idea whether it was or not.

Dad straightened and hung the cue back on the rack. "I'm out of practice."

Eloise took the final few steps into the room and over to Dad's side of the table, where she leaned back, careful not to bump the final ball out of place. She cradled her coffee in her hands, unsure of how to breach the conversation she knew they needed to have. She'd wanted to protect his privacy by not asking about his enhanced abilities, but after yesterday... Well, she was the leader of LIO, wasn't she? She couldn't skirt around the issue just because she was his daughter. She needed to know what was going on.

Still, she sipped her coffee, stalling. "Sleep OK?" she asked.

"Sure, when I wasn't worried about that EAEA woman

busting the door down."

Eloise sighed. "Same. Maybe tonight will be better."

"We can't stay here forever."

No, they couldn't. But Eloise needed to gather all the information she could before calculating their next move. Back to HQ? Rendezvous with Mary? Eloise still needed to let Mary know where she was, and what had happened. With her phone destroyed, she needed a secure way to contact people. It was something she should have done last night; as soon as she was done here, she'd head upstairs and ask Holland.

She was half tempted to go talk to him now, to further stall this moment. Maybe stall it forever. Instead, she took a deep breath to steady herself. "I have to ask, Dad. About your powers. Are they gone?"

Dad picked the cue back up off the rack, rubbed the end in chalk, then held onto the thing like it might offer him some escape. "No. They're not gone. I just..." He lifted his shoulders, shook his head. Embarrassment? "I can't use them anymore."

"Are they painful?"

"No, nothing like that. They're dangerous."

Eloise just looked at him. Dad's powers had always been dangerous. Fire powers tended to be. She thought of Jenna, and the havoc she'd wreaked with hers. Eloise didn't doubt that she could have done much, much worse.

Dad set the pool cue on the edge of the table and brushed off his hands, holding the palms out flat. "Your mother controlled my powers for years, El. For so long that I don't know where the line is between what she did and what I did."

With the Knife's aid, Eloise had held the LIO retirees' powers, briefly, during the fight in the L.A. hotel. She didn't know what it was like to be on the other end, to have your own abilities worked through you—or even simply held hostage, as Eloise had done—without your permission.

Although... she did know, in a way. Didn't she? The Pearl Knife communicated with her, often obeying her commands but sometimes taking its own direction. Couldn't she say the same thing, then, about her own enhanced abilities? That the Knife controlled them as much as she did? Unease crept up her spine, and she tamped it down. This was not the time to lose faith in herself, or the Pearl Knife. Not when they'd just begun to reach an understanding. Not when the Knife needed rescuing.

"Dolly's gone," Eloise said, with more confidence than she felt. Dolly *was* gone, but where? They didn't know. "She won't get the Knife back. I can protect you, Dad."

Eloise hated that she was the one who made his eyes shine with tears. She wasn't even sure which part of what she'd said made him shake his head like that. The memory of Dolly? Of the horrors she'd worked through him? Or was it the sight of his daughter promising to protect him?

Dad took a shaky breath. She wanted to save him from this conversation. She wished she could. "I proved I wasn't strong enough to protect others from my power," he said. "I could control my actions, but not my abilities specifically. I was conscious while she tortured people, burned them, forced false confessions using my fire."

"Because you wouldn't do it for her."

He nodded, rubbing the back of his hand across his nose. Neither of them stated the obvious: that refusing to use his powers now would not stop the Knife's new wielder—if it had one, and if they knew what the Knife could do—from forcing his abilities back into action.

"It feels like tearing," Dad set a hand on the pool table as though to steady himself, his voice barely more than a whisper. "Like... like the Knife is cutting you off from a piece of what makes you who you are. What if I'm tainted now? What if my abilities are somehow corrupted?"

Eloise shook her head. "It doesn't work that way."

Dad closed his eyes, opened them again. She could see the pain reflected in them, a reflection of her own. "You can't know that."

Yet another reason she wished for Agnes's help. If science could even assess a situation like this. Even if it couldn't, Eloise knew that Agnes, in her LIO days, would damn well have tried to figure it out.

"I know that you're you," Eloise said, the words coming out with more heat than she intended. She gritted her teeth, trying to control her tone, but the anger and grief she felt at the way he'd been treated... It was too much to contain. "You're kind, and you're a hero, and you didn't hurt anyone. Dolly did that. Your powers belong to you, Dad. Not to her."

Dad bobbed his head, reaching out to give her shoulder a squeeze, as if there was nothing more to say. And maybe it was true. Whatever Eloise believed, Dad got to choose what he did with his enhanced abilities. Not Dolly, not Eloise. Not anyone else.

He was helping her to retrieve the very artifact that had allowed Dolly to control him. By wielding the Pearl Knife, Eloise would be able to control his powers. Even if she chose not to. But what about the Knife itself? She still suspected the blade of deliberately hurting Dolly—suspected it more and more as her own physical strength returned. She didn't know what it might decide to do on its own. She didn't meant to question her own return to health, but she couldn't help feeling unnerved by it.

But Eloise didn't dare voice any of her doubts. She held Dad's gaze for a moment, then straightened. "I should go freshen my coffee."

Dad picked up the pool cue. "And I should get back to practicing."

"Right." On instinct, Eloise raised onto her tiptoes and gave her father a peck on the cheek. "We've got this, Dad. We'll figure it out."

He gave her a brief hug, and she hurried back up the stairs before she could betray her emotion. How she could leave a conversation about Dad trusting his own powers feeling more uncertain than ever about her own... It wasn't right.

But Dad's powers were different than the Knife's. The Knife was a sentient thing that lodged itself into her thoughts, talked to her, sang to her, responded to her commands—mostly. It was hers only in that no one else could wield it, except maybe this person who seemed to be hunting it.

Dad's abilities were different. With Dolly gone, with the Pearl Knife gone—for now, and soon to be returned to Eloise's control—the power belonged to him alone. She had to believe that.

Eloise breathed deeply, trying to reframe her thoughts with a healthy dose of oxygen. She could analyze the Knife all she wanted, as soon as she got it back. Maybe even find a way to communicate with it more effectively. For now, she needed to establish communication with Gail and the team. She needed to contact Mary.

A few hours out of lockup, and the items on her to-do list were already piling up.

As she reached the top of the basement stairs, though, she heard a familiar pair of voices thundering down from the second floor. The sun was barely up, yet Steve and Ire were already fighting. Loudly.

Enough. Eloise met them in the entry before they could argue their way into the kitchen, arms folded across her chest. The two fools were so focused on each other that they didn't notice her until they were both mere inches from stepping on her toes. Ire reared back, startled, and Steve clamped his mouth shut.

Eloise pointed back toward an alcove at the entrance. She doubted it would keep Holland Gold from listening—she wasn't sure it mattered—but it was the best she could do with anger pulsing in her ears. "A word."

The two men moved as if she'd grabbed them each by the ear and dragged them toward the alcove, which turned out to be a small parlor-type room. It was gratifying, really, to find that she was still intimidating enough to get two grown men moving that fast. Especially given the way Ire towered over everything in his vicinity.

Eloise eased the sliding door shut with more patience than she felt, before turning to face them. The men didn't even have the grace to look ashamed by their behavior. Instead, they were glaring at one another as if trying to see if one had developed killer laser-eye abilities overnight.

"You've been awake for thirty seconds," Eloise said, "and already you're giving me the headache of the century. What is it now?"

Ire tilted his head toward Steve. "He thinks we should have stayed at the facility. Waited it out."

Eloise lifted an eyebrow. Steve just shrugged. "I think the league would do better to work with the authorities, rather than against them," he said. "I think it would have played out all right."

Or they would have vanished overnight.

"They were going to throw us in a pit," Ire said, as if reading Eloise's thoughts. "Make us disappear."

Steve shook his head. "At which point we could have escaped. We acted too early. Now we've confirmed we're the criminals they want people to believe we are."

In the past, Eloise might have agreed. But it was more than obvious that Travis and his minions had no intention of treating league members fairly. Travis acted like a man with a vendetta. He let a bigoted organization hulk at his sides, validating their fear of enhanced abilities, throwing the doors of his government wide open to their influence.

Steve had been stuck in the situation, the same way she had, and he was certainly entitled to his views. If he couldn't see the larger ramifications of what had happened to them—what could have happened to them—she wasn't sure how to reason with him. He clearly had strong opinions on how the league ought to run, but he also wouldn't commit to staying.

"I don't usually advocate for rash action," Eloise said, choosing her words carefully, "but this was the right thing to do."

Ire smiled, looking far too satisfied, but Eloise raised a hand before he could speak. "It isn't about who's right and who's wrong. It's about the fact that you two are acting like children. Sooner or later, it's going to lose us a fight."

Steve opened his mouth, but Eloise shook her head. No matter how much she liked the man, she didn't have time for him to come trailing after her today. Asking about her health. Acting like he cared. And hating every choice she made.

"No excuses," she said. "No explanations. Find a way to get along."

With that, she turned on her heel and eased the sliding door open with careful control. She had too much to do without babysitting contentious men. She needed to get in touch with Mary. And she needed more coffee, damn it.

Eloise found Holland in the same spot where she'd left him, a cup of orange juice at his elbow. If he'd overheard her conversation with Ire and Steve, he gave no sign of it. "I was just wondering," she said, "can you help me make a call?"

NATHAN HALF EXPECTED the alien women to be gone when he and Mary headed for their door, first thing in the morning. But if Sloane and the others had slipped past the team's surveillance setup, he and Mary would find them. If more armored aliens came, he and Mary would fight them. *Together.*

He hadn't dared to wish for this, but as they made their way to Sloane's door, Mary looked... Well, she didn't look like she hated him, or like she regretted last night, and that was enough to make the motel seem like a paradise, chipped paint, musty carpets, and all. Even the questionable coffee he'd made in the room for them this morning—for *both* of them—tasted perfect.

Nothing could ruin today. Nothing.

And apparently the aliens had pegged Mary and Nathan as their best chance of survival, because Alex cracked the door open as soon as Mary knocked, peering out over the flimsy security chain.

"That's what the peephole is for," Mary said as the scientist opened the door to let them in.

Alex frowned at it. "I thought it was some kind of a data port."

"I think they'd be more comfortable at HQ," Nathan said. It seemed to him that HQ had data ports every few steps. Mary just shot him a look over her shoulder, as if these people were a far cry from earning enough trust to even mention the league's headquarters.

Nathan followed her into the room, where the other two waited. They sat together at a round table by the window, curtains drawn, untouched pastries in front of them. He hoped they hadn't swiped the food from the lobby's questionable continental breakfast. Definitely not the strongest representative of Earth's cuisine.

Alex shut the door. "This planet is weird. We're going to need help charging our tech at some point."

Mary pulled herself up to sit on the cheap bureau. "Already handled. I sent specs on your gear back to our engineering team last night. Everything but the hover boards, because we don't need you slipping away again."

"I think we know better than that by now." Sloane sat with her cheek propped against her hand. She flicked a crumb across the table, earning a sour look from Hilda.

"You should at least be able to recharge your tablets," Mary said.

Nathan stayed with his back to the door. It was becoming a habit, that guard's position, but he rather liked the full view it gave him of a room without removing him from the conversation.

From this angle, it seemed like the space travelers had barely slept. Sloane wore half-circle bruises stamped under her eyes, and with her head in her hand, it looked like she could hardly sit up straight. Hilda had her arms crossed, and Alex's eyes couldn't seem to rest on anyone for more than a second or two.

They looked exhausted. Scared.

If Mary noticed it, she didn't let on. "We need a game plan," she said. "I need you to tell me everything you know about this Sever character so we know how to fight him."

Sloane barked a laugh. "You don't fight Sever. Even I know that. You fight Sever, your entire world ends up a charred crisp of its former self."

"Well I'm not just going to let him waltz in here like he did at the comic convention," Mary said.

"Sever wasn't there," Alex murmured. "If Sever had been there himself, you'd have known."

As if it hadn't been bad enough. Mary held on to the edge of the dresser, leaning forward and keeping her attention on Sloane. "Then what do you suggest?"

Sloane flicked the pastry again, sending flakes of hardened croissant ricocheting across the table. "I *suggest* that we contact Sever's people, give him the Blade of Starlight, and ask humbly that he allow us back through our ship's wormhole. Which he currently controls. If we beg enough, he might leave us alone."

Like Mary would agree to just hand the Pearl Knife to this guy. Guy? He sounded more like a god. At this point, Nathan only half believed that he existed, but he'd seen too much to risk writing the threat off as some myth.

Mary looked ready to knock some sense into Sloane—they weren't going to give the Knife to anyone—but it was Hilda who spoke. "You don't understand. Giving him the Blade would be... irresponsible."

It sounded like the understatement of the century. Sloane sat up, flipping her long hair back over her shoulder, but something about the gesture smacked of false bravado rather than real confidence. "Have you not learned anything about me? Irresponsible is my go-to move."

"We don't know what he wants with it," Alex said, her voice soft. She'd taken a seat on one of the beds, her legs tucked up under her. "It can create wormholes. He's already powerful without that capability."

"He *has* that capability," Sloane said. "He has our ship."

"The Pearl Knife does more than create wormholes," Mary said. She was taking a back seat to the conversation, but Nathan could see her analyzing everything these people said. She gave Eloise all the credit for excelling in these kinds of conversations, but she wasn't bad at it herself.

Sloane twisted her hair behind her neck, then sat back in the chair and looked at the ceiling. "All the more reason to give it to him and stay on his good side. It's not like you have the resources to fight him."

Nathan shifted against the door, tucking his fingertips into his pockets. "We might."

Everyone turned to look at him, Sloane's lips parting in surprise—as if she'd thought he was a silent bodyguard type— her friends wary. He focused on Mary as he collected his words. Carefully. She was watching him expectantly.

"We need to pool our allies," Nathan said. "Our potential allies."

Sloane was blinking at him, and he wished he could read her mind. Part of him thought she underestimated Earth as a whole, along with its people. The other part, though... the other part thought she might be cataloguing everything he said. To what end, he didn't know.

"Eloise called. They're free, at least for now," Mary said. "Who else is there?"

She knew who else. She had to be waiting for him to say it. Nathan held her gaze, aware of Sloane's eyes still locked on him. "Wave. They've far more enhanced humans on their side than we do."

"Enhanced humans," Sloane repeated. "Like cyborgs?"

"Like superpowers," Nathan said.

Sloane mouthed the word, like it was completely foreign to her. Hilda shrugged, and Sloane's eyes moved back and forth like she was reading something in the faux-wood tabletop. Maybe she was. She did have some kind of a translation software running.

"Wave has a full arsenal of enhanced humans working with them." Nathan addressed his comments to Mary, who had her palms pressed against the bureau beside her. At least she wasn't crossing her arms. She had to have known this would come up again. "We could call a meeting. Everyone together, in one neutral spot."

"El will never agree," Mary said.

The aliens exchanged questioning glances, but thankfully none of them interrupted. This was Mary's call, not theirs. Sloane, though, leaned her forearms on the table, watching them intently. She, at least, had a stake in this. And she didn't hide it well.

"Eloise doesn't have to agree," Nathan said quietly. "You're calling the meeting. All these factions, all these supposed enemies, we at least need to have a conversation. Do LIO and Wave even know why they're fighting anymore?"

Mary blinked. "LIO framed them for terrorism, for starters. Then forced them into hiding. And threw a bunch of them in jail, until you released them unlawfully."

"It was the right thing to do."

Mary shook her head, the reflection of the dingy hotel lighting streaking through her hair. She made every room beautiful. "Obviously, but still. They like *you*, Nathan. They don't like the league."

"I don't like the league so much, either," Sloane muttered.

"Why not?" Mary asked. "We're just the ones who saved your asses."

Hilda waved a hand. "She doesn't like anyone."

Nathan chose to ignore the exchange. *Someone* had to stay on topic. "We need to all sit down together. A phone call to Dr. Gordon, and he can try to arrange it."

Nathan couldn't promise Wave would be any more open to negotiation than Eloise was. Dr. Gordon and Jo would do their best, though. He knew they would.

Mary licked her lips, pressed them together. He could see the indecision, the lack of confidence in her instincts. He could see her fighting with herself. She'd moved so decisively last night—he still couldn't quite believe it—but her struggle was all too obvious today. She was afraid of leading them all into danger, but they were in danger either way. If Alex and Hilda were right about this Sever guy, the whole world might be.

Yes, Nathan could make the call himself. Yes, he could take the lead. He wanted Mary to do it, to believe in herself again. And he thought Eloise would be more likely to listen—to show up—if Mary asked her to.

Mary pushed off the bureau abruptly. "We can't make any sudden moves. Maybe we should just get the Knife to El, go back to HQ, and forget the whole thing."

Nathan shook his head. They were clearly past that point. Mary had to know that.

"Sever won't let you forget it," Hilda said, confirming his fears. Her voice was soft. Frightened. "You're in this, whether you like it or not."

Mary shook her head, and Nathan stepped aside as she made for the door. "I need some time to think this over. I'll be back."

Sloane stared after her, eyes wide, and Alex rested her cheek against her hand.

"She'll help us, right?" Hilda said. "You'll help us?"

Nathan nodded. He couldn't speak for the league, or for Wave, but he knew Mary would help. She just needed to take that final leap, to trust herself again. And if he could help her do that, he would.

MARY WANTED TO RUN AGAIN. As far as she could. As fast as she could. Back to HQ, back to Malibu. Maybe as far as her apartment in Paris, or farther—Thailand, or Australia. She longed for Aries, her mountain sanctuary, and its quiet forests, its lakeside pier, its feeling of isolation. Because of her choices, Aries had burned to the ground. Like the rest of her life.

She wanted to run, but that wasn't an option. Not when those armored soldiers could slice a hole in the air any second, when Nathan was the only other person here with half an idea of how to throw a punch. Not when Sloane and the others were counting on her to help.

So she settled for running as far as the pool. It was too early to open, but she vaulted the fence easily and settled on the end of a lounge chair, propping her head in her hands to watch how the morning light danced across the water. Intermittent traffic on the street rumbled through the back of her mind, carrying the occasional thrum of bass-heavy music with it, but she let the sounds fade into white noise as she watched the water and thought about how nice it would be to jump in, to swim, to ignore all the problems these people had brought.

But they hadn't brought the problems, had they? Someone

from Earth had stolen the Pearl Knife from this Sever guy a century ago, or so it seemed. Despite what the aliens warned, Mary couldn't quite think of him as a bad guy. Not when she hadn't even laid eyes on him. Wasn't that what had gotten LIO into all this trouble in the first place? Maybe the new guy just wanted his property back.

And maybe that was wishful thinking. Alex claimed he'd burned entire worlds, which certainly made him sound like a bad guy. And it wasn't as if he'd shown up and asked politely. He sent teams of thieves, and killer soldiers. Not the most diplomatic.

She wasn't sure why Sloane was suddenly advocating returning the Knife to Sever after the way she'd described him last night. She recognized the woman's fear, though.

If only Mary could make a decision. If only she could act. A phone call. A battle plan. But every choice she made led to disaster. No matter how long she let her thoughts circle, she already knew she wasn't up to this task. She couldn't be trusted.

She'd only been seated by the pool for a few minutes before the fence rattled, announcing Nathan's presence as he climbed over it to join her. As she'd known he would. He probably would have come after her even if they hadn't made up last night, though perhaps he'd have left the fence between them to respect her boundaries.

Now, though, he settled on the lounge chair next to Mary's, facing her with his elbows on his knees. And said nothing. Just waited, like he knew she'd speak first. Another bass-blasting car passed, and she resisted the urge to throw her grapple hook at it. Not something she should get in the habit of doing. Even as the joke passed through her mind, she cringed. The more she tried to deflect her pain with levity—even when she didn't speak it out loud—the harder it became to ignore what she was trying to forget.

Nathan stayed where he was, casual. Smelling like pine and cedar. Mary sighed. "Eloise said no to calling Wave."

He didn't move. Didn't twitch. He knew all her arguments before she made them. "That was before."

Before the EAEA had attacked, before she'd annoyed Government Travis into turning against them, before Sever's soldiers'd tried to kill them all. Before. "Wave refused to help in L.A. when we were fighting Diana." Who Mary had antagonized into a fight by chasing after the LIO retirees. Another example of her astoundingly bad choices. "Why would they help now?"

Nathan smiled, and Mary wanted to run again, this time back to last night. Back to their private world. "Because now they have Dr. Gordon and Jo, and a dozen other operatives who did come to L.A., because they trust me," he said. "You're not in this alone, Mary. I can make phone calls, too."

That was the point of the league. Had always been the point. That this vigilante whatever-it-was life revolved around partnerships. Backup.

Yet Nathan wouldn't make the call without her go-ahead, or so he seemed to imply. No; she was sure he didn't mean to act without her. He'd freed the prisoners on his own, though. "Why don't you just make the call yourself, then?" she asked.

He studied her face, as if he could find the answer written there. "Because I trust your instincts. And if your gut tells you not to involve Wave, then we shouldn't."

Her gut. She'd trusted it, too, once upon a time. Lately, it was a faulty compass. She bit her lip, thinking. "What about Chloe? She can make temporary powers. Maybe we should call her, too."

Her instinct was that the EAEA would harm more than they helped, and that calling them would mean inviting them-selves directly into a trap. But she wanted to hear him say the words. She wanted confirmation that her gut could still pull her in the right direction. What did *his* instincts say?

Nathan steepled his hands, thought for a moment. "I'd say better not."

She nodded. OK, he agreed with that, and *his* compass didn't seem faulty. Still, it was easier to withhold action than to take it. "Meeting with Wave could be the wrong call."

"It could."

"They could side with this... Sever guy. They could decide we're worse."

"It's a possibility." Nathan scooted his chair closer, reaching out to take her hand. "We can't guard against every eventuality, Mary. You couldn't, either, when you went after them."

Them. The LIO retirees. She wasn't sure she could ever get past the shame of that crusade. Goldi's screams echoed in her nightmares, alongside the excruciating pain of Diana's poison burning through her bloodstream, and the guilt that told her she deserved it. She'd kidnapped at least one innocent person, held him in a cell. And Flick had ultimately decided to save her life, anyway.

Mary tensed, not wanting to face that conversation. She didn't deserve absolution. As usual, though, Nathan kept talking.

"You regret rounding up the retirees," he said. "I get that. But Mary, they *did* participate in your parents' deaths. And they helped lock up dozens of innocent Wave operatives for over a decade. They deserve to face justice."

"I nearly killed Goldi."

"An accident."

"I imprisoned Flick, and he was on our side the whole time."

Nathan lifted her hand to his cheek. His palm felt warm against her skin, a comfort. "I'm not saying it was perfect. I'm saying it's complicated. We were lucky yesterday. These guys... they're beyond the two of us. They're beyond Eloise and Ire, too. We need help."

Help. When had she ever asked for it? When had the *league* ever asked for it? She drew him closer, letting her lips brush against his.

As far as she saw it, Mary had two choices before her. A fork in the road, one she wasn't ready to face. But since when did the world care about what she was ready for? She could continue this life, and continue working with LIO. Or, she could disappear for good. Fade into the shadows—with Nathan beside her, or so she hoped—and live quietly in the woods. Or by the beach.

If she chose LIO's world, she needed to choose it for good. No hedging. No avoiding a conflict. When she decided to retire from vigilantism, it would be on her own terms—not because she was afraid.

Would Wave really form an alliance with them? Would Sloane and her friends trust LIO enough to help? Or would Eloise find a way to shut it all down?

Mary had no idea. But she needed to act, anyway. She pulled away from Nathan's embrace and pressed her phone into his hand. "Make the call."

When Nathan gave her that tilted smile, she wanted to pull him to his feet and back upstairs. But then he said, "And Eloise?"

Mary sighed. "Get a hold of this doctor of yours. I'll handle Eloise."

AGNES WAS CLEANING tools and contemplating a coffee break
—perhaps at home with Tam and Lucy, who'd surely be
studying this afternoon—when the lab door opened and Fran
strode in, leaning on her cane. The old woman wore a flowery
dress and a pinched expression, her dark eyebrows practically
meeting in the center of her brow and giving Agnes the impression of a well-dressed hawk. Her heart thumped into action,
and she set down her tools, wiping her hands carefully on a
towel. Was the island in danger? Had someone's powers taken a
toxic turn? She hadn't seen that, not yet, but she'd feared it.

"The league has reached out," Fran said.

Agnes blinked, her fear draining into sudden numbness.
"How?"

"Via Dr. Gordon, interestingly." Fran's deepening frown
told Agnes that the woman intended to find out exactly how he
and Nathan had managed that—it had to have been Nathan—
without setting off any surveillance alarms. "We've got a
meeting to attend."

Agnes drew in a breath, relieved. Not a disaster, then.
Though why they wanted a meeting, she couldn't begin to
guess. "A meeting. Where?"

Fran lifted a shoulder. "They sent coordinates. Bradley's looking up the location now."

Could Eloise actually have approved this? She'd reached out twice to ask for help, once in L.A., and once through that mysterious message, the one Agnes had never answered. Surely she wouldn't try to reach out again. "Are you here to ask if we ought to go?" she asked.

Fran lay a hand on one of the lab tables, looking around. "I'm here to request your assistance. It would be helpful. To have you there."

So they'd already decided. Of course they had. Agnes was supposed to be a window to understanding the league and their actions; it was the Committee who made the decisions.

It could be a trap. Another way to push Wave down, to clip the competition's wings. Agnes would have thought the league had more important matters to deal with, and yet... No matter what Eloise said, or what help she asked for, she still mistrusted Wave. Agnes had felt that anger when they'd faced each other in Vegas, even though it was LIO who'd done all the sneaking around, all the framing and terrorizing. Eloise's requests for help afterward had been entirely one sided. She expected Agnes to trust her without reciprocation.

Agnes wiped her hands on the towel again, though they were already dry. "Are we sure this is a good idea?"

Fran gave her a dry smile. "Nope, but the helicopter's waiting. You coming?"

ELOISE PRESSED the phone so close to her ear that it hurt. She wanted to pretend she hadn't understood Mary's words, but they'd come through loud and clear.

Dad, Steve, and Ire pretended to be focused on their breakfasts as they sat around Jeff's dining table, but Eloise knew better. She could practically feel them straining to hear Mary's end of the call. She wasn't sure where Holland Gold was hiding out this morning, but it was a relief not to have him at the table; somehow, Eloise knew the lawyer wouldn't try to hide his interest.

"Say that again?" Eloise said, her throat dry.

"I know, I know," Mary said. "I swore off going rogue. But El, you didn't see these guys coming through the portal."

Actually, she had. It was the only thing playing on every news channel, the videos lifted out of social media accounts as comic-convention-goers filmed the alien soldiers while they ran. Some still seemed to think it was some kind of a hoax, but Pete had pulled additional footage from the hotel's cameras. So far, LIO had detected no sign of video doctoring.

Besides, Eloise had seen that fiery portal before. It was all too real.

"Sloane has the Knife," Mary said. "She's ready to turn it over to you. Meet us. Talk to us."

Sloane. Mary named her as if they were old friends. Allies. Eloise pressed her fingers into the table, trying to control the tone of her voice. To sound calmer than she felt. "And to Wave. You want me to stand in the same room with Wave."

Steve jerked his head up, and Dad's eyebrows lifted toward his hairline. Ire took a bite of his blueberry muffin, as if he hadn't heard.

"Don't be ridiculous," Mary said. "I'd never set an indoor meeting between LIO and Wave. Haven't we wreaked enough material damage?"

Pain lanced through Eloise's stomach, following by roiling nausea. She wanted the Knife back, or... or did she? The more she thought about her conversation with Dad in Jeff's pool room, the more the truth of the Knife's power gnawed at her. Frightened her, even, if she were being honest with herself. For days, it had made her almost too sick to function, or its absence had. It had chosen, she was sure, to punish Dolly.

She knew all this. She'd been over every angle a thousand times. But with the Knife so close, the questions brimmed to near obsession. Dad still felt that he couldn't trust his power because of the Pearl Knife. Why should Eloise trust it? Why should she trust herself, while she wielded it?

And yet, the hole where its mind had melded with hers... it hadn't quite closed. She needed it back in her life, if only to better understand. If only to keep it from those who would abuse it.

Eloise swallowed, wishing she'd stepped out of the room to hold this conversation. She wanted to be angry with Mary, but at least her sister was out here. Taking action. It almost felt like old times.

"All right," she said. "Send the coordinates."

FOR THE FIRST time since her uncle's beater of a spaceship had shown up in her life—crashed into her life, really, via an unauthorized bay at the med school spaceport—Sloane wasn't thinking about money, or how to make enough of it to get *Moneymaker* and its crew out of her hair. All her thoughts were bent on that ghostly hologram of the soldiers looming over her family. How long had they been there? Were Mom, Dad, and Lissie allowed to eat? To sleep in their own beds?

Morik had asked her to gather all the Earth enemies into one place, and a single probing comment from Sloane had prompted Nathan to suggest just that. It was almost too easy. But was it enough to exonerate her in Morik's eyes? In Sever's?

Because no matter what she'd suggested to the others, she couldn't turn the Blade over, even with fear for her family clamped like a vise around her throat. Not to Sever. But if she wasn't there to *keep* it from him, this little drama would play out on its own, and Sloane wouldn't be culpable. She liked Alex and Hilda, she did, but they'd gone all hero on her. That wouldn't save her family.

So while Alex and Hilda gathered their things, ready to sprint off to this meeting the others had cooked up between factions Sloane would never understand—exactly as Morik had been hoping for—she dropped the Blade of Starlight on the bed. And then she took the opportunity to leave.

Yes, she'd be stuck on a backward planet, with no access to a proper medical school or decent technology. It stung, sure, but what better place to fade into obscurity? Without the Blade, no one would bother to come after her. It was the best chance she had to help her family. Or so she kept repeating to herself as she closed the hotel door behind her, as if the mantra could force wishful thinking into reality.

She didn't want to be the bad guy, and she couldn't be the good guy. Better to run. Let Mary and her punch-happy companions handle this.

Sloane got as far as the stairs, where she found Mary waiting for her. Or so it seemed. The woman stood with her back to the rail, looking all too casual, her golden curls pulled back in a loose ponytail.

Well, Sloane could look casual, too. She'd crashed more than one party by sauntering in through the kitchen. She'd snuck past girlfriends, debt collectors, and her own father. She made straight for the stairs, meeting Mary's eyes as she passed. She even smiled, though the stretch of her lips felt tight. Fake.

"Headed out?" Mary asked, as she reached the top of the steps.

The fizzy drinks. The ones that came out of machines in disturbing tones of orange, purple, yellow, and, most frequently, an undefinable brown color. She didn't have a translation for it, and the app took a moment to supply one. "Soda?"

Mary pointed down the hall. "No need to go downstairs. There's a machine there."

Sloane nodded, remembering how Morik's face had reflected so disturbingly in the vending machine glass last night. Surely there'd be an exit over that way.

Only, the woman followed her. "Need some change?"

Change? Sloane needed the entire situation to change. She frowned at the translation app, which stuttered before beaming another definition across her vision. Change also translated as metal coins.

Sloane hated Earth and all its finicky little definitions. "No, thanks. I'm good."

Mary slipped in front of her, not quite barring her passage. "I think you might have an idea of how to beat this Sever guy and his friends."

His friends? His army, more like. Sloane brushed her hair out of her face. If she was going to keep it long, she should probably think about braiding it the way Hilda did. As it happened, she did have an idea. It involved sacrificing her ass for the sake of this planet which, if she was being honest, could smell a lot better. No, thank you.

Mary took Sloane by the arm. Sloane had seen the woman fight; any moment, she was sure to get slammed into a wall or flipped over Mary's shoulder. Had Mary seen her talking to Morik? What did she suspect?

Sloane really needed to invest in some kind of self-defense training, or at least remember to carry a weapon.

Instead of attacking, Mary just gave her arm a squeeze. "Don't do this. Don't be like me."

"Self righteous, nosy, and violent?"

Mary tilted her head and gave Sloane a searching look. "Don't run away because you're scared. You'll regret it forever."

This woman, scared? Sloane couldn't imagine it. She snorted. "What are you afraid of? Losing your stylist?"

She meant it as a put-down, though the woman really did have excellent hair. Mary didn't look offended, and she didn't smile. "Don't leave your friends when they need you."

Sloane sagged back against the wall, and Mary let go of her

arm. "Would you let me go even if I wanted to? Which I don't. I just wanted a fizzy drink. That's it."

"No, I wouldn't let you go," Mary said. "But I'd prefer your cooperation. We're not going to get it from any of our other... guests."

Great. Just great. Sever was after them, and from what Sloane could tell, their potential allies were more likely to start pummeling each other than stand against him. She cursed her uncle for what felt like the millionth time, wondering where in the stars he'd landed himself.

Well, she still had options. She could tell Mary the truth, let her be prepared for the fact that this meeting was exactly what Morik had asked for. But that would mean no last-minute side switching to save her own hide—or, more importantly, her family's.

Alex had mentioned a way to jam the case's resonance, hadn't she? Maybe Sloane could push her on that. Find a way to keep Morik and his goons from finding the Earthers while they negotiated. Give them their best shot. And if the fight went south, well, Sloane would have done all she could to keep the Blade out of Sever's hands.

If she kept repeating that, it too might come true.

Mary was still waiting, that serious look on her face. As if she could read every treacherous thought running through Sloane's mind. Until she admitted it, though, Sloane would pretend she knew nothing. She just sighed, making it as dramatic as she could. "Fine," she said. "Let's get this over with."

Mary's coordinates brought Eloise and the others to the middle of nowhere. As in, nothing but sand and cactus plants and dry grasses. If anyone else had tried to send her to a location like this, in fact, Eloise would have assumed it was a trap.

God, she hoped this wasn't a trap. But Mary hadn't used any of the passwords or warning terms during her call. Whatever her mistakes, she was back in the league, and Eloise had to believe Mary wouldn't let them walk into a bad situation under any circumstances.

From the passenger seat of the van that Holland Gold had somehow procured for them—though he'd stayed behind in Malibu, ostensibly to work on their case against the government —Eloise watched the California hills flatten into flat brown desert until Steve pulled the car off the highway and onto a dirt road where their tires kicked up enough dust to be seen from space.

"Are we sure this is the right way?" he asked. It was a fair question, except for the fact that he'd asked it a dozen times since they'd left civilization behind. Eloise could practically feel Ire glaring at him from the back seat. When they got back to HQ, she was going to lock these two in a room to work out their differences.

Eloise glanced at Steve. He was gripping the wheel, attention laser-focused ahead, as if he expected an attack at any moment. "I'm starting to think you're not just asking about the road," she said.

But what *was* he asking about? If he wanted the league to operate above board, an open meeting should seem like a good way to do that. But the way he'd latched onto that wheel, knuckles whitening around it, he didn't appear to see it that way.

"I just thought any meeting with Wave would be something that happened on your terms," Steve said finally.

She wanted to reach out to him, to squeeze his shoulder. Offer some kind of support. Steve was still half in the old world, his father's world. And his father didn't trust LIO, or Wave, or anyone. There was a reason they hadn't seen Flick since that fight in the L.A. hotel. Eloise didn't know how to combat Steve's doubts, or reassure him when she hardly felt assured herself.

So instead of reaching out, she just nodded. What was she supposed to say? Yeah, Mary had gone rogue again. Kind of. But Eloise trusted her, and she'd learned LIO's leadership could benefit from a group effort rather than Dolly's despotic tendencies.

Ideally, sure, a meeting with Wave would have happened on her terms. But Wave—or Agnes, at least—had failed to respond to any of her requests.

Like Steve, Eloise didn't trust them. In fact, she'd be surprised if they even bothered to show up to Mary's little gathering. If Eloise was half-braced for a trap, they must be outright expecting one.

Steve turned right at an old sign, its borders rusted out, the paint chipped almost beyond legibility. Eloise thought the last word was 'airfield' but she wasn't sure—until an equally rust-pocked airplane hangar rose out of the desert before them. Its roof had caved in, and one of the walls tilted dangerously as if it planned to follow suit. What the hell was this place?

Steve pulled to a stop, the wheels spewing dust, and Eloise stepped out into the desert evening before he could voice any further doubts. Just a few hours of driving, and the warmth of L.A.'s sun felt far, far away. Why did they have to meet in the desert, of all places? Eloise grabbed her jacket out of the front seat and shrugged it over her shoulders, sincerely hoping that Mary didn't mean for them to meet her inside that rotted building.

As Ire and Dad hopped out of the back seat, Steve pointed to the tarmac. If the crumbling strip of a runway still counted as tarmac. There, Mary stood waiting for them, with Nathan at her side. And the woman who'd stolen the Pearl Knife.

Technically, she was the woman who'd announced her intention to steal it, before her colleague had jumped the line and run off with it. As far as Eloise was concerned, it was the same thing. A few early stars were already pecking their way into the sky as she shut the car door and made her way to the tarmac, keeping an eye out for scorpions. This seemed like the kind of place that would have scorpions.

Mary had been serious about choosing an outdoor location. She obviously wasn't sure how this meeting would go, either.

"Are we *sure* we trust Mary?" Steve asked, falling into step beside Eloise. They'd grown up together, in a way, and though Steve's presence had been intermittent, he should know they could. But there was much more of his father in him that Eloise had originally thought, his easy charm and ready smiles hiding a mind in turmoil. Well, Eloise could relate to that.

Why *would* Mary do this? Why would she partner with

these thieves? Eloise knew her intentions were good, but the woman's reckless streak... She just hoped this wouldn't evolve into another Jenna Carpenter situation, with Sloane and her friends turning on the league.

"Of course we trust Mary," Eloise said. After everything that had happened, she refused to do otherwise.

They stopped in the middle of the tarmac, a few meters from where Mary waited with Nathan and Sloane. Behind them, the other two women who'd come through the golden portal hung together like nervous shadows. Mary had left her car's headlights on, and Eloise could see why; darkness was coming on quickly.

"I'd better not step on any scorpions," Eloise said.

Mary grinned, all confidence. Eloise noted her close proximity to Nathan, and the lack of glaring between them. Had those two finally made things right? Eloise could only hope.

"I've got something for you," Mary said, nodding to Sloane.

Sloane sighed and produced a box from her bag, one Eloise recognized all too well. The case her friend had used to steal the Knife was white as ivory, with strange carvings in the sides, and Eloise itched to snatch it out of the woman's hands. Sloane glanced at Mary, who gave her another encouraging nod, before stepping forward.

Instead of offering the box to Eloise, though, she popped the top open and held it out.

Inside, the Knife gleamed. Eloise felt it reaching for her, tendrils of musical emotion rushing through the desert air to coil themselves into her mind. She reached back, fingers closing around the edges of the box.

Sloane pulled back, still clutching the case, and Eloise felt Steve tense as she let the other woman pull it away. Where could Sloane run, in the middle of the desert? "Don't tell me you have conditions," Eloise said.

"No conditions," Sloane said. "Except that I need to keep the box."

A very serious condition, actually. Eloise nearly laughed. She suppressed the reaction with such force that she nearly choked. "You can't be serious."

Sloane blinked at her with wide, dark eyes. Eloise had a feeling that innocent look had gotten her far in life. Up to a point. "I need it."

Eloise shook her head, anger lancing through her stomach. This was what Mary had called her here for? She wanted to grab the box. She wanted to run. "To steal the Knife again whenever you please? I don't think so. I'm locking that box up where no one else can access it. Ever."

This whole situation was a warning, from the stolen Knife to the fighting league members to the alliance of Travis and Chloe. What if the EAEA got its hypocritical hands on this box? They could take the Knife. Study it. Find a way to control it. Or Wave could, or the still-MIA Dolly, or some other enemy that had yet to announce itself. These days, new enemies popped up so fast she could hardly keep track of them all.

The Knife reached for Eloise's thoughts, tapping at the closed doors of her mind, but she hadn't touched it yet. It couldn't communicate with her, not fully. She wanted it to. She also wanted to wall it off. The tumult in her mind felt like it might cleave her in half. The Knife beamed a message of concern, of worry, and Eloise gritted her teeth as she blocked it out.

Behind her, Dad cleared his throat, but Eloise remained immobile. First Mary didn't trust herself, and Dad didn't trust his powers. Now Eloise doubted her own. It would be foolish to leave the Knife behind after all she'd gone through to capture it back from these people. Indecision seemed to be catching around here.

"I should be taking you back to HQ for questioning," Eloise said. She was stalling—she knew she was stalling—but she couldn't help herself. She also couldn't take her eyes off the Knife.

At least it was safe. It was within her reach.

Mary stepped forward. "Take the Knife, El," she said gently. "Let Sloane have the box, and we'll explain."

Since when had Mary ever been gentle? Eloise glanced at Nathan, but he just stood there with his hands in his pockets, casual as anything.

Eloise folded her arms, leaving the Knife where it was. Sloane twisted her lips, like she didn't want to hold onto it any longer than she had to. After a moment, she set the box down on the tarmac and stepped back, as if she expected it to leap out and bite her.

Knowing the Pearl Knife, it might.

"OK," Eloise said. "Get explaining."

Mary and Nathan exchanged a glance. Definitely something happening there. A week ago, Mary hadn't even wanted to look at him, and now they were conspiring. Maybe it was better when those two *didn't* team up.

Nathan cleared his throat. "We have to wait until everyone gets here."

Eloise shook her head. "You might as well tell us whatever plan you've concocted. They're not going to show."

Timing, she'd learned, had a way of biting a person in the ass. As soon as the words left Eloise's mouth, helicopter blades broke through the silence of the desert, descending out of the darkening heavens as if from nowhere. The lights grew brighter, until Eloise had to shield her eyes. Where were they coming from? Where had they been hiding—and how?

Dispersing dust and whipping the dried grasses into a frenzy, the helicopter landed and deposited its passengers on the tarmac. Bradley Archer descended first—because of course the lightning-haired weirdo would show up here—and offered his hand to an old woman, who accepted his help before striding across the old runway with the help of a cane, her dress fluttering behind her in the copter-stirred wind. Behind him came Nathan's friend, Dr. Gordon, his glasses riding precariously on the edge of his nose.

There was a beat in which nothing else happened, and Eloise nearly sighed in relief. No Agnes. But as the helicopter blades slowed to a stop, the old woman paused and turned back. She said something to Bradley, who darted back to the helicopter to offer a hand to someone else.

Eloise suspected that Agnes hadn't needed his hand. Just a moment to collect herself. Maybe come up with some excuses as to why she'd ignored Eloise's latest attempt to reach out, her plea for help.

Agnes stepped down from the helicopter, ducking beneath the stopped blades, and followed Bradley across the runway. Her eyes went to Mary, and Eloise realized the two hadn't seen one another since the showdown with Wave in the warehouse last fall, a fight that felt like an eternity ago. Where Mange had died. Where Jenna had announced Coral's secret identity to the world, unmasking Mary and starting a chain reaction they were still trying to clean up.

And where, after learning the truth about LIO's past, Agnes had betrayed the league for Wave.

THE LOOK on Eloise's face made Mary want to second guess this whole rendezvous. El had obviously convinced herself that Wave wouldn't show—she might even have been counting on it —and for some reason, the majority of her rage seemed to be channeled toward Agnes. With a slice left over for Bradley Archer who, Mary had to admit, probably deserved at least a small helping of that vitriol.

Mary, for her part, couldn't help the relief that swept through her at the sight of Agnes. She'd known her friend was alive, that she'd been working with Will and that El had seen her mere weeks ago. Still, the sight of her slight figure walking across the tarmac was a strong relief. Mary hadn't been at all sure that Agnes would come. That Wave would want her to, or that Agnes would even agree.

Mary offered her a smile, which Agnes returned briefly before her eyes flickered to the Pearl Knife, sitting in its box. The centerpiece of this party, the blade lay unclaimed in the middle of the crumbling runway. Sloane stood above it like she was still considering making a break for it, and Eloise—to Mary's surprise—seemed hesitant to pick up the Knife.

Which meant any one of these people could scoop up the

box and make off with the damn thing. Mary half thought she ought to do it herself.

Night blanketed the abandoned airfield now, the headlights beaming double spotlights on the crowd as the stars glinted above like threats. Out here in the desert, they seemed so close, and yet Mary knew they were closer still, much closer than she'd ever imagined. The Knife could lead her straight to them. The golden portal flashed across her mind like a ticking time bomb, and yet... Something about it was intriguing, too. Robo-soldiers aside, there was a spaceship waiting on the other side. And gadgets. So many gadgets.

She'd never cared much for first contact stories, though, and this situation explained why. In the case of first contact, who'd be stuck cleaning it up? The league. Including Mary.

Who was she kidding? The way they were all glaring at one another, there'd be a full-on brawl in a minute. Before anyone had said a word about aliens, portals, and potentially world-charring enemies.

And then Nathan peeled away from her side, striding across the tarmac to offer his hand to an older man with glasses who had to be Dr. Gordon. The man smiled, shaking Nathan's hand with both of his. For a moment, Mary's heart swelled practically to bursting, the sentiment warm and much too sweet for comfort. Nathan had formed a bond with these people. He'd released them from unfair imprisonment, and now he represented the strongest tie between their two organizations.

With his movement, the staring-contest spell seemed to shatter. But not in the way Mary had hoped for.

"You shouldn't be here," Eloise said. She was looking directly at Agnes, as if she could shoot actual knives from her eyes. Which Mary wouldn't put past her, honestly, though she'd never seen the Knife do anything like that. She knew El and Agnes had clashed in Vegas recently, but she wasn't sure that fight could fully explain the level of anger pulsing between them now. Had something else happened?

Agnes shook her head and hugged her arms around herself. "None of us should be here. This is ludicrous."

"We can't trust you," Eloise said.

Agnes scoffed, brushing a wayward curl out of her face. "Of course you'd see it that way."

"How many secrets have you told them?" Eloise took a half step forward. What was she going to do, grab the Knife and fling it at Agnes? Mary sincerely hoped she wouldn't. "How many secret entrances and formulas and surveillance systems have they catalogued since you betrayed us?"

Agnes's eyes flashed in indignation, and Mary fully expected her to deny the accusation. Instead, she said, "And what if I did share what I know? What could you possibly do about it?"

It was hard to believe that Agnes would have betrayed the league's secrets. Unless her morals made it impossible to do otherwise, which, Mary had to admit, suddenly felt all too likely. Still, wouldn't Wave have come crashing into HQ by now, and hijacked the league's safe houses, if Agnes had given away every secret?

Given what they now faced, Mary wasn't sure it mattered.

Never in her life had she acted as a peacekeeper. Not effectively, anyway. People tended to step in and keep the peace with *her*, not the other way around. But Sloane was worrying her bottom lip between her teeth, panic practically eking out of her pores as she looked to Mary to sort this out.

Sloane could have run, and she hadn't. She'd come here of her own volition. How could Mary ask her to trust the league, or Wave, or any of them, when they refused to trust each other?

Mary took a breath and stepped between Agnes and Eloise. They were separated by meters of space, each group carefully situated on their own point of a ragged triangle—with the glowing Pearl Knife at its center—but they weren't here to battle. They were here to form a treaty. They didn't have to like each other to do that.

These two would have to fight it out later.

"You've seen the news," Mary said.

It wasn't a question. The comic con videos were everywhere, shaky social media recordings replayed ad nauseam. That vendor with the LIO figurines had been interviewed on one channel, slipping an ad into his eyewitness account by claiming he'd sold out of everything.

So Mary wasn't surprised when they responded with reluctant nods. Eloise, Will, Steve, Ire. The old Wave woman, who seemed to be in charge yet allowed Agnes to speak for her. Bradley. Dr. Gordon.

Even Agnes clenched her jaw and inclined her head in a single angry nod. "It's not a hoax?"

Mary held Agnes's gaze, determined to keep her friend's attention. "Not a hoax. The people who came through the portal? They want the Knife."

Bradley pushed a hand through his white-blond hair, making it stand up more than ever. "And *they* are?"

"Aliens," Mary said.

"We're *humans*," Alex protested from behind her. "Our species, at least, matches sufficiently with yours to assume so."

Implying that there were other species out there that didn't? Like... space slugs? Sentient squid? Walking plants?

Mary set the questions aside. She had a tendency to be flippant in moments like these—who didn't like a little comic relief?—but with Eloise ready to attack, it fell on Mary to focus. "Fine, those *people* are coming for the Knife."

Silence. The Pearl Knife glowed brighter, as if energized by the weight of everyone's attention on it. And maybe it was.

"Then let them come." The old Wave woman lifted her cane and planted it back down with a loud *thwack*. "Give it to them, if that will protect Earth. We're not going to defend your weapon."

The weapon that had been used to torture her people. To murder Wave members, including Mary's parents, and to frame their operatives for LIO-perpetrated crimes and throw them into prison cells. Mary wasn't sure what to say. How to convince her of the danger.

It was Sloane who spoke. "Giving them the Blade won't protect your planet. Once Sever has it... well, we don't know what he'll do."

"Take over, probably," Alex said.

"Or destroy your world as punishment," Hilda added. "He likes that kind of thing."

Blunt. But right now, they needed blunt. There was a long pause, and Mary half expected everyone to start yelling again.

Instead, the old woman leaned forward on her cane, lips pursed. "All right. Assuming that's not complete lunacy, what do you propose?"

Everyone was watching Sloane. Mary glanced back to see Alex and Hilda's eyes pinned on her, too. She had a sense Sloane hadn't filled them in on this part.

Sloane let out a long breath. "We bait them. They say they're tracking the Blade's resonance, but I think..." She swallowed, looking around, as if she wasn't used to showing her cards. "They're tracking the location of the box. At the moment, anyway. It's how they find us."

How Sloane could know that for certain, Mary wasn't at all sure she wanted to know. Sloane had been adamant that Alex disrupt the box's resonance, had pushed her to work on it the whole way here, which she'd done with gadgets balanced on her knees in the back seat of the car.

Sloane paused, looking around as if to make sure everyone had heard. Eloise raised her eyebrows. "So we bait them, and then what? We get slaughtered?"

"And then we get my ship back. They need it to reach you. That's where the wormhole generator is."

"The *only* wormhole generator," Alex said.

Mary wondered how she could know that it was the only wormhole generator in the entire universe. Especially with the Knife sitting right there, looking all innocent and moonlight-y. It could create wormholes, too, couldn't it? Or was that something else?

"So we help you get your ship back," Mary said, "and this problem goes away?"

Sloane twisted her hair behind her neck, giving it a tug. "For a while, at least."

Mary felt sure they weren't seeing the whole picture, that Sloane knew more than she was saying. Was she holding back a piece of her plan, or did her nerves only make her seem like she was hiding something?

The old woman leaned on her cane, watching Sloane with a shrewd expression, as if she might be wondering the same thing. Her people, including Agnes, watched her carefully. "So what is it you want us to do?"

Sloane glanced at Mary, who offered her the most encouraging nod she could muster. This part, she thought she could predict. And no one was going to like it.

"Distract them," Sloane said. "Fight them. And help us get control of our ship."

Which was where the wormhole machine thing was. Mary would have liked to see that. Maybe she'd get a chance, before all this was over. Did Sloane mean to destroy it? Somehow, Mary didn't think Alex would go for that.

Sloane pointed at Eloise. "But she can't fight. The real

Blade needs to disappear." She chewed her lip. "Maybe you can send your strongman and your fast guy through the portal to help us. And your spy couple."

Spy couple? Mary glanced at Nathan, who rolled his eyes. He was smiling, though.

Sloane fluttered her hand in Wave's general direction. "And these other people can distract the soldiers who come through the portal. Though maybe you have someone who looks more like they can fight. No offense."

Mary wouldn't have discounted the old woman so quickly. She had a feeling that cane might be pretty painful, when applied to the top of one's skull. Still, Wave could call upon far more resources than this little group represented. It would help to have them on the ground, an army of enhanced humans on their side.

But Eloise frowned. "Leave Wave in charge of the Earth-side of the fight? I don't think so."

"It makes sense. We have more operatives than you do," Agnes said.

"We can mix and match," Nathan said. "Pair Wave agents with league members."

That could definitely work. As long as Eloise and Agnes stayed far, far away from one another. But before Mary could say as much, Eloise stepped forward and snatched the Knife up out of its case. The box top snapped closed, as if of its own volition, and Eloise shoved the Knife into the empty sheath at her waist.

"I won't be led into a trap," Eloise said. "I won't sacrifice my people, or trust Wave to back us up. I can't."

"El," Mary said. "We have to do something."

Eloise took a step back. "Yes. We have to get back to HQ and secure the Knife."

If these people could really track the Knife's resonance, it wouldn't stay secure for long. Sloane claimed it was the box, but the two items were clearly linked somehow. If the Knife had belonged to Sever, he'd know all about how to use it. How to contain it.

"And what about us?" Sloane asked.

Eloise looked at her for a long moment, her expression unreadable. "I suggest you bury that box and run," she said. "Make the most of your new home on Earth." And with that, Eloise turned on her heel and marched back to her van, with Steve and Ire at her sides.

Will, though, hesitated. He stood there, clearly uncertain, and Mary remembered that he'd been working with Wave, too. They'd saved his life by faking his death, and he was caught squarely in the middle. She could certainly understand that feeling.

For a moment, Mary thought he might actually stay. But he just shook his head and turned to follow the others back to the van. Mary couldn't tell if he was apologetic, defeated, or simply disappointed in all of them, but she supposed it would have been too much to expect him to side against his daughter. Still, didn't he owe Mary some measure of fatherly feeling, too?

She watched her friends go, defeat rising painfully in her own chest. Of everyone she'd invited here, she'd thought El would be the one to side with her. To go along with the plan.

Mary looked to the old woman, and the Wave leader wrenched her birdlike gaze from Eloise's retreating figure to meet Mary's eyes. Mary wondered if this woman had known her parents, if they'd ever worked together.

If so, the woman showed no sign of it. "We can't risk our people to save your weapon."

The weapon which was currently speeding away from the airfield in Eloise's van. Mary wanted to scream at all of them, to drag them back and make them understand what they were risking.

"You did hear what she said." Mary inclined her head toward Sloane. "This isn't just about the Knife. It's about Earth."

"And at least two galaxies," Alex added.

The old woman shook her head, her eyes sad. Mary looked to Agnes, but her friend averted her eyes. She wouldn't fight for them, either. She refused to understand. And when the old woman turned back toward the helicopter, Agnes followed, Dr. Gordon and Bradley Archer falling in behind her.

This meeting had just been another mistake. Mary could see it in Sloane's eyes, the way she frowned after the two groups. "What is your role on Earth again?" she said.

This time, the mistake wasn't Mary's. She'd done all she could. LIO and Wave couldn't move past their differences, their ancient grudges. But Mary could still act.

Sloane was still looking at Mary, like she actually expected an answer. Only trouble was, Mary didn't know what to say. She sighed. "We're supposed to be its protectors," she said. "Come on. Let's see how we can adjust this plan of yours."

Agnes watched the dusty country roll by below, the helicopter blades a constant churn in the background. The desert had always unnerved her. From the sky, it presented itself as a barren wasteland. On the ground, it bustled with life. Energy. It wasn't to be trusted.

When she tore her gaze away from the window, she found Fran sitting directly across from her, the old woman observing her with sharp interest. Beside her, Bradley Archer leaned his head against the window with his eyes closed, while Dr. Gordon stared at his hands in the seat beside Agnes's. She supposed that meeting had not gone the way he'd hoped it would.

But the doctor was overly optimistic. Agnes was a pragmatist. She looked back to Fran. "I know why I stepped away," she said. "Why did you?"

Neither Bradley nor Dr. Gordon so much as twitched, but she knew they were listening. How could they not? The helicopter wasn't that loud.

Fran's expression didn't change. She still reminded Agnes of a hawk, with that sharp nose, those all-seeing eyes. "I stepped away because you did."

Agnes blinked. Not the response she'd expected. Bradley's lips tipped up in a slight smile. Someday, Agnes would make it a point to learn his story.

"That shouldn't surprise you." Fran leaned back in her seat, eyes still locked on Agnes's face. "You're the Committee's inside connection to the league, the only way we have to understand them. If an ex-operative that we happen to trust doesn't trust them, well, we'd be fools to go against her advice."

She spoke as if the Committee had made the decision together, though Fran had been the only one present. Well, perhaps they had. Perhaps the others had authorized Fran to act according to Agnes's suggestion. They could be consulting in her ear right now, watching through one of the buttons on Fran's dress. Who could tell?

Agnes looked back out the window, as if the landscape could offer some sort of answer as to whether she'd made the right decision. She could only think of Lucy, so afraid of the league that she was prepared to run from her home at any moment. Or give herself enhanced abilities, to try and save her family.

And yet LIO had defined the role of independent operatives to the world. The public didn't see all the tangled chains that held LIO in the past, their misdeeds piled upon their mistakes. They didn't know the truth. Agnes did.

That, more than anything, was why she'd walked away. She only hoped she'd made the right call.

"Do you think those people are really aliens?" Agnes asked. She kept her eyes out the window this time; she didn't want to see Bradley smirking, or the doctor clenching his hands in his lap.

Fran blew out a breath. "I don't know. But if they are, I imagine we'll be hearing about them again."

Like it or not. Agnes leaned her head on the window, letting the vibrations settle into her head as she closed her eyes, wondering how long she could keep Wave from tangling in this mess—and what she would do when the fight came to them.

THE PEARL KNIFE settled into a cozy corner of Eloise's brain, nestling close as the LIO jet hurtled them across the country once again. She rested the blade on her knee, watching the familiar threads of light as they pulsed across its surface and trying to feel the same camaraderie she'd felt for the weapon before.

Dad had worried about his powers, worried so much that he refused to use them anymore. But he was autonomous now; no one could rip his control away.

No one but Eloise. She held the power right here in her lap. The Knife stirred as the thought crossed her mind, as if sitting up in alarm. She felt its music turn strained, concerned. No, Eloise had no intention of using the blade for ill. Having the Knife back... It was a relief, truly. To the hole in her mind, to the concerns about her health, even to the part of her that had worried about its safety. It was, after all that had happened, a friend.

Mostly, though, it was a relief because no one else—least of all this Sever person—would have the power to control others' enhanced abilities.

It still unnerved Eloise to think that *she* did.

A question spiraled through her feelings, laced with worry. As if the Knife wanted to know what, exactly, she intended to do.

Eloise wasn't sure. She sighed, tucking the Knife into its sheath at her waist, and headed to the back of the plane to pour herself a drink. After all this, she figured she'd earned one.

Steve met her at the bar, leaning an elbow on the cherry wood countertop as Eloise added ice to a glass. "Let no one say that LIO keeps cheap accommodations," he said.

Eloise smiled, though she felt tired, her eyes dry and papery when she blinked. She was pretty sure she could sleep for a whole week.

Instead, she had to have a conversation. A difficult one. Was there any other kind? Contention seemed constant at this point. She poured a mini bottle of bourbon into the glass and swirled it around. Stalling, with Steve's eyes on her. As if he knew what she was going to say.

"I need you to commit to the league," she said finally. "I need you to commit or go. You want a say in the way we operate, but you refuse to join. So join. Otherwise, I'll have a second car waiting when we land in Niagara. It'll take you to Boston, or anywhere you want to go."

Steve leaned in closer, his dark eyes searching hers, bringing the heady scent of spiced coconut with him. "You want me to leave."

Eloise set her glass down on the counter, clenching her hand into a fist to hide its shaking. *Want* him to leave? She wanted the opposite. But it didn't matter what she wanted, and this conversation, this decision, was long overdue. "Is that what you got from what I said? That's what you boiled it down to? No, I don't want you to leave. I'm giving you a choice."

"Ire—"

"Has no part in this conversation," Eloise interrupted. "And whatever little rivalry you two have developed, he's not the reason I'm talking to you. I'm not choosing him over you."

She just... couldn't keep trying to mediate when Steve wasn't even technically part of the league. She couldn't keep wondering if she'd wake up one morning to find him gone.

Steve rubbed a hand over his chin, drew in a deep breath. "I don't like the secrecy, El. I never have."

Eloise wanted to laugh. Sometimes it seemed the league was nothing *but* secrets. And for good reason. With their cover blown, she'd agreed to work with the government, and look where it had gotten them. Working to keep her voice level—and therefore devoid of judgment, or any other inconvenient emotions—she said, "Then why are you still here?"

Steve lifted his thumb to her cheek and dragged it lightly along her jaw line. Eloise wanted to glance around the plane, to make sure no one was watching, but she couldn't wrench her eyes away from his. He leaned in closer, brushing his lips lightly against hers. An answer. A question, too.

Eloise wanted to say yes, to lean against him, to breathe him in.

But she couldn't make league decisions based on her personal feelings, no matter how strongly the desire burned in her throat. So instead, she forced herself to step back, her heart thrumming a dissonant argument, the Knife taking up a corresponding melody. Eloise pushed them away, silencing them as best she could.

She stood up straight, assuming the heavy, comforting posture of LIO's leader. She'd do what she had to do. "I take it that means you're leaving," she said. "I'll call the second car."

THEY'D OPTED to stay at the airfield, rather than tearing off to a more populated area. Or, to be more specific, Mary had spat the order at them after the meeting went south, and since Sloane didn't know how to drive their vehicle—and thought it unlikely she'd be able to steal the keys from the woman in the first place—she didn't bother to argue. What would be the point, anyway? Alex's jamming whatever-it-was couldn't last forever. Sever's guys would find her wherever she went, until she ditched the case.

The window of opportunity for that maneuver was closing. Rapidly.

So she stayed, tucked against the rotting wall of the old airplane hangar and watching the stars tick by above the desert. Where, when the fight came to them—and it would, soon—innocent people wouldn't get hurt.

Of course, Sloane had already hurt people. Mary sat curled against Nathan's side, trading soft conversation with him. Every time they looked into each other's eyes, shame rose through Sloane's chest. By withholding what she knew, and by telling herself she could still play both sides, she'd endangered them.

And she'd endangered the crew she was supposed to protect. Alex and Hilda sat on either side of her, as if to grab her if she tried to escape. Escape to where, she didn't know. But they were clearly ready to prevent it. Maybe they understood her better than she'd thought.

After a long time—hours, probably—Alex turned her head to look at Sloane. She had her knees pulled up to her chin, her curly hair gone wild in the gentle desert wind. "How did you know?" she asked. "That they'd been tracking the box and not the Blade itself?"

Ah. So that was the giveaway. There was dirt under Sloane's fingernails, an unacceptable amount of it. She'd have to scrub them for an hour to get it out. "One of Sever's guys told me. He's been... in contact."

On her other side, Hilda just snorted. As if she'd expected no more. "He offered me a deal," Sloane added. "I didn't take it, in case you're wondering."

Though maybe she should have. Where was her family now? Did Sever consider her part of the deal fulfilled, or... Sloane didn't want to contemplate the other option. She couldn't.

"Why didn't you tell us?" Alex asked.

Why had she betrayed them, like Oliver. Why had she kept it a secret. Why. Sloane scanned the landscape, as if she might be able to see Sever's guys coming. An abandoned airplane hulked in the distance, its wing crushed against the dried grasses.

"He has my family," Sloane said, the words gumming uncomfortably in her throat. Why was it so hard to admit that she was vulnerable? "I thought I could leave the door open, in case things went wrong here. In case I could still save them."

She should probably add an apology in there—the burning shame in her chest said it was the least she could do—but she doubted they'd believe it, anyway. In their eyes, Sloane was the selfish one, the reluctant captain hellbent on getting back to her normal life.

Not too likely. At this point, she wasn't even sure she could get through the night.

To Sloane's surprise, Alex lay a light hand on her arm. "That's what Sever does. He's all fear and violence. That's why we have to keep this Blade away from him, whatever the cost."

Sloane swallowed back a bitter comment that Alex's family was not currently lined up to pay that cost. Instead, she said, "He'll find a way to get it. You know he will."

"You didn't have to help him along," Hilda pointed out, but her voice sounded tired. Far away. Sloane risked a glance in her direction, looking away quickly when she saw tears glistening in the pilot's eyes.

All at once, Sloane wished she'd found a way to send Alex and Hilda to safety, at least. To hide them away until this was over, for better or worse.

But it was too late to send anyone to safety now. A thread of golden light ripped through the pre-dawn sky, rending the air in the middle of the runway, and Mary leapt to her feet as Sever's soldiers poured through the portal. Helmeted, as they'd been at the convention center, with their weird half capes. Sloane pressed her back against the rusting hangar, as if it could protect her. More likely it would topple over.

Rather than launching into an immediate fight, Mary sauntered toward the soldiers with Nathan at her side. The woman was too brave for her own good.

"Hey," she said. "Maybe we can talk this out."

If Mary could be that brave, Sloane could at least stand up. She got to her feet, brushing off her hands. Did Mary really think a parley was likely to work here? That the soldiers would stop their raging to chat, perhaps over a cup of tea?

Apparently so. She waited, Nathan standing stock still by her side. Sloane wondered how fast he could draw a weapon, if he decided to. For the little good that any Earth weapon would do against these oversized insect-robots.

"Tell us where to find the Blade of Starlight."

The voice that answered was deep, robotic, and Sloane wondered if there were actual people inside those shells or just machines. The Fleet banned the use of drone soldiers, unless operated by humans from afar. Sloane had no love for the Fleet —bunch of killjoy bullies, in her experience—but at least they had rules. Sever would adhere to none.

Whether human or machine, the one who'd spoken was a leader, with blue paint splashed on their elbows and shoulders, while the others had only silver.

Mary raised her hands to her shoulders, casual. "I would, I swear. But I have no idea."

The soldier struck out, fast, with an arm like a metallic scythe. But Mary must have expected it, because she threw herself to the ground while the blade-arm whistled through empty air, Nathan mimicking the move beside her. The soldier didn't falter, the suit absorbing any upset in balance. In the second that the soldier retracted their arm, Mary scattered an arch of silver coins at the robots' feet. While Sloane wondered what that was supposed to do—they didn't seem the type to grab for tokens—Mary crawled to her feet and ran toward the hangar, hands over her ears, with Nathan staggering at her side.

The coins... pulsed. It was the only word for it. One moment they lay inert on the pavement, and in the next, waves of energy poured from each one. It was visible, too, like watching heat waver from metal in the summer, and Sloane could feel the vibration in her chest like an explosion. No fire, though. No smoke.

But there was power. The pulse knocked half the soldiers

off their feet, and they struggled to rise, kicking on the pavement like bugs trapped in glue. Sloane wasn't sure if the coins had done something to their suits, or to the people inside them —if there were people inside them—but either way, she watched in awe as Mary spun to face the portal.

Because there was no time to celebrate. A wave of standing soldiers vaulted over their companions, and Mary must have run out of magic coins, because she was already dodging punches, throwing herself into the fray. Nathan had somehow stuck to her side, where he fended off the soldiers with a pair of blue-tipped sticks. Sloane wasn't sure what they would do against these soldiers. There were too many of them. But the coins proved Earth had a few worthy tech tricks up its sleeves. Or at least, Mary did.

Sloane was suddenly aware of the hangar wall behind her, the fact that she still stood in its shadow. "We need to help," she heard herself say.

Alex, who hadn't yet stood—wisely, Sloane thought— straightened now and pressed something into Sloane's hands. Sloane looked down at it. The Blade's box. It was latched shut now, though it still glowed, as if hoping its contents would return.

And suddenly, Sloane knew how to end this battle. She turned to Hilda, hands shaking as she clutched the box. "Do you still have the fake Blade? The one from the convention?"

Hilda nodded.

Sloane's eyes drifted back to the fight, a sick feeling rising in her stomach. Was this what it felt like to commit to the good guys? If so, she was going to need an immediate supply of antacids. "I've got an idea," she said. "But first we need to make it to the portal."

METAL CLASHED on every side as Nathan did his best to hold off his opponents. Plural. Because one robo-soldier was clearly not enough; these things were pouring through the hole in the sky like an infestation. He'd been lucky so far, with most of the clashing metal representing missed hits that cracked into the runway, or into another soldier.

At some point, he'd get tired. And then the robo-fists would crack into his all-too-human skull.

At least he had tasers. Nathan managed to plunge the tip of one of them into a soldier's armpit, and the robot staggered back as blue light fizzled through the suit's electronics. The soldier froze in place, but Nathan had no time for satisfaction as another plunged toward him. How many were there? How long could two un-armored, unenhanced humans hold out against an alien army?

Nathan felt Mary dancing beside him as he swung his second taser toward the new opponent. She was fast, as always, ducking and dodging and even landing the occasional kick. At any moment, though, one of these guys could send her spinning. He tried to wipe away the image of her flying into the side of the hangar, falling unconscious to the ground. There was no room here for a split-second of distraction.

The soldier in front of him clamped metal fingers around the taser, and Nathan tried to fry the suit as he had with this one's friend. But the soldier snapped the end of the weapon, sending sparks fizzling to the ground. Nathan couldn't see the person's face, but he felt certain it was grinning at him. Smug. Did these soldiers even know what they were fighting for? Or did they just like to break things?

The soldier swung for him, and Nathan dropped to the tarmac, rolling back toward the hangar. As he pushed to his feet, he caught sight of Sloane. She waved frantically at him, jumping up and down and pointing straight at the portal.

Nathan's soldier clomped toward him, and he fended the thing off with the broken end of the taser. It was still spitting blue sparks, though he couldn't say how much good that would do. The soldier clearly didn't know, either; they avoided the strikes.

Nathan risked a glance at Sloane, who was still gesturing to the portal. She obviously wanted to reach it, but how? And *why?* Even if she reached it, her ship must be overrun with these soldiers. And maybe worse. Maybe that had been the plan before, when they'd hoped to have enhanced operatives on their side. Now, it would be a suicide move.

He didn't understand the plan, but Mary trusted her. That had to be enough.

Nathan swiped the fizzling stick at the soldier, clipping their neck with a lucky stroke. The soldier staggered back, and for a moment, there was a breath.

Nathan ducked to Mary's side, grabbing her arm. "We need to clear a path to the portal," he said.

She was breathing hard, a bruise already darkening her left

cheek, but she nodded, fire blazing in her green eyes. "Is that all?"

"No problem, right?"

Except there was, because the soldiers she'd mowed down with her disks were overcoming their shock—or, more likely, their systems had rebooted—and they were lurching to their feet like huge robot-zombies. In capes.

And then Mary was darting to the left. One soldier followed her; another followed Nathan to the right. The rest stayed in the center. They'd learned their lesson about getting separated, clearly. All he could do was watch—and dodge this soldier's attempts to grab him by the neck—while the reanimated soldiers headed straight for Sloane and her friends. By trying to draw off the soldiers, Mary and Nathan had cleared a path straight to the women. An inevitable path—this fight had never been one they could win—but still.

There was nothing he could do. He tried to duck under the soldier's arm, but his opponent was too fast, closing any potential gaps with a clang of metal. Well, sure. If you had a computer to help you, which these guys surely did, anticipating your enemy's move would be all too simple. Across the way, Mary somersaulted away from her soldier. They couldn't keep this up.

If Eloise had stayed, or Wave... but there wasn't any point in regretting the outcome of the meeting. Except, perhaps, that Nathan hadn't said any goodbyes.

The rest of the soldiers closed the gap, clomping steadily toward Sloane and her friends. Twenty feet, fifteen. As he once again darted out of his own opponent's reach, Nathan knew he was trapped, with no way to help the others.

A deluge of sparkling droplets rained down on the advancing soldiers, and the group lurched practically as one, grasping at their necks, at the elbow joints of their suits.

Nathan shielded his eyes as sparks nipped at his own sleeves, looking up to find the source of the raining fire. A new invention of Mary's, maybe? Nathan scrambled back toward the hangar and out of the literal line of fire, still squinting upwards.

It was Will who descended from the sky, flame pouring out of his hands like dual blowtorches. Blasting the soldiers until they fell back to the pavement, writhing, Will cleared a path to the portal, the sight nothing short of biblical.

Jenna had shot fire from her hands, and that had been powerful. Nathan remembered it all too well. Will, though... Will's entire body was engulfed in flame, his eyes glaring red behind the wall of heat. Nathan had thought his powers might have dried up, that he was somehow without them. But here he was, in the middle of the fight. Defying LIO. Defying Wave. Defying every law of physics Nathan understood, and probably a good number that he didn't.

He could see why they called this man the Inferno.

Sloane didn't pause to gape, or to question his intervention. She ran, with her friends right behind her and the Knife-snatching box clutched against her chest.

That was when Nathan realized the soldier he'd been fighting was running, throwing himself across the runway to intercept Sloane at the portal. They'd been on the fringe of Will's attack, and the suit obviously still worked. Nathan sprinted forward, pushing his legs as fast as he could, but he was too far to do anything but watch as the soldier reached for Sloane.

Mary got there first. She launched herself off the pavement, flying kick-first into the soldier's chest and knocking him straight through the portal. As Nathan ran, chest burning for air, Mary's momentum took her after the soldier and through the gap in the universe. Sloane, Alex, and Hilda leapt in after her.

And then, as if sated after a large meal, the portal zipped shut.

Nathan stumbled, falling to his knees where the portal's golden edges still burned behind his eyelids, raking his hands through the air as if he could somehow call it back. There was no sign it had ever been here. And Mary? Mary was gone.

MARY BARELY REGISTERED the fact that she'd landed on a spaceship, which was honestly such a shame. She could practically smell the technology chugging around her, the toys waiting to be examined.

Unfortunately, there was still a massive robot-suited asshole trying to punch her into oblivion. Whoever was in that suit punched fast, and they punched hard. She needed every bit of concentration—already wearing thin after the airfield fight—to keep from losing a limb, or worse.

Mary avoided a punch and tried for another kick, vaguely registering Alex's protective stance in front of a table packed with tech and bubbling potion-type things. The scientist stood with her arms stretched to the sides, as if she could protect the fragile tubes and bottles with her body. Like a mother bear protecting her cubs.

One metal-fisted punch in the wrong direction, and that machine would be toast. Mary understood that this had to be the wormhole technology that Alex had spent her life developing.

One blow, and Mary would be stuck here. One blow, and she wouldn't be going home.

The robot growled, swinging a vise-like fist toward Mary's neck. Before she could dodge, Sloane ripped something off the shelf and threw herself between them with a roar, meeting the robot's fist with a shield that looked like some kind of a metal door. The robot's fist landed, denting the metal with a blow that seemed like it should have broken Sloane's arm. But the other woman held the onto the makeshift shield, baring her teeth as if coming home had given her some kind of new strength to fight.

"We need to get them off the ship," Sloane said.

Mary only saw the one soldier, but she didn't disagree. Where were the others? Surely there had to be others, unless they'd all jumped over to Earth. "Count of three?"

Sloane nodded, and together they rushed their opponent, slamming their shoulders into the metal-armored chest. Mary's arm objected strenuously as they knocked the soldier out of the room and into the opposite wall. Before Mary could wonder what the plan was now—that soldier would be up in a second, plucking them off its body like ants—Sloane slammed the shield down between the shoulders and head of the armor.

The soldier twitched, electric light fizzling through its neck, and went still. For a heart-seizing moment, Mary thought Sloane had broken the person's neck; she half expected to see the head roll away.

"Stop looking like I just murdered a puppy." Sloane jammed an index finger against the side of the fallen soldier's helmet, indicating a green light. "They're alive. Not sure why you want them to be, but whatever. I just killed the suit."

Hands shaking, Mary nodded. Sloane beckoned for Hilda and Alex, who rushed out of the lab looking as startled by Sloane's actions as Mary felt. Up until now, the woman hadn't exactly acted like the take-charge type.

"Remove this one's armor and restrain them," Sloane said. "Then Hilda, get up to the pilot's deck."

"What if the armor is password protected?" Alex asked, frowning worriedly at the fallen soldier. Was the person awake? Knocked out? There was no way to tell.

"You're the genius," Sloane said, standing up. "Figure it out."

She started down the hall, and Mary followed, rushing to keep up while also trying to take in every detail of the ship. The halls were narrow, everything made of metal. She looked around for a window, but they were just in a hall full of closed doors. Cabins? Stock rooms? Mary wanted the full layout. And she wanted a glimpse of the stars.

But Sloane was already rushing down a set of clanging metal steps to get to what looked like a cargo area. Without actual cargo, at least for the moment, but large enough to carry plenty of crates. What sort of goods made the rounds in this galaxy?

"Tell me what you're thinking," Mary said. "I don't see any more soldiers. Why can't Hilda take off now?"

Instead of answering, Sloane pressed her lips into a grim line and lifted a rust-pocked panel on the right of the doors. She pressed a few buttons, and the metal doors shifted aside to show a wide, clear window.

For a moment, Mary's heart leapt, thinking she might see the stars.

Instead, she saw the wall of a ship. An enormous one, hulking close enough that it was hard to see how far its sides extended in any direction. A tube-like passage connected it to Sloane's ship, to this door. An airlock, if Mary had to guess. "We need to break the connection," Sloane said.

As Mary watched, the airlock door creaked open. She might have little practical experience when it came to space—OK, she had none—but it didn't take an expert to know that breaking that passage away without a sealed airlock would be very bad, for all of them. She thought of Nathan, trapped back on Earth, waiting for her to return. She *had* to return.

"How are you going to do that?" she asked.

Sloane shook her head, her face grim. As if she'd somehow expected this. She stepped away from the panel, centering herself in the cargo bay. Ready to face whatever came through.

"Tell me you have a plan," Mary said.

"Oh, I have a plan," Sloane said, her words barely audible behind the screeching airlock doors. Mary had the distinct impression that this ship had seen better days. Sloane looked at Mary, meeting her eyes. "I'm thinking I'll lead them on a chase."

Mary couldn't possibly have heard that correctly. Because this woman, who'd been ready to abandon them all less than twenty-four hours, couldn't possibly be suggesting... "You're going to sacrifice yourself?"

Sloane clutched the box, but her hands weren't shaking now. "I seriously hope not. But either way, a chase won't hold them for long. Even if we lose them, they've seen the wormhole tech. They'll copy it." She twisted her hair behind her neck, securing it with a tie. "Get your teams on the same page. The fight's coming back to Earth."

Mary grabbed her arm as the airlock doors shuddered, paused, started up again. "I should stay. I can help."

A crowd of figures stepped into the airlock, waiting for the doors to finish parting. Some robo-soldiers, but also a man in a long cloak, with black sausage curls cascading over his shoulders. With a jolt, Mary recognized him from the hologram she'd seen in L.A.

"Just tell Hilda to be ready to fly," Sloane said. "Alex can reopen the portal for you. If you want to save your planet, you need to leave. Now."

The doors shuddered into their slots in the wall. Mary hesitated, her feet ready to run and her heart loath to leave these people behind. "Where will you go?"

Sloane grimaced. "If we shake these guys, I fully intend to find my uncle. I owe him a piece of my mind."

Again, Mary wanted to pause. Wanted to help, to say something more. Sloane and the others might not be able to evade Sever. Even if they did, Mary doubted she'd see them again; it felt wrong to leave them this way.

But Sloane was right. If Mary wanted to save her friends, and the rest of the world, she needed to go. She cast one more glance toward the airlock, toward the shiny-haired boss—Sever himself?—and then, she did as Sloane instructed. She ran.

SLOANE WAS COUNTING on Morik to have more interest in the Blade—or, in the box that supposedly held it—than in the retreating Earth woman. If he ordered his soldiers to chase after Mary, there wouldn't be much Sloane could do.

He didn't. He just stood there, unsmiling, those unsettling cheek lines drooping lower than when he'd appeared to her on Earth. She wasn't sure if that meant something. As *Money-maker's* doors gasped open at last, he seemed to be waiting for her to speak.

Sloane counted herself a pretty good actress. She'd spent her entire teenhood saying things like 'No, Dad, I wasn't at the party where they busted everyone for g-dust possession' and 'Yes, Dad, I slept here all night' and 'No, Dad, he's just a friend.' And she'd only gotten busted once or twice.

But now there was more on the line than a stern lecture or a cut-off allowance. Her life. The lives of her crew, her family. The lives, maybe, of an entire planet. One she hadn't even heard of a week ago and wished she didn't care about.

Sloane drew herself up, tipped her chin as high as she could while still looking Morik in the eye, and slipped her right hand slowly into her pocket. "Get off my ship," she said.

Morik's ears twitched at the ends, ruffling his hair, and his eyes drifted to the box in her hand. "Do you have something for me?"

Sloane fingered the remote in her pocket. It looked like Morik was focused on the closed box, but there were soldiers behind him, and they supposedly had eyes, too. She couldn't trust any of them. She pushed the button in her pocket, using the remote control to guide the fake Blade out of her back pocket, until it hovered in the air between them.

If she could distract them with it, get them to back their asses back onto that ship of theirs, then she'd be able to trick them twice. Once with the toy Blade. Twice with the box. These soldiers didn't know the case was empty.

That was the part that made her sweat. She didn't exactly relish the idea of being chased through space by Sever's hulking ship, but there was no backing out now. Hilda *had* claimed to be a racing champion. Now she could prove it.

For a moment, she thought the near-silent—but not completely silent—buzz of the Blade-drone's engine would call attention to it as a fake. As Morik's gaze snapped away from the box to land on the Blade, though, he licked his lips. And Sloane realized.

Morik hadn't seen the Blade of Starlight. Or, if he had, it would have been over a century ago. She didn't know how long his race lived, but she'd be willing to bet it wasn't as long as Sever.

"What payment do you demand?" Morik asked, his voice quiet.

"Just get off my ship."

One of the soldiers leaned in to speak quietly to Morik, and Sloane's heart hammered a frantic beat against her chest. Sever might be the only one who'd seen the Blade of Starlight, but these robo-soldiers had seen the toys. Morik's thick brows drew together, and he looked up at the Blade more sharply as it turned lazy figure eights between them.

"How do I know this isn't a fake?" he said. "Perhaps I'll take the Blade *and* the ship."

"And perhaps I'll blow it all up," Sloane said. She drew her hand out of her pocket, holding the remote up like a detonator. The Blade continued its circles.

She counted herself a pretty good actress. But was she good enough to pull off this kind of improv? She only hoped that Mary, at least, had managed to get home. That she hadn't decided to stick around to help. Her planet needed her, and would need her more in the days to come.

"We know the Blade is strong," Sloane said, "but can it withstand an explosion? The vacuum of space? Everything has its limits."

And Morik clearly didn't know what the Blade's might be. He licked his lips again—those things must get chapped like crazy—his eyes flickering between the 'detonator' and the Blade. "All you want is the ship?"

"And my family's safety."

Morik slipped a tab out of his pocket and made a call. When he was finished, he held up the screen to show her the image of a trio of soldiers leaving her family's home.

They'd surely return, as soon as Morik realized what Sloane had done. But maybe her parents would have the presence of mind to run. It was the best she could do.

Sloane nodded, and Morik took a step back, inclining his head. Sloane grinned the best, most arrogant grin she could manage, relief pulsing through her upper body as she flew the Blade over Morik's head and onto his ship. She hurried to the panel, willing the airlock doors to close fluidly this time. Before he could figure out her ruse.

The doors slid to a close, with only a slight stutter. The ships parted with a jolt.

As Morik's face receded into the black, Sloane smiled at him. She waved. And then she held up the box that could hold the real Blade of Starlight but didn't. As if to say 'haha, got your real Blade right here.'

Because for some reason, Sloane had decided to be the idiot of a wild goose that saved Earth. Or at least bought them some time. For their sake, she hoped they'd use it well.

She hoped her family was already running.

Morik's face turned a satisfying shade of red. But it was too late.

"Hilda," Sloane said. "Time to fly." And with that, *Money-maker* took off into the black.

MARY PRACTICALLY FELL through Alex's hastily opened portal as the spaceship lurched under her, landing her on her hands and knees on the airfield pavement. As soon as she landed—crashed, really—the portal disappeared behind her, and she couldn't help but wonder if she'd ever find a graceful way to pass through one of these things.

Maybe El would let her practice that.

The airfield was littered with prone robo-soldiers, their visors lifted to reveal actual flesh-and-blood faces. The air smelled of fried electronics, but no burning flesh. Maybe the suits had taken the worst of Will's onslaught. He was crouched over one of them, apparently working to loosen the suit.

No matter who these people were, Mary never had a desire to see anyone dead. Will wouldn't, either. And maybe, with the portal gone, they'd be able to get some answers about Sever, and the Parse Galaxy, and how Sloane's little translation app could have known so much about Earth.

In any case, LIO's prison level would be full again tonight.

Mary pushed to her feet, taking in the remains of the battle as she scanned the airfield. Because really, there was only one person she wanted to see.

Nathan was staggering toward her, his face streaked with tears. She met him halfway, and he pulled her into his arms, kissing her lips, her neck, her face. His whole body was shaking. "Do not do that again," he said. "Ever."

His voice was rough, as if he'd been screaming. As if he'd thought she was lost. Never once had he issued such a command, or deemed anything too dangerous for her to handle, and she couldn't resent it. Not when he might as well be laying his heart bare for her to read. Not when he was so overcome with grief.

Mary lay a hand on his cheek and kissed him back, tears stinging her own eyes. "What? You expected me to resist the chance to visit another galaxy?"

She'd been gone for half an hour, at most, and all she'd seen was the inside of a spaceship. Not much of a tour. Well, the way things seemed to be going, maybe she'd have a chance to go back someday.

For now, she'd never been gladder to be home.

ELOISE WAS glad to have everyone back at HQ, back underground. Mary and Nathan had returned today, along with Dad and more than a dozen alien soldiers—supposedly employed by this Sever character—who currently resided on the prison level with Diana and the other LIO retirees.

Eloise had a feeling the storm had only just begun. It was a relief to have her people here, where everyone would be safe.

Well, almost everyone. As soon as the plane had landed, Steve had taken the car back to Boston without protest, and Ire had watched him go, looking surprisingly conflicted. Eloise had tried to keep similar emotions off her face as the car pulled away, and already she missed Steve's presence here. He'd felt like an ally. A friend. She didn't want to reduce their numbers even further, but this had been the right call.

After a quick debriefing over a sandwich spread, during which Eloise regretted her emotion-fueled choice not to help them in the fight, Mary and Nathan had retired—together, because apparently wonders never ceased—and Dad had followed Eloise back to her office.

There'd been no word from Travis Bertram, or the EAEA.

If they knew what had happened in the desert, they weren't calling to chat about it.

Now, Dad was watching Eloise from the chair across from her desk, his dark eyes calm. He'd changed his mind not an hour after they'd left the meeting on the airfield, and truthfully, Eloise hadn't been able to hide her relief. She'd felt, every moment after leaving, that though she had a responsibility to get the Knife as far from these invaders as possible, she could have at least left Ire and Steve behind to help. Her grudge against Wave had made her too angry to see straight.

Or maybe it hadn't been the grudge at all. The Pearl Knife pulsed gently in her mind, glad to be back, yet practically vibrating with an undercurrent of nerves, and Eloise couldn't separate its thoughts from her own. The way it had reached for her mind back at the airfield, the way she'd responded... Even the memory left her feeling off balance. No, more than that; she was completely lost. Unable to focus. Unable to trust. Had her own misgivings convinced her to betray Mary—it *was* Mary she'd betrayed by leaving in anger, not Wave—or had it been the Knife, somehow? Confusion trailed through her thoughts, and she pressed a finger to her temple.

Dad waited, legs crossed, as if they were here to hang out over drinks. But he was clearly here to check on her.

"How did it feel?" Eloise asked finally, fingering the edge of her desk. "To use your powers again?"

Dad's smile was gentle. "It was just as you said, El. I'm in control. It felt right."

Eloise nodded. Good. That was good. Wasn't it?

"What will you do?" Dad asked.

Eloise knew what he was asking, that he understood they'd been discussing more than his powers back at Jeff Hayes's house in Malibu. "I don't know," she said.

Dad nodded, got up from the chair. "Long day," he said. "Get some rest."

She watched him leave, unsure whether he knew it was a lie. It didn't matter. She did know what she planned to do, but she needed to do it on her own. No discussions. No outside influences. She drew the Pearl Knife out of its sheath, and it fluttered hopefully in her mind as she balanced the milky white blade on her finger. A thing of the stars. It reached tentatively toward her, hope and anticipation brimming through its melodic thoughts. Like a child.

A dangerous child. Eloise steeled herself against it as she locked her thoughts within an impenetrable cage. A wall. She still sensed the Knife on the other side, its keening protest, but she knew what she had to do.

Eloise got up and crossed the room to the cabinet where she kept all her throwing knives. She didn't hesitate as she placed the Pearl Knife gingerly on its shelf, as she locked the cabinet and stepped back. The Knife gleamed as if in protest, begging her to listen, but Eloise shook her head. She thought she'd understood it—for a few blessed days, she'd been so *sure*—but she'd only just scraped the surface. Until she learned more, and until she could trust what it told her, she had to leave it alone.

Eloise left her office and locked the door, ignoring the Knife's pleas.

IF TRAVIS HAD HIS WAY, this would not be his last time standing in the Oval Office. If he had his way, in fact, he'd someday take his place behind the desk where President Caldwell was currently poised to sign an executive order—one that had come about because of Travis.

And because of the Enhanced Abilities Enforcement Association, he supposed, whose representatives—Chloe Pearce, the American representative whose name Travis couldn't recall, and EAEA founder Simone Laurent—stood beside him to witness the signing. Along with Senator Jones, of course, and the rest of the enhanced abilities liaison committee. In mere moments, the liaison committee would become the oversight committee, and Travis's power would trounce Eloise Reyna's into the dirt.

President Caldwell paused, pen poised over the paper, and Travis's heart skipped a nervous rhythm as the old man looked over the committee. The President wouldn't raise his doubts again now, would he? With the press looking on? He could, of course. He could delay the signing, ask for more information, insist the measures run through Congress. He could alert

Eloise, who would no doubt sweet-talk him into trusting her corrupt league again.

After a beat, though, President Caldwell returned his attention to the paper, added his signature with a flourish, and set down the pen. "The League of Independent Operatives now answers directly to the Enhanced Abilities Oversight Committee," he said. "Furthermore, unassociated enhanced humans will be required to register their status with the federal government."

Oh, there would be lawsuits. Protests. Travis understood that. He could picture the anger, the signs. But he also understood that those protests would fail, and that the public's ire would turn to rage against the league, as soon as they understood the true nature of their so-called heroes.

The photographers herded everyone behind the President's desk, and Travis positioned himself toward the front. The cameras clicked, and he smiled. He stood on the right side of history, and nothing could stop him now.

S<small>EVER HAD FELT</small> the absence of the Blade before Morik's ship had attached to his station. The hole had gaped in his consciousness for the last hundred years; he'd have known if its companion were near. Without hope, he'd watched the ship's approach from his favorite spot on the station's viewing deck, the stars laid out before him like needle points. Tiny flares of pain in the darkness.

Now, as his advisor stood trembling before him, all his arrogance stripped to naught, Sever had never felt more frustrated by the Blade's absence.

His people kept coming close. They kept failing.

"These Earthens," Sever said, "they go to extraordinary lengths to protect the Blade of Starlight."

Morik looked up, as though hopeful he might lay the blame elsewhere, and Sever sensed it was nearly time for another court cleanse. He did not abide weak companions, or those who were too afraid of him to be useful.

Morik held up the false blade. A mere toy, yet it had fooled him. Twice. "They practically worship it. They create these idols, you see? They'll do anything to keep it safe."

Anger rippled through the calm Sever worked hard to

maintain, squeezing at his chest, threatening to cleave him in half. The Blade of Starlight was the most dangerous article known to the universe. For a century, he'd wanted nothing more than its destruction.

Whether Earth had stolen it, or whether some misguided creature had deposited it there, Sever didn't know. Yet in the meantime, much had happened.

"You think this beat-up ship with the wormhole generator also has the blade?" he asked, mostly to gauge his servant's loyalty. Still, a good leader knew anyone could miss an important detail.

Morik shrugged, his cloak nearly slipping off his shoulders. "Maybe. But that woman's tricked us before. I don't trust it."

Neither did Sever. He would know, would he not, if the Blade touched the Parse Galaxy? He felt certain that the wretched thing was still on this... Earth.

"You sent a pod after the ship?"

Morik bobbed his head in a frantic nod. "To cover all avenues."

Fine. Let them think he'd taken the bait. "And our own wormhole generator?"

"It's nearly there, Sever. It's nearly there."

Sever looked out at the sea of stars, imagining he could make out Earth's star among them. Imagining he could crush them from where he stood. He gripped the viewing deck rail. When the soft metal crumpled in his grip, Morik whimpered.

"Good," Sever said. "As soon as it's ready, we return to Earth. Clearly it is a planet in need of supervision."

Thanks for reading!

Curious about what exactly happened in Reykjavik? Or the origins of the EAEA?

Sign up for my VIP reader list at www.katesheeranswed.com to get *Power Struggle*, a free LIO prequel novella!

ABOUT THE AUTHOR

Kate Sheeran Swed loves hot chocolate, plastic dinosaurs, and airplane tickets. She has trekked along the Inca Trail to Macchu Picchu, hiked on the Mýrdalsjökull glacier in Iceland, and climbed the ruins of Masada to watch the sunrise over the Dead Sea. Kate currently lives in New York's capital region with her husband and son, and two cats who were named after movie dogs (Benji and Beethoven). She holds an MFA in Fiction from Pacific University.

You can find more of Kate's work, and pick up a free novella, at katesheeranswed.com.

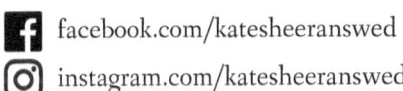

facebook.com/katesheeranswed

instagram.com/katesheeranswed